Also by David Lubar

NOVELS

Hidden Talents

True Talents

MONSTERRIFIC TALES

Hyde and Shriek

The Vanishing Vampire

The Unwilling Witch

The Wavering Werewolf

The Gloomy Ghost

The Bully Bug

NATHAN ABERCROMBIE, ACCIDENTAL ZOMBIE SERIES

My Rotten Life

Dead Guy Spy

Goop Soup

The Big Stink

Enter the Zombie

STORY COLLECTIONS

Attack of the Vampire Weenies and Other Warped and Creepy Tales

The Battle of the Red Hot Pepper Weenies and Other Warped and Creepy Tales

Beware the Ninja Weenies and Other Warped and Creepy Tales

The Curse of the Campfire Weenies and Other Warped and Creepy Tales

In the Land of the Lawn Weenies and Other Warped and Creepy Tales

Invasion of the Road Weenies and Other Warped and Creepy Tales

Wipeout of the Wireless Weenies and Other Warped and Creepy Tales

Extremities

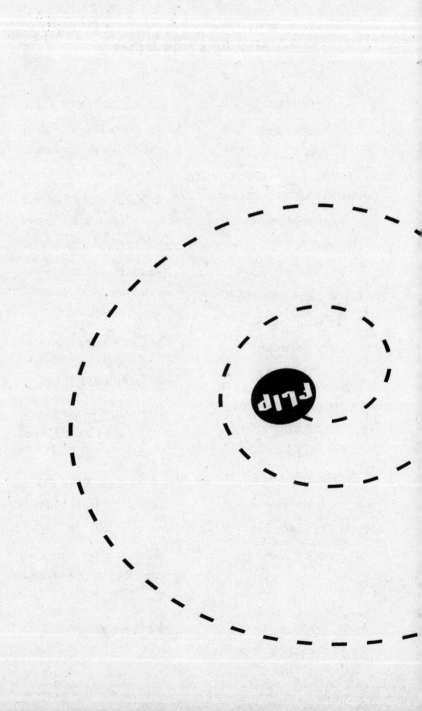

FLIP

David Lubar

STARSCAPE

A Tom Doherty Associates Book
New York

FLIP

A Tor Book
Published by Tom Doherty Associates, LLC
175 Fifth Avenue
New York, NY 10010

www.tor-forge.com

Tor® is a registered trademark of Tom Doherty Associates, LLC.

The Library of Congress has cataloged
the hardcover edition as follows:

Lubar, David.
    Flip / David Lubar.—1st ed.
        p. cm.
    ISBN 978-0-7653-0149-9 (hardcover)
    ISBN 978-1-4299-6234-6 (e-book)
    1. Twins—Fiction.   2. Peer pressure—Fiction.   3. Science fiction.
    PZ7.L96775 Fl 2003
    [Fic]

                                                    2003278250

ISBN 978-0-7653-7843-9 (trade paperback)

Tor books may be purchased for educational, business, or promotional use.
For information on bulk purchases, please contact the Macmillan Corporate
and Premium Sales Department at 1-800-221-7945, extension 5442,
or write to specialmarkets@macmillan.com.

First Edition: July 2003
First Trade Paperback Edition: March 2015

Printed in the United States of America

0   9   8   7   6   5   4   3   2   1

For Doug Baldwin, because

A. he's a good friend

B. he reads my rough drafts and gives me
great suggestions

C. he helped keep the wolf from the door

D. he doesn't take either of us too seriously

E. all of the above

ACKNOWLEDGMENTS

I need, first of all, to thank everyone at Tor for their support, and for their patience while I figured out how to write this book. That includes Tom Doherty, Kathleen Doherty, and Jonathan Schmidt, to name just a few.

Through the generosity of Tor, I had the privilege of speaking at a YALSA event in San Francisco on science fiction. I met a group of brilliant teens there, and later asked two of them to read a large chunk of this book at a point when I needed some fresh feedback. They both found the time to do this and to offer some excellent comments. Thank you, Jil Christian and David White. (If anyone wants to read the talk, it's posted on my Web site at www.davidlubar.com.)

Other folks were kind enough to read various drafts of this book and offer suggestions. They include Joelle Lubar, Alison Lubar, Doug Baldwin, Heather Baldwin, Fern Baldwin, Dian Curtis Regan, and Marilyn Singer. I am a lucky guy.

Nazareth, Pennsylvania
Early in the 21st century

Before

On Earth, they call Hollywood the entertainment capital of the world. In space, they call Nexula the entertainment hub of the universe. Like planet-hopping locusts, Nexulan talent scouts search the galaxies for new material. When they discovered the human race, they knew they'd found a winner. For eighteen months, a Nexulan production team gathered information about Earth's heroes and legends. They also created a spectacular ad to promote the resulting product.

Finally, their work done, the crew headed home, bringing with them a series of small silver disks. When a Nexulan, or any similar species, activated a disk, he'd experience great moments in the life of a legend.

Two hundred miles above the surface of the Earth, as the ship prepared to enter hyperspace, it collided with an orbiting wrench that had been dropped by a Russian technician during one of the early Mir missions.

The combined speed of the ship and the wrench ripped a gash in the main cargo compartment, spilling out the disks. The crew returned to Nexula with empty tentacles.

Most of the disks fell into the ocean. A handful of the disks and a gel-sphere recording of the ad ended up in the woods near Ferdinand Demara Middle School. If humans were like Nexulans, none of this would matter. But when a human activates a disk, he gets more than an experience.

He becomes a legend.

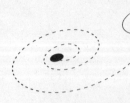

Still Before
and 200 Miles Below

The garlic-powder shaker was clogged. Ryan frowned and shook it harder. Nothing came out.

"Tap the bottom on the table," his sister, Taylor, said. "You need to dislodge the granules."

You need to dislodge your brain, Ryan thought. Ignoring Taylor's advice, he leaped from his seat and shot his arm down full speed. That worked. Sort of. The lid flew off, dumping a pile of garlic powder over his pizza.

"Crap." Ryan stared at the miniature mountain that rose from the cheese.

"Sit down," Mr. McKenzie said. "Do you have to ruin every meal?"

"Somebody has to," Ryan muttered. He picked up the slice and brushed it off. Grains of garlic ticked against his plate, but so much stuck to the piece that it looked like a sandy beach towel. Still standing, he reached for another slice.

"What—are—you—doing?" His father fired each word across the table like a shot from a large caliber pistol.

"Getting some pizza," Ryan said.

"Eat what you have, first. And sit down. This isn't a barn."

"But that one's got—"

"Eat it!" his father shouted, jumping to his feet so fast his chair toppled over.

Ryan turned to Mrs. McKenzie. Sometimes—rarely—she took his side. But not this time. "Listen to your father," she said.

He glanced at Taylor, who wouldn't look up from her food. *All out of brilliant advice?* It figured. She only had answers for things that didn't matter, like homework and tests.

Ryan knew his father wanted him to beg for another piece. No way. He sat and took a bite, flinching as his taste buds went into shock. He managed to choke down half the slice before the garlic won. "Can I go now?" he asked his mom, fighting the urge to gag.

She nodded, and Ryan headed up the stairs. Behind him, he heard his father say, "Hard to believe they're twins."

Bits of garlic crunched between his molars as he gritted his teeth. *I'm not the one who ruins everything.* He spent the rest of the evening in his room, reading one of the few books his parents hadn't taken away yet, then went to sleep.

Late at night, a powerful thirst woke Ryan. After he got a drink, he thought about starting his math homework, but quickly dropped the idea. It wouldn't make any difference.

I'm dead no matter what I do. School was like quicksand. With each step, he sank deeper. Ryan expected to be completely buried before he reached high school. He saw himself repeating eighth grade forever, like a poor imitation of a ghost, a doomed spirit who eventually became invisible to his teachers.

At least it was Friday. Just eight periods lay between him and freedom. He sighed as he thought about his classes. Social studies was the mental equivalent of a trip to the dentist. He didn't get algebra. English put him to sleep. Science, which should have been so cool, had turned into a mind-numbing series of biographies. Art was bearable. So was lunch. But gym was torture and wood shop was terror.

What's the point? Ryan gazed out his window at the dark sky above the treetops, as if an answer had been hidden there in a code known only to a lucky few. High up, a star flickered, then grew impossibly bright. Ryan watched as the star broke apart and the pieces fell to earth.

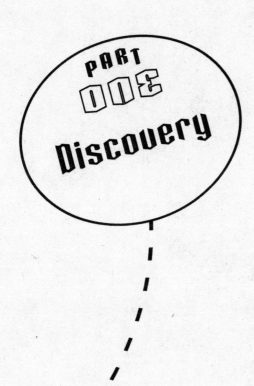

PART
ONE

Discovery

Speak roughly to your little boy,
And beat him when he sneezes;
He only does it to annoy,
Because he knows it teases.

—**Lewis Carroll**

Halfway into the Woods

Taylor shut off her alarm clock and blinked the bedroom into focus. As the morning light filled her eyes, the memory of a flash flittered through her mind. *There must have been some lightning last night,* she thought.

The slight chill of the hardwood floor felt nice against her bare feet when she shuffled down the hall to the bathroom. On the way, she paused by her brother's door long enough to knock and say, "Seven o'clock. Time for school, Ryan."

No answer. No surprise. They were twins, but far from identical. He was blond with blue eyes. Her hair and eyes were light brown. But the real differences lay beneath the surface. Ryan did everything at the last minute, if he did it at all. She finished every assignment as soon as possible. He dangled near the bottom of their class. She hovered at the top. He acted out every thought. She thought out every action.

Taylor knocked again on the way back from the bathroom. "Get up. You can sleep as late as you want tomorrow." Still no answer. *I tried.*

She dressed in the clothes she'd laid out the night before, checked her backpack to make sure she had everything ready, then sat at her desk and wrote in her journal until seven-thirty.

Yogurt, she decided as she capped her pen and closed her journal. That's what she usually had on Fridays. Blueberry. With one tablespoon of wheat germ. A good source of vitamin B.

After breakfast, Taylor left for school—allowing herself enough time to arrive fifteen minutes early, as always. She enjoyed the walk, especially now that spring was so close. The school was only eight blocks from her home, including the long stretch that bordered the park.

When she got there, she spotted a familiar figure wandering along the edge of the woods by the football field. Even from behind, Taylor recognized the black sweatshirt with the bright green alien face, the electric-blue sneakers with the dangling orange laces, and the blond hair in that ridiculous ponytail.

What's he doing? Taylor jogged around the side of the school and across the field. By the time she reached the woods, Ryan had disappeared among the trees, but she had no trouble following the snap of branches that marked his passage.

"Hey," she called when she caught sight of him.

"Hi," Ryan said. "What are you doing here?"

"What are *you* doing here?" Taylor asked. She glanced nervously over her shoulder in the direction of the school.

"Looking for the alien ship," Ryan said.

This wasn't even close to any of the thousand excuses she'd expected from him. "What alien ship?"

"The one that exploded over the woods. I saw it last night. Couldn't sleep after that. So I got out of bed early."

"Don't be absurd," Taylor said. "You saw lightning—probably a distant flash which you misinterpreted due to your overactive imagination. That's all."

"I'm not stupid," Ryan said. "I know what I saw. It wouldn't hurt for you to believe me once in a while. I saw a spaceship."

"Then you were dreaming." Taylor checked her watch. There was still plenty of time before school started.

"No way. I was awake. I had a killer thirst. Remember what happened at dinner?"

"Every detail, unfortunately." The scene was fresh in her mind, the newest entry in a collection she thought of as "Explosions at the McKenzie Dinner Table." Of course, if Ryan had listened to her, there wouldn't have been any trouble. All he had to do was tap the stupid shaker. But he never listened. It was like his brain was clogged.

"I got up for a drink of water. That's when I saw it. Had to be an alien ship. As long as you're here, you can help me look." Ryan waved an arm at the woods around them. "I'll bet we find pieces all over."

"You're wasting your time," Taylor said. It drove her crazy. He wouldn't spend five minutes on things that really mattered like homework or studying, but he'd squander hours chasing after some fantasy. "There aren't any alien spaceships."

"There's one less than there used to be," Ryan said. "That's for sure. Come on, help me look for stuff. If they're smart enough for space travel, they've got to have all kinds of equipment. You know—alien artifacts. And weapons. They'd definitely need protection against hostile earthlings. Wouldn't it be great if we found a disrupter beam?" Ryan squatted and fired at a nearby tree.

Taylor wondered which hostile earthling was Ryan's real target. A list of possibilities scrolled through her mind: Dad, Ms. Gelman, Coach Ballast, Mr. Zorn, Principal Guthrie, Billy Snooks. Maybe even her. The list, like the universe, was endlessly expanding.

While space was growing larger, time was growing shorter. She glanced at her watch again. "We'd better head back, or we'll be late."

Ryan shrugged. "So?"

"So we'll get in trouble." Taylor wasn't about to blow a hole in her perfect attendance record.

"I don't care." Ryan spun away from her and charged deeper into the woods.

"Travel between the stars is virtually impossible," Taylor called after him. "I learned all about that when I did my report for the science club last month." No answer. But she could hear him crashing around the underbrush. "Faster-than-light travel is prohibited by the laws of physics. If you maintain a sub-lightspeed velocity, it'll take forever to get anywhere. Okay, not technically forever, but well beyond the lifespan of any imaginable being. The nearest star is . . ." Taylor let it drop. She realized it was pointless trying to influence Ryan with facts.

If a physics lesson falls in a forest, and nobody listens, does it make a difference? With Ryan, Taylor had learned, nothing seemed to make a difference.

Taylor checked her watch again. *I should leave him. I should just go to school and let him wander through the woods all day.* She glanced toward the school, took two steps in that direction, then sighed, turned, and ran to catch up with her brother. "Come on!" she hollered. "Let's go."

He was standing still, staring down at the ground. *Now here's a curious anomaly. He's no longer a body in motion.* Maybe he was actually paying attention to her for once. "There aren't any interstellar spaceships," she said, resuming her lecture. "There aren't any aliens. And there aren't any artifacts."

"Really?" Ryan raised one eyebrow and gave her an odd smirk.

"Really."

"No artifacts?"

"None." Taylor was glad he was listening to her. There might be some hope for him after all.

"Then what's this?" Ryan asked, pointing at a bed of weeds near his feet.

Meanwhile

illy Snooks opened his eyes the slightest crack and checked across the room. The other bed was empty. No reason it wouldn't be. Adam had been gone for nearly three months, leaving nothing behind but a torn NASCAR poster and a thousand bad memories. He'd slunk off to an army base in Oklahoma, thanks to a judge who'd given him a choice between serving time or serving his country. Still, it was a hard habit for Billy to break. He'd been Adam's punching bag for as long as he could remember. He'd spent his whole life looking out of the corners of his eyes.

Seeing that he was safe, Billy sat up, arched his back, flexed his arms, and let out a satisfied groan. He loved the way his biceps bulged. *Rock solid,* he thought.

Across the room, his door inched open and his mother peeked in from the hallway. "Billy, do you want your breakfast now?"

"Yeah, sure," he said. It was weird the way she always seemed to know the exact second he got up. Almost like she waited there all morning.

She dashed off. Billy heard pans and dishes clattering in the kitchen, followed by the crack of eggs breaking. A couple of minutes later, his mother scurried back with a tray. "Ham 'n eggs, just the way you like," she said. "Fresh juice. I squeezed it myself. Biscuits and jelly, too."

He breathed in the sweet aroma of fried ham. "I think my clock's broke." It was almost time for school to start. Not that he minded missing a class or two.

"Your clock's just fine. You looked so tired last night, I turned the alarm off," his mother said, tucking the napkin around his neck. "You're a growing boy. And growing boys need lots of sleep. I'm sure your teachers will understand. I'll write you a nice note."

"They don't like me," Billy said. He shoveled a forkful of eggs into his mouth, then washed it down with half a glass of orange juice.

"Hush that nonsense," his mother said, reaching out to ruffle his hair. "Everyone likes you. You're my Billy Boy." She poured more juice for him.

Billy dug his spoon in the jar and plopped a glob of strawberry jelly on the open face of a steaming biscuit. As he lifted the biscuit to his mouth, the jelly quivered like a frightened child.

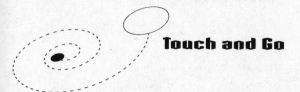

Touch and Go

Taylor stared at the shimmering glob. Bits of color darted beneath the surface like miniature tropical fish, and the whole glob quivered rhythmically as if someone was stamping hard on the ground nearby.

"It's from outer space," Ryan said.

"Sure. Absolutely." Taylor had heard more than enough wild fantasies for one day. "An entire spaceship explodes, and this is all that's left. One piece of gook the size of a golf ball. Good thinking, Ryan." She knelt for a closer look, taking care not to get her knees dirty. *Probably some kind of insect slime,* she thought. Bugs made all sorts of icky globs. Or it could be tree sap. That's how amber started out. Maybe even a fungus. Or a slime mold. For a second she imagined the thrill of discovering a new species of myxomycete. She'd probably be the youngest scientist who ever made such a find. She pushed aside a fern that was blocking her view.

"Hey, I saw it first," Ryan said, reaching over her shoulder to grab the glob.

"Don't touch it!" Taylor tried to block his arm but Ryan bumped her and she toppled forward. Her hand shot out and landed right on top of the glob.

"I said it's mine. Let go."

Taylor tried to let go. But the glob spread over her fingers, covering them with a flickering film that chilled her flesh like rubbing alcohol.

"Get it off!" She yanked her hand away and scuttled back. Too late. The film raced up her wrist and vanished beneath her sleeve. A cool tingle flowed past her elbow, then washed across her shoulder. A rainbow flashed above her hand as she raised it closer to her face.

"Ryan?" she cried. She saw that his hand was also engulfed in the flowing film. The coolness spread over her body and, worse, upward toward her head. It covered her neck and chin.

"No!" Taylor shouted. She slammed her mouth shut and fought the urge to scream again as the film invaded her lips, her eyes, her ears.

A crazy thought shot through her mind: *I've never seen the Grand Canyon.* There was so much she hadn't done. So much she wanted to do. She had her whole life planned out. This wasn't part of it.

The world turned black, silent, cold.

The cold, flowing film covered Ryan. Faint music drifted toward him through the darkness. *Cool,* he thought, turning his mind over to the sensations. The music grew louder. He realized it wasn't coming from the woods. It was coming from inside his head.

The music blared like he was surrounded by an orchestra of trumpets and violins. Light filled the space between his eyes and mind, swirling in formless colors. This was definitely cool. He wished his friend Ellis was here to share the fun instead of Taylor. Ellis would think this was great.

"You hear that?" he called.

No answer.

Ryan figured all of this was probably wasted on his sister. She didn't do well in new situations. She liked things to be the same all the time. Which was impossible. Stuff changed. It was changing right now for sure.

He forgot all about Taylor as a deep voice entered his consciousness, spewing a rapid stream of words.

They're new! They're stunning! They're unlike anything the universe has ever experienced. From the creative team that brought you Andromeda Adventures *and the smash hit series* Sensations of Sirius *comes the latest extravaganza of exotic aliens from unknown worlds.*

The swirling colors focused into an image. Ryan found himself face-to—*face?* with a giant worm. Dozens of waving tentacles rippled along the segmented body. Ryan agreed with the announcer—this was definitely an exotic alien.

The creature spoke from an opening near the bottom of its

middle segment. *Yes, friends. They're finally here. Legends of Earth. Our finest assortment ever.* An image of Earth, streaked with bands of clouds, appeared next to the creature.

You heard me right. Earth. Filled with unbelievably strange and alien life forms. They're amazing, they're amusing, they're virtually indescribable. And indescribably virtual. Once you've experienced them, you'll know what we mean.

Several of the tentacles braided together, then waved at a spot beneath the slowly spinning planet. As the trumpets went wild, a man with bulging muscles appeared, wearing an animal skin and gripping a club. Ryan smelled sweat, along with a musky animal odor and a whiff of blood. *Behold Hercules,* the voice announced. The tentacles whipped toward another spot. There stood Cleopatra, grasping a dark red fruit. The air filled with the scent of perfume. Ryan's mouth watered as the sharp flavor of pomegranate invaded his taste buds.

The next wave of the tentacles brought Robin Hood stabbing a slab of venison with his knife. Meat juices flowed across Ryan's tongue. *Wave.* Albert Einstein. *Wave.* Leonardo da Vinci. *Wave.* Billy the Kid, Amelia Earhart, Abraham Lincoln, Annie Oakley, Wolfgang Amadeus Mozart, Eric the Red. Each one was announced by name as dozens of smells, flavors, and sounds flooded Ryan's senses.

Yes. All these and hundreds more. Legends of Earth. The wildest creatures that ever walked on two feet or breathed through one nose.

A tentacle snapped toward Ryan, releasing a spinning disk the size of a quarter. It sailed forward, expanding until the shimmering surface filled the entire field of vision in his mind. The disk vanished with a pop, and he saw the creature again, along with all the legends. They waved at him and smiled. Lincoln winked. Cleopatra blew him a kiss. Mozart wiggled his ears, and Eric the Red did a trick with his thumb. The colors and shapes grew soft, then faded like a microscope image spun out of focus.

"Awesome," Ryan said. It was almost too cool for words.

Another voice, far less grand and impressive, but far more familiar, drifted in from near by. "What in the world . . . ?"

wesome . . ."

The sound of her brother's voice was like a beacon guiding Taylor back to reality. She blinked and stared at the woods that surrounded her. "What in the world . . . ?" The sounds and images that had tried to invade her mind were gone now. She'd managed to fight them off by giving her brain the Herculean task of alphabetizing the elements of the periodic table. During those awful moments, she'd squeezed her eyes so tight, her face hurt. But, by the time she'd reached molybdenum, she knew she'd won.

"Too cool," Ryan said. "That was better than when we went to the 3-D movie."

"Cool?" Taylor uncurled her fingers and looked at the crescents her nails had etched in her palms. "What are you talking about?"

"Didn't you see the ad?"

"I didn't see anything," Taylor said. *Nothing real.* She tried to think of a logical explanation for the incident. Maybe there'd been a chemical in the glob that produced hallucinations. Cautiously, she sniffed her fingertips. All she detected was a faint scent that reminded her of fresh laundry.

"We have to find some more of that globby stuff. And the disks they told us about. I bet they're way better than movies." Ryan dropped to his knees and began pawing through the weeds. "You going to stand there? You're always telling me to stick with things I start. Everyone's always telling me that. Well, I'm sticking with this. No matter how long it takes."

How long? "Oh my God." Taylor's stomach clenched as she

checked her watch. The rising wave of panic fell back when she saw she still had time to get to homeroom. But barely. "Let's go. The bell's about to ring."

Ryan shook his head. "No way. I'm tired of everyone telling me what to do. Mom, Dad, my teachers, and especially my know-it-all sister. I feel like a freakin' puppet."

"Come *on*. If you wait until after school, I'll help you look. Okay?" She'd promise anything just to get him moving.

"I'm looking now." Ryan crawled deeper into the bushes. "Hey, if a spaceship blew up, would all the stuff fall in one place, or would it spread out? Come on, you're the family brain. How about putting some of that knowledge to good use for once in your life?"

Taylor ignored the insult. "I'm not helping you until after school," she said, her attention focused on a familiar-shaped leaf near her feet. "And I'll give you a great reason to go inside."

"Like what?" Ryan asked.

"Like you should wash your hands right away because you've been digging through poison ivy."

"Oh crap!" Ryan yelled as he leaped to his feet and charged out of the woods. "I'm doomed!"

Taylor sighed. She had never seen her brother so anxious to get to school. She just wished it had been for the right reason.

Better Late than Clever

No need to rush, Billy thought as he strolled to school. He had a note. A block from home, he spotted a couple of dorks in business suits heading his way. Even from far off, he could read the signs in the way they moved. They acted like zebras when the lion shows up for dinner. *They're scared of me*, he thought. That was cool. Fear meant respect. He hadn't put in endless hours at the weight room because he liked how it smelled. He'd pumped all that iron to make himself into a human fortress. Unbeatable. Untouchable. Nobody worked harder. Nobody was tougher. Except maybe Ace. And Ace was five years older.

Wait 'til I'm eighteen. He'd have his own wheels by then, for sure. A white Ford truck, with a bed liner and a tool box. His own job. His own place. No more crap from anyone. Especially not teachers. The good life waited just down the road.

The dorks shifted wide of him on the curb side as they passed. Billy wondered what would happen if he shouted, "Boo!" *Probably wet their pants.* The thought made him smile. But the smile faded when he reached school.

In the office, the secretary didn't even bother to read the note. She handed him a slip of paper.

"What's this?" Billy asked.

"Saturday detention." She pointed to the clock. "You're nearly an hour late. Again."

"I got a note."

"You always have a note. It doesn't matter. You know the rules," she said. "It has to be a doctor's excuse."

I'll send you to the doctor. Sweet as it would be to see fear on her face, Billy kept his mouth shut. It wasn't worth the crap he'd have to deal with when she started screaming for the cops. That was one lesson Adam had never learned.

"Why are you standing there? Get to class," she said.

As Billy left the office, he thought about the guys in the suits. "Should have scared those dorks." Halfway down the hall he punched a locker hard enough to dent the metal. That felt so good he punched another.

S hoot," Taylor said as she struggled with the latch on her locker after school. The metal was dented. It looked like some idiot had whacked it with a sledge hammer.

When she finally got the door open, she grabbed her jacket and yanked her backpack free from the narrow space, then headed out front to wait for Ryan. As the crowd thinned, her friend Ariel appeared, trailing a small group of girls. *Oh great,* Taylor thought. *What's she doing with them?*

"Want to come over?" Ariel asked, stepping away from the pack to join Taylor. "We're going to hang out at my place."

"I can't." Taylor tried to read the faces of the girls. Kara, Tara, Danielle, and Tiffany. They looked bored, with that empty, pouting expression she'd seen on so many fashion models. "I have to help Ryan with something."

"Is it them?" Ariel whispered after the other girls had walked ahead. "Is that why you don't want to come?"

"No," Taylor said. She and Ariel had been best friends since kindergarten. Taylor still had clear memories of the first day of school, when she'd stood by the coat closet after her mom had left, studying all the unfamiliar faces. She didn't even have her brother there. Ryan was in a different class. She'd spotted another pair of nervous eyes in the far corner of the room. It was like discovering a magic mirror that reflected her own feelings. *Want to be friends?* she'd asked. *Sure,* the girl had answered. Taylor and Ariel. Friends forever.

But things had changed this year. They didn't get together to study like they used to, or walk across town to the library to work on papers. Ariel had even talked about trying out for cheerleading next fall, though they'd planned for years to play soccer together when they got to high school. And Ariel had started hanging around at the fringes of the popular crowd.

"Come on, Ariel," Kara called. Her expression shifted from bored to annoyed. "Let's go."

"I'll be right there," Ariel said, speaking over her shoulder to Kara. She reached out toward Taylor, but her fingers stopped short of Taylor's sleeve. "You sure?" she asked. "It'll be fun."

Taylor nodded. "I'm sure. Honest. I really do have to help—" She didn't get a chance to finish her sentence.

"Ryan has detention," Ellis Izbecki said as he stumbled down the steps and dashed over to Taylor. "He wanted me to let you know. As soon as he gets out, we can look for the spaceship."

"He *told* you?" Taylor asked through clenched teeth, tilting her head back so she could look up at Ellis, who was the tallest kid in the eighth grade. He reminded Taylor of a stick figure. The fact that portions of his uncombed red hair usually stuck straight up in the air added to the effect.

"Spaceship?" Ariel's confused gaze bounced from Ellis to Taylor.

"Ryan told me all about it," Ellis said. "Ryan tells me everything. And, if anything ever happened in my incredibly boring life, I'd sure tell him. But you know me. Ellis the Uneventful. My life is dull, dull, dull. I could write my biography on a grain of sand. If my life was any less interesting, I probably wouldn't exist. But things will get a lot more exciting when we find the spaceship. Did I mention that my life was dull?"

Ariel grabbed Taylor's arm. "What spaceship?"

"There's no spaceship," Taylor said, laughing nervously. "You know Ryan. It's just some stupid joke." The last thing she needed was to have the whole school find out her brother believed in aliens. Especially when people seemed determined to swallow the myth that all twins were alike in every way. *Ryan's crazy. So Taylor must be crazy, too.*

"Arie*lllll*," Kara called in a voice that dripped irritation. "We're *going*." She glared in their direction, standing with one hand on her hip and her head cocked to the side. The pose reminded Taylor of a mother trying to extract her toddler from the toy aisle at a discount store.

Ariel shuffled a step toward Kara, then turned back to look at Taylor.

"Go ahead," Taylor told her. "This thing with Ryan is just a wild waste of time. I'm only tagging along to keep him out of trouble. That's me—the perpetual nanny. I'll tell you all about it later. I promise."

"Great. I'll call you tonight." Ariel rushed away.

As the group moved off, Taylor heard the word *loser* drift her way in Kara's cutting voice.

"Airhead," Taylor muttered.

"This is just too awesome," Ellis said.

"You didn't tell anyone else, did you?" Taylor could picture him running down the hall shouting *"The sky is falling!"*

Ellis shook his head. "Nope. Wouldn't matter if I did. Nobody listens to me. Ellis the Unheard. I'm just background noise. Human static. Audible wallpaper. Talk, talk, talk. You think we can find some of those disks? It would be really extraordinary. I'd love to watch a Viking movie in my head. Do you suppose that's how it works?" He flexed one skinny arm, then shouted, *"Ellis the Red!"*

"Shh." Taylor glanced around to make sure people weren't staring at her.

"Relax," Ellis said. "Nobody is tuned to my frequency. I could stand here and shout all day. Watch this, I'll prove it." He

backed a step away from her and yelled, "Hey, I found a hundred dollar bill! Anyone lose some money?"

Taylor realized nobody even glanced in his direction.

"See? It's a rare talent. I think it expands to cover anyone I'm
talking to. So tell me all about the disks."

"There aren't any disks," Taylor said. "It's just Ryan's imagination. Even if there were disks, they'd be useless. Think about
it. What if someone on another planet found a DVD or something? They couldn't do anything with it. Right? Not without
a disk player."

Taylor didn't get an answer from Ellis. At that moment, he
was busy turning from Ellis the Red into Ellis the Chicken. "Oh
no. Hide me," he squawked, dropping into a crouch by her side.
With his long arms and legs, that was about as effective as trying to hide a fistful of uncooked spaghetti inside a thimble.

Taylor spun around as a large shadow fell across the walkway at her feet.

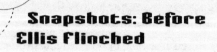

Kara frowned at Ariel. "I can't believe you kept me waiting."

"Sorry," Ariel said.

"Were you trying to make me look stupid? I had to call you *twice.* Maybe it was a mistake to let you hang out with us."

Ariel lowered her head. "I said I was sorry."

"You know who stands around waiting for people?" Kara asked. "Losers. That's who." *Like that pathetic McKenzie girl.* She glared over her shoulder and called out, "Loser." Then she turned back to Ariel and smiled. "Hey, I'm glad you understand. I'm sure you wouldn't want someone to keep you waiting around, either."

"I guess not," Ariel said.

"What was so important back there, anyhow?" Kara asked.

Click

Ryan couldn't believe he'd gotten detention. He'd made it to homeroom in time, even though he'd stopped to scrub his hands. But during first period, when he'd tried to tell Ellis about the spaceship, Ms. Gelman had warned him to be quiet. And then she'd slapped him with a detention. She never missed a chance to punish him.

He'd tried to make a deal with the teacher in charge of detention. "Look, can I come on Monday? I'll even do a double detention. Okay?"

The teacher pointed to a desk. "Just sit down and be quiet. I don't like being here any more than you do. Four years of college, two years of graduate school, and they have me baby-sitting a bunch of delinquents. Besides, there's no such thing as a double detention."

Ryan sat and watched the clock.

Click
Billy threw his English paper in the garbage on the way out of class. He couldn't believe his teacher had given him an F. To make things worse, the teacher had bored everyone with a stupid essay by some idiot girl from another class.

"That's the sort of work you all should strive for," the teacher had said when he pinned the paper to the bulletin board.

On his way out, Billy glared at the perfectly formed letters, lined up in neat rows of words that didn't look anything like his own messy scrawl. The name *Taylor McKenzie* sat dead center under the title. He'd never heard of her. Probably some goody-goody smart kid who sucked up to all her teachers and brought home wonderful grades. Billy hoped something bad would happen to her.

As he left the school, he decided that something bad was definitely going to happen to someone. He just hoped he could find at least one kid who'd fight back. It was a lot more fun that way.

Taylor had no trouble spotting the source of Ellis's panic. Billy Snooks rumbled out the front door, moving like a human bulldozer through the scattering clusters of kids, his muscle-bound arms swinging wide of his sides in a way that reminded Taylor of a cheap plastic action figure.

Behind her, Ellis scrunched into a tighter bundle. It didn't make any difference. Snooks seemed able to smell fear as easily as flies could smell road kill.

"Hey, freak." Snooks gave Ellis a hard shove on the shoulder. Ellis responded with an ear-piercing yelp as he flopped to the ground and sprawled out like a pile of scattered pickup sticks. Snooks shook his head in disgust and lumbered off, obviously in search of more challenging targets.

"Leave him alone, you big bully!"

That's what Taylor wanted to shout. But the words froze somewhere between her brain and her throat.

"I hate that guy," Ellis said as he unfolded himself back to his natural height. "Snooks is the human equivalent of air pollution. No, make that water pollution."

"I hate him, too," Taylor said. "I wish he'd go away, and take his whole gang with him." She shuddered at the thought of those thugs. Some of the crowd who hung out with Snooks were in high school. A couple were older, including a guy called "Ace," who was even tougher than Snooks. According to the rumors, Ace had spent time in prison. Taylor had never seen him up close, but she'd heard he was scary looking.

"Hey, what's the difference between Billy Snooks and a gorilla?" Ellis asked. "Give up? The gorilla's almost human. What's the difference between Billy Snooks and a big steaming pile of dog crap? The crap started out as something useful. And crap doesn't smell nearly as bad. Hey, I thought of another one . . ."

As Ellis talked, Taylor passed the time by filling out her application for the summer engineering program at the Huntington Museum. Her science teacher had given her the information after class, and it sounded perfect. The program would also look good when she applied to college. Just as she finished the last section on the bottom of the page, a handful of detention victims escaped through the front doorway of the school.

"Where's Ryan?" Ellis asked as the last of the students emerged.

"A familiar question," Taylor said. She scanned the three-story building without finding any clues hidden within the windows. "Maybe he got double detention."

Ellis gave her a puzzled look. "Do they have that?"

"Probably not, but they might invent it just for Ryan."

The instant detention ended, Ryan rushed from the classroom. He was eager to get going, but he needed to make one quick stop. As he passed the empty science lab, he ducked inside and grabbed a pair of tongs from a drawer. His parents constantly complained that he never planned ahead. That wasn't true. When it came to important stuff, he liked to be prepared. The sad truth was that most things his parents cared about weren't very important.

"You okay?" Ryan asked when he got outside. He noticed that Ellis's face was redder than usual.

"Yeah. I'm fine," Ellis said. "I just stepped in some dog crap."

"Snooks," Taylor said.

"Forget about him. We've got adventures awaiting us." Ryan headed around the side of the school.

"Try not to touch any more plants with three shiny leaves," Taylor said when they reached the trees. "Okay?"

"Don't worry. I learned that lesson." Even though he'd scrubbed his hands, Ryan could feel them starting to itch.

"Poison ivy?" Ellis asked. He froze in mid-step. "Don't tell me there's poison ivy here. I'm really allergic to it. Ellis the Itchy. I blow up like a pumpkin on steroids. I look like the loser in a heavyweight fight."

"Relax," Taylor said. "Just follow me and you'll be okay."

Ryan followed Taylor, too, until they reached the area where he'd discovered the glob.

"What exactly are we looking for?" Ellis asked.

"Anything unusual," Ryan said as he dropped to his knees. "If it's not green, check it out."

Ellis laughed. "And if it's brown, flush it down."

"That's gross," Taylor said.

"Sorry. Once a thought leaves my mind, there's not much I can do to stop it. It's sort of like a verbal diarrhea. Oops—there I go again. Excuse me while I clean my mouth." Ellis pushed a finger against his nose and made a flushing sound.

"Seriously," Taylor warned, "be careful. Don't touch anything weird."

"Now you sound like my mom," Ellis said, poking in the bushes with a stick. "But you're right. It could take control of our minds." He dropped the stick and backed away from the bush. "We could end up frozen here while some movie plays over and over in our heads."

"Whoa!" Ryan shouted when he spotted a flash of gold amongst the leaves. But when he got closer he saw it was just the wrapper from a chocolate bar. "Never mind," he said, but that wasn't necessary. It was pretty obvious nobody was paying any attention to him.

"Or what if it's real scary, and you can't stop it?" Ellis said. "That would be like getting trapped in a haunted house."

Ryan crawled to the other side of the trail and let out a loud sigh. "Uh, hello? You going to help, or just stand there?"

But Ellis seemed to need to list every possible way the disks could destroy him. "Imagine if you can feel it? I mean, it would be great to fly a jet or walk on the moon. But I wouldn't want to be some guy from the French Revolution who ends up in the guillotine." He made a swishing sound, like a falling blade, then moved his head up and down as if he was watching a ball bounce away. "*Boing, boing, booooiiiiinnnng, splat.*"

"Ellis, none of that is going to happen," Ryan said.

"Wait," Ellis said, rushing over to Ryan. "What if it's a trap? Maybe the disks are some kind of alien fishhook. They could snag our minds and drag us off. Ellis the Abducted." He hooked his lip with an index finger and started thrashing around like a fish on a line, then grabbed his butt with both hands. "Man, I don't want some alien inserting probes into me. That's gotta hurt."

Ryan spotted another glimmer. He dropped to his stomach and crawled carefully under a thorn bush.

"Stop scaring yourself," Taylor said to Ellis. "We aren't going to find anything. Whatever Ryan saw when he touched the glob was just his imagination. If objects really had fallen from outer space, most likely they would have burned up in our atmosphere. Besides, these woods are huge. No way any ship could crash without strewing wreckage over a vast area. The odds against success are literally astronomical. There's no way we'll find anything—"

"I found something!" Ryan shouted. *I knew it,* he thought as he wriggled forward. A silver disk the size of a quarter lay half hidden in the leaves.

"Don't touch it," Taylor warned.

"Don't, don't, don't," Ryan said, mocking Taylor's nervous tone. "Maybe when you grow up you can get a job as a *Don't Walk* sign." He reached under his sweatshirt and pulled the tongs from his rear pocket. "*Don't* worry. I came prepared." He pushed the tongs through the branches and clamped them on the disk. Then he backed out from the bush.

"Careful," Taylor said.

Ryan had heard all the warnings he could take. "Look out!" he shouted, shoving the tongs toward her face.

Taylor squealed and jumped backwards. "Not funny," she said.

"Sorry," Ryan said, though he couldn't keep from grinning. She'd really gotten some good air time.

"You could have poked her eye out," Ellis told him.

"Like this?" Ryan asked, jabbing the tongs at Ellis.

Ellis yelped and leaped away.

"Knock it off," Taylor said as she stepped back over to Ryan. "Is the other side blank, too?"

"I don't know." Ryan turned the tongs over. Tiny, irregular markings covered the surface of the disk. *Oh my God.* Ryan's scalp tingled as he realized what he was looking at. "Alien writing. Fantastic."

"Or Japanese," Taylor told him, "or ancient Greek, or a Russian code, or just about anything. It could be random scratches. For that matter, it's probably something you put here for a joke."

Why did she have to try to spoil everything? "It's alien writing," Ryan said. "It has to be. And we're the first Earthlings to ever see any. Got something to carry it in?"

"I thought you were prepared," Taylor said.

"Jeez, Taylor, just shut up and give me your backpack."

"Hey, you don't have to get nasty." Taylor slipped off her backpack and unzipped the small pocket in front. "Here," she said, pulling the opening wider. "I never use this part, anyhow."

Ryan dropped the disk into the pocket. "Let's keep looking," he said, clicking the tongs together a couple of times. "There could be tons of them. There could be all kinds of other stuff, too." He still hoped to find a spacesuit, or some awesome alien artifacts.

They searched as far as the creek, then doubled back toward the school. By the time the sun settled behind the high hills to the west, they'd found, according to Ryan's count, fifty-one disks.

"I told you there'd be disks," Ryan said. "That proves I wasn't imagining anything."

"You probably saw them this morning, before you touched the glob," Taylor said. "Maybe you didn't even notice them, but your subconscious did. The mind works that way, you know. It's called 'subliminal suggestion.' Besides, why didn't we find anything else? No wreckage. No big pieces of mangled hull. Explain that, if you can."

"Biodegradable saucers?" Ellis guessed. "They could be ecological aliens. There's probably this big triangle on the bottom of the saucer with a number in it, like on a ketchup bottle. Except the number's probably higher."

"I don't care what we didn't find," Ryan said. "The cool thing is what we did find. We've got alien disks. Come on, let's take them home."

Billy's Club

Billy failed to find anyone willing to put up a decent fight. No problem. He knew someone would get in his face sooner or later. He went home and spent a couple of hours in his backyard, working on the dirt bike he was rebuilding, then decided to head toward the south side of town. He couldn't do much more, anyhow, until he bought a chain-and-sprocket kit. And he couldn't do that until he got some money.

"You're so good with your hands," his mom said as he put away his tools. "You should think about being a doctor. Can I make you a sandwich before you leave?"

"No thanks." Billy wiped his hands on a rag, tossed it on the lawn, then stepped toward the side gate.

"Adam called," his mom said. She picked up the rag, folded it, and put it in the pocket of her apron.

"That's nice." Billy lifted the latch. He really didn't care about anything Adam had to say.

"He's out of the army."

Billy froze. "He's out?"

"He hurt his back. Poor boy. He's a lot more fragile than you. I never should have let him join up. I'm sure I could have explained everything to the judge if they'd let me. Adam's such a good boy. People just don't understand him. I guess because he's so big."

"When's he coming home?" Billy asked.

"Not right away. That's why he called. He needed money to help get a place to stay. He told me he likes it out there."

"Super," Billy said. He brushed a drop of sweat from his forehead with the back of his hand. *As long as he stays there.* It figured Adam would fake being hurt to get out of the army. He'd never done a bit of work around the house. *Damn.* Billy kicked open the gate.

"Have a good time." His mother waved cheerfully as Billy walked away.

He found Jimmy, Rick, and Lance on Filmore Street outside the 7-Eleven.

"What's up?" Lance asked, pulling a bag of chips from under his jacket.

"Nothing." Billy took the bag and turned toward the YMCA, which was on the other side of town. He didn't need to say anything. They'd follow him. That's the way it was. If he told Lance to walk out in the road with his eyes closed, Lance would do it. Jimmy and Rick, too. They'd do anything he said. They respected him. In return, he protected them. That was the leader's job. Nobody messed with his friends.

They rounded the corner near the park. Three kids were coming their way. *Runts,* Billy thought gloomily. Not worth the effort. He had more important things to deal with.

"You seen Johnny around?" Billy asked. "He owes me twenty bucks."

"Not since last week," Lance said.

"You got Johnny's number?" Billy asked.

"Yeah." Lance told him the number.

Billy felt in his pocket for a pencil. Nothing. Did that idiot expect him to remember the number?

A Pack of Trouble

Taylor zipped the front pocket of her backpack, then slipped a strap over her left shoulder. *That was a waste of time,* she thought as the three of them left the woods.

"This is awesome. We should call the FBI," Ellis said. "No, wait. The FBI is for stuff inside the country. Right? The CIA is for foreign stuff. Are aliens foreign? I'll bet there's some special secret group for outer space."

" 'Men in Black,' " Ryan said.

"Yeah," Ellis nodded. "Guys like that. A top-secret government agency. We should call them. But we can't if they're secret. I mean, it's not like they'd be in the phone book. What do you think we should do?"

"I don't think we should tell anyone," Ryan said.

"I promised I'd tell Ariel what I was doing," Taylor said.

"Real promise?" Ryan asked. "Or was it like 'I promise I'll pick up my dirty laundry'?"

Taylor wasn't sure what kind of promise it had been. Until recently, anything she said to Ariel would have been as binding as a sacred oath. But their relationship had changed and Taylor hadn't figured out the new rules yet. Besides, there really wasn't anything to tell.

Past the park, Taylor spotted Billy Snooks and three other thugs cruising toward them. "I'll bet they're not on their way to a tea party," she said. She noticed Ellis's eyes had filled with panic, like a bunny that had hopped into the path of a sabretooth tiger.

Relax, Taylor told herself. *Just keep walking and they'll leave us alone.* But her confident expression masked a fear that she suddenly had morphed into something that dwelled near the low end of the food chain.

Ellis groaned. "We are so toast."

Ryan was several paces in front of Taylor and Ellis. He didn't seem concerned about Snooks and his buddies. Taylor squeezed in front of Ellis, like a sheepdog herding a lamb away from a dangerous cliff.

"You got Johnny's phone number?" she heard Snooks bark to his buddy. His voice was deep and hoarse, like the growl of a large carnivore.

"Yeah." One of the others told him a number.

Taylor jumped. There was a smack like an ax hitting a tree. Snooks had whacked the kid on the shoulder. "I can't remember that!" he growled. "Write it down." The three boys were just ahead of them now. Taylor edged close to the curb, nearly forcing Ellis into the street as the thugs kept jabbering.

"Ouch," the boy whined, rubbing his shoulder. "I ain't got no pencil. You got a pencil?"

"No. And I ain't got no paper."

"Me either."

Idiots. Taylor would never even think of leaving home without a pencil or a notepad. But that was his problem, not hers. She felt the muscles in her back relax as Snooks lumbered past her down the sidewalk. She took a slow, deep, relieved breath. *We made it,* she thought.

Before she could even exhale, a sharp tug on her shoulder nearly yanked her off her feet.

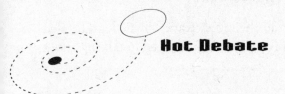

Hot Debate

What a hunk." Kara gazed down at a gorgeous photo of her favorite actor in Ariel's copy of *Teen Stars*. "As my mom says, he could sweep me right off my feet."

"He could sweep me anywhere," Tiffany said.

Kara put the magazine in her bag. "You mind if I take this?"

"I guess not," Ariel said.

"Great. Hey, you know who's really hot?"

"Who?" Ariel asked.

"Ryan," Kara said. "Except for that ponytail. If he got a haircut, he'd be truly delicious." She licked her lips, then made a kissing sound.

"Yeah," Tara said. "But it sure doesn't run in the family. His sister's such a loser."

"One of them must be adopted." Kara hated the way that girl always sucked up to her teachers.

"She's so weird," Tara said. "Probably lives in the library. Bet she asks for books for her birthday."

"Some day her head's going to explode," Tiffany said. The girls giggled in agreement, except Ariel.

What's with her? Kara thought. She stared at Ariel. "I'll bet Taylor still plays with dolls."

Ariel didn't answer.

"Probably plays house, too," Tiffany said.

"You aren't planning to hang out with losers like her next year, are you?" Kara asked. "They'll drag you down in high school."

Ariel bit at her lip and shrugged. Kara frowned, and rolled her eyes. Fine. She really was more interested in talking about herself anyway.

"Who's got a mirror?"

Ripped Off

"Hey!" Taylor shouted as she spun around. Whatever else she'd planned to say died in her throat as she found herself face to face with Billy Snooks.

Next to her, Ellis let out a high-pitched yelp that sounded frighteningly like a Yorkshire terrier getting stomped.

"Where's the pencils?" Snooks asked. He had wrestled the pack roughly off Taylor's shoulders and was reaching for the front pocket.

"Other pocket," Taylor said. She didn't want him pawing through everything. Taylor liked to keep her backpack as neat as possible. "There's a memo pad, too." She hated the way her voice trembled. *Just give him what he wants.* Maybe he'd take a piece of paper and a pencil, and that would be the end of the problem.

But Snooks carried the pack into the park, heading for the benches in the center section where the main paths from the four corners met.

"That's mine," Taylor called after him. She'd tried to shout, but the words left her mouth with no more force than a handful of thrown grass. "Mine . . . ," she said again, more quietly.

She turned back toward Ellis, who'd grown as pale as overcooked pasta. "I'd love to smash him," she said.

"Me too," Ellis said.

"Someday, somebody is going to tear him up. I just hope I'm there to see it. And you know what? I don't care if that brings me down to his level." She'd happily visit the basement of human emotions long enough to see Snooks stomped, and then crawl back up to a more civilized level.

"We need to get the pack right now," Ryan said. "What if he finds the disks?"

Taylor shook her head. "He'll leave it when he's done." But the thought of Snooks trashing her notebooks sent a wave of panic through her. She kept everything so carefully organized.

"If I can get him to leave the backpack, can you grab it?" Ryan asked.

"I guess . . ." Taylor didn't see how that could happen. There was no way Ryan could get Snooks to do anything.

Ryan had no plans to tear up Snooks, or to give Snooks a chance to tear him up. "Get ready to grab the pack," he said. "I'll meet you back home."

He hoped Taylor could handle her part. She seemed sort of stunned. So did Ellis, who was clutching a street sign, welding himself to the pole as if they'd been joined since birth. "Why don't you go on ahead to my house," Ryan said. "I might need you there." He knew this didn't make sense, but he wanted to give Ellis an excuse to leave.

"Good thinking." Ellis hurried off.

Ryan figured it wouldn't be smart to approach Snooks on the lighted part of the path. Instead, he snuck along the darkened side of the park by the old tennis courts. The net was long gone, but someone had built a ramp last summer out of scrap plywood. Ryan had spent a lot of time there before his parents took away his skateboard. His friends usually hung out there, too. Unfortunately, none of the skaters were around right now. Not that it mattered. Ryan wasn't planning to start a fight with Snooks. For that, he'd need a whole army.

When he reached the end of the fence by the tennis courts, he cut across the old playground, angling toward the benches. There wasn't much time. If those thugs opened the front pocket of the backpack, he knew he'd never see the disks again.

Just be careful, Ryan reminded himself. He had no desire to become a hero.

Taylor watched Ryan stroll past the tennis courts and cut across the carpet of wood chips that surrounded Old Rottensides. Years ago, the town had built a play area with slides, ladders, and climbing nets. Once, it had looked like a ship, complete with a mast and a big wooden wheel. White letters on the prow said, "S.S. Happy Time." They'd never taken care of it, and now everything was falling apart, earning the ship a new name in the process. A large piece of plywood from the side had already been dragged off to the tennis courts, leaving a gaping hole.

Taylor tried to guess Ryan's plan, but quickly gave up. His mind worked so differently from hers that he might as well have fallen from a spaceship himself.

"Oh no. Don't do that," she groaned as Snooks opened her backpack and dumped the contents of the main compartment onto the concrete pathway. He tossed the backpack aside, where it crumpled to the ground like an empty cocoon, and ripped a page from one of Taylor's notebooks. Even from a distance, the sound of tearing paper made her flinch.

The sun had set, and the park was deep in shadows. Two of the three lights near the benches were broken. The third flickered weakly, casting barely enough light for Taylor to pick out Ryan in the darkness.

He was ten or fifteen yards from the benches now. "Hey ugly!" he shouted at Snooks. "Did your mother have you in the zoo or were you born in the wild?"

Oh no! Taylor couldn't believe Ryan had mentioned Snooks's mother. That was definitely over the line.

Snooks and his pals tumbled from the bench like a load of boulders bouncing off a dump truck. As Ryan spun away and dashed across the grass, his flapping ponytail reminded Taylor of a dancing snake. Beneath it, the alien face on his sweatshirt, caught in the flickering lamplight, seemed to smirk at his pursuers.

In an instant, Ryan was swallowed by the shadows beyond the pool of light. The scene reminded Taylor of an antelope fleeing a pack of jackals. Win, and you get to live another day. Lose, and you're an unhappy meal.

Fear Itself

I should have *stayed,* Ellis thought. Just once, he'd like to do something brave. Stand up for himself. Or if not brave, at least not so afraid. All his life, he'd scurried away from danger. Never toward it.

"Ellis the Pathetic," he sighed as he shuffled along the sidewalk.

Voices to his right startled him. Across the street, a group of chirping girls—Kara and her crew—strutted down the front porch of a house and jostled their way into the passenger seats of a Volvo that waited for them at the curb. *Ariel's house,* Ellis thought, remembering how she'd gone off with that group after school.

Ellis wasn't sure who was scarier, Billy Snooks or Kara Henkle. Maybe Kara. She could tear him apart with a glance. Any damage Snooks inflicted on his victims would eventually heal. Even the ugliest bruise fades over time. Kara's daggers stayed in place forever. He'd seen her mock one girl last week for wearing the wrong brand of jeans. Kara hadn't let up until the girl was sobbing. For all her money, for all her clothes and friends and fancy hairstyles, for all her surface beauty with its layers of expensive makeup, Ellis didn't think she was very pretty. Not that his vote counted. Most of the guys in the school chased after her.

His brother had told him life got better as you got older. Right now, Jake was backpacking through South America. Ellis's sister, Lisa, was in vet school. She seemed happy.

I guess two out of three isn't bad, he thought.

A half block later, he spun around as he heard footsteps racing toward him. His heart beat like a rabbit's.

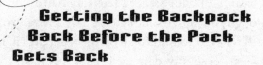

Getting the Backpack
Back Before the Pack
Gets Back

s prey and predators disappeared beyond a hedge, Taylor remembered she had her own role to play. She rushed to the bench, swept up the books and papers from the ground, and shoved everything into her backpack. This was one moment when neatness and organization did not count. In her haste she almost missed the application, which had fallen under the bench. She grabbed it, zipped up the backpack, then raced off, taking the long way around the park to avoid any chance of bumping into Snooks.

"It's not worth it," she said to herself as her brain invented a dozen different scenes of Snooks destroying her brother—ripping Ryan the way he'd ripped her notebook. Ryan shouldn't have risked getting hurt for some stupid disks.

When Taylor cut over to Mayhew Street, she spotted a kid walking along with his head slumped down and his hands in his pockets. Ellis. Even a deep slouch couldn't disguise him. He kicked at a pebble, missed it, kicked another, missed that one, too, then finally connected with a third one, sending it skittering into the road. As she jogged toward him, he spun and let out another of his unmistakable yelps. "Oh my God!" he gasped, clasping his chest. "You scared me. I thought it was them."

"Take it easy," Taylor said. "We're okay. But I'm worried about Ryan. He got them to chase him."

"Snooks is chasing Ryan?"

Taylor nodded.

"Then he's dead," Ellis said. "That's all there is to it. They caught him. They killed him. You're now officially an only child."

"Thanks," Taylor said. "I feel way better."

Though she didn't completely share Ellis's grim outlook, she was still relieved to find Ryan on the front porch. He didn't seem to have suffered any damage during his dash to freedom. He wasn't even breathing heavily. "Hey, you got it. Good job," he said. "I'll tell you something—those guys can't run at all. They were pathetic. I had to keep slowing down so I wouldn't lose them. It was like playing tag with a two-year-old."

"Are you crazy?" Taylor slammed the backpack to the ground. "Are you out of your mind? Do you have the slightest idea what you did?"

"What?" Ryan's expression told her he didn't have a clue.

"You went too far. You're doomed! Billy Snooks is going to smash you."

"You think so?" Ryan asked.

"Why did you have to say something about his mother? Do you want to die?" Taylor figured Ryan might as well have spat in the bully's face. Snooks would never let him get away unpunished, especially since the insult happened in front of his fellow thugs. "Don't you know those words are guaranteed to start a fight? What were you thinking?"

"There wasn't a whole lot of time for thinking." Ryan leaned forward and patted the backpack. "And it worked, right? Besides, he'll forget all about it by Monday."

"His brain's not *that* small," Taylor said. "You are so doomed. Is he in any of your classes?"

"Nope," Ryan said. "I'd bet he doesn't even know who I am."

"A risky bet," Taylor said. She tried to calculate the odds. Four different elementary schools fed students into the middle school. There were too many factors involved to make a good estimate.

"Doomed," Ellis moaned. "You're going to need bodyguards. You're going to need an army. This is big trouble. Your life is over. You can't even risk going to the boys' room now. If he catches you alone, you're dead. You're going to have to carry around your own little toilet, like the ones they take camping. Maybe you can get one with wheels so you can roll it down the hall."

Ellis stuck one hand back and leaned forward like he was pulling a heavy wagon. An instant later, he abandoned the pantomime. "Oh no . . ." His eyes grew wide. "No . . ."

"What's wrong?" Ryan asked.

"Do you think he knows I'm your friend? Oh man, I'm probably doomed, too. I'll bet he's searching for us right now. He's going to turn me into an organ donor." Ellis scanned the street in both directions with rapid, jerky head motions, doing a perfect imitation of a terrified parrot.

"Let's get inside," Taylor said. She grabbed the backpack and carried it into the house. "We're home," she called.

"Dinner's in an hour," her mom called back. "Your father had to work late." The familiar aroma of beef stew drifted through the air, the sixth meal of a fourteen-day menu cycle her mom had devised. Every second Friday, they had beef stew.

Taylor went to the kitchen and pulled the application from her backpack. "Can you sign this? It's for a summer program at the museum."

"Sure." Her mom signed the form, then handed it to her. "I wish your brother had some ambition."

He does, Taylor thought, remembering Ryan's obsession with searching the woods. *But never for anything important.* "Thanks, Mom."

Ellis and Ryan were waiting for her at the top of the stairs.

"I could change my appearance," Ellis said, still plotting survival techniques. "Maybe I should dye my hair. I've heard that people treat you nicer if you're blond."

"Yeah, that would make you less noticeable," Taylor said. She could just picture it: instead of a matchstick, he'd look like one of those extra long cottonswabs that her doctor kept in a tall glass jar next to the tongue depressors and tissues.

In her room Taylor dumped the disks onto her desk. They jangled like a slot machine jackpot. *No prizes here,* she thought, making sure not to touch them. After her experience with the glob, she didn't want any more surprises.

She opened the main part of her backpack and carefully transferred her books and papers to her bed. With a grateful sigh of relief, she realized everything was there. Of course, everything would have to be reorganized, but that was no problem. It could even be fun.

"Now what?" Ellis asked.

"I'll get my magnifying glass. I'd like to do a closer analysis of the disks." She opened the door of her closet. She kept small scientific instruments in the plastic box with the purple lid, right next to the green-lidded box that held her fossils and rocks. She turned back just in time to see Ryan reach toward her desk.

"This is the best way to find out," he said as he plucked a disk from the pile.

Ryan clutched the disk between his thumb and forefinger. The cold metal warmed quickly at his touch. "Amazing!" He jerked his body like he'd been jolted with a massive surge of electricity, then grabbed his forehead with his free hand and staggered backward.

Taylor slid to a halt. "Drop it, Ryan!"

An evil grin spread across Ryan's face as he returned her stare. "I am Alkazar, the Conqueror of the Universe! I must wipe my enemies from this puny planet." He spun toward Ellis and let out a villainous laugh. "*Mwwaahhhh hhhaaaa hhhaaa hhaaaa.* Die, Earthling!"

With a yelp, Ellis dived behind Taylor's bed, wedging himself between the side of the mattress and the wall.

Ryan turned his attention toward Taylor. "You cannot escape me."

She backed away. Fear flickered across her face. But the expression didn't last. It was replaced almost immediately by annoyance. "Knock it off, Ryan."

"Call me Alkazar!" he demanded, taking a stiff-legged step toward her. "Honor me, Earthlings. Resistance is futile. Your fate has been sealed. Your planet is mine. Bring me all your chicken beaks and bottle caps."

Taylor's bed thumped across the floor as Ellis tried to crawl beneath it.

"Knock it *off*, Ryan," Taylor said again. "Right now. You are *so* immature. Do you know that?"

Ryan let out another evil laugh. He enjoyed the sound.

Taylor glared at him. "This is *not* funny. Okay?"

"Sure it is," Ryan said. "If you have a sense of humor." He hadn't expected anyone to take him seriously. He peeked behind the bed. "Ellis, you can come out. It's me. I was joking."

Ellis's muffled voice rose from the cramped space. "You sure?"

"He's sure," Taylor said. She shook her head. "Alkazar the Conqueror? Give me a break, Ryan. That sounds like something you take for an upset stomach."

"Or constipation," Ellis muttered as he joined them.

Ryan grinned. "Hey, it was kinda funny, wasn't it?"

"Not really," Taylor said.

"So nothing happened when you touched it?" Ellis asked. "It's not like the glob?"

"Nope." Remembering the end of the ad, Ryan flipped the disk with his thumb, spinning it toward Taylor.

"Watch it." Taylor jumped aside and let the disk fall to the floor.

For an instant, the metal surface seemed to flicker. Ryan realized it was just a reflection from the lamp. He snatched up the disk and dropped it on the desk, then stood aside while Taylor leaned over and peered at it through the magnifying glass.

She was concentrating so hard that Ryan was going to shout, "BANG!" but he figured Taylor was already pretty upset with him. And he didn't want Ellis to jump out the window. After Taylor uttered her seventeenth variation of *hmm, interesting,* Ryan had enough. "Let me see."

"Here." Taylor handed him the magnifying glass. He moved the lens until the writing was as large as possible. It still made no sense. He checked several other disks. "Hey, they're all different."

"We should make copies," Ellis said.

"Go right ahead," Taylor told him. "There's a drawing pad in closet. Left side, second shelf, where I keep all my paper larger than eleven inches. Help yourself. I need to straighten out my backpack. And I've got to study."

"Study?" Ryan said. "It's the weekend."

"Exactly." Taylor picked up a book from her bed and brushed off the cover.

Ryan got the pad, being careful not to mess up anything in the closet while Taylor was there to yell at him. Everything she owned was neat and clean and lined up perfectly. Sometimes, he'd slip into her room and tilt one of the framed prints on her wall just a little bit. The next time he looked, it was always straight.

Ryan and Ellis spent nearly an hour copying the markings and trying to make sense of them. The thrill of finding alien items soon ran headfirst into the frustration of not understanding anything about them.

"I give up," Ryan said. His eyes felt fuzzy from staring at the meaningless squiggles. "We'll never figure this out." He gathered the drawings and offered them to Ellis. "These things are giving me a headache. You want them?"

"Sure," Ellis said. "Okay with you, Taylor?"

"Go right ahead," she said.

As Ellis took the papers, Mrs. McKenzie called up the stairs: "Dinner!"

"Feel like staying?" Ryan asked.

Ellis shook his head. "No thanks. I was in social studies with you this morning, remember?"

Ryan sighed. "Yeah, I remember." He could still hear Ms. Gelman's angry voice.

"I know what you've got in your pocket." Ellis patted Ryan on the back. "Good luck." With that, he headed out.

"How many do you have?" Taylor asked.

Ryan had to think for a minute. "Three."

"Three? Oh man, they're gonna flip."

Stewing over Dinner

Other families start a meal with Grace, Taylor thought as she took her seat at the table. *We start with mail.* She stared at her bowl of beef stew, knowing it would be a while before she'd get a chance to taste the first mouthful.

"Did you bring anything home from school?" Mr. McKenzie asked Ryan. He still wore his white shirt and tie from work, though he'd removed his suit jacket and had draped it across the back of his chair. A half empty glass with his traditional after-work scotch and soda sat by his right hand.

Ryan dug into his pocket, then reached across the table, offering three crumpled envelopes. Opposite Taylor, Mrs. McKenzie shifted her fork slowly a quarter inch lower, centering it on top of her napkin. Taylor adjusted her own fork.

"Talking in social studies class again," Mr. McKenzie said after he opened the first envelope.

Ryan shrugged. "Everyone talks. Nobody else gets detention. I guess that means I'm her favorite. Aren't you proud of me?" He winked at Taylor and whispered, "Imagine that. I'm a teacher's pet."

Here it comes, Taylor thought.

Instead of shouting, Mr. McKenzie drained the rest of his drink, then reached back and pulled a pen from his jacket pocket. He signed the letter and passed it to Ryan. "Make sure you turn that in."

"And try to be a little more attentive," Mrs. McKenzie said as she adjusted the position of her water glass.

Taylor wondered why anyone bothered with this ritual. The teachers wrote the letters. Ryan brought them home. Her parents read them and signed them, then handed them to Ryan who carried them back to the teachers. Nothing changed. She gripped the sides of her chair and waited as her dad read the second letter, about a series of missing homework assignments in algebra. The third letter warned that Ryan was in danger of failing gym.

"Gym?" Taylor said, mouthing the word toward Ryan. *How could anyone fail gym?* Even her friend Susan, who barely did more than show up, managed to pass. It was bad enough Ryan was already in danger of failing English. She knew he could be a good athlete if he had any interest in sports. She remembered him playing on a baseball team when they were little. And he was a pretty good skateboarder. That took a fair amount of coordination.

"Yeah, gym," Ryan said. "I suck at it."

Taylor waited to see what her dad would do. Sometimes he lectured Ryan. Sometimes he shouted. Other times he didn't say a word. She'd never been able to discover a pattern to his behavior. Finally, he said, "You're grounded this weekend."

Ryan shrugged and started eating.

"And how was your day?" Mrs. McKenzie asked Taylor.

"Okay." Taylor didn't tell them about the perfect 100 she'd earned on her spelling test. Or the A+ on her English essay. Not right now. It would only make Ryan look worse. Which meant it would probably make her dad angrier. If she avoided that, she figured there was a chance of getting all the way through dinner without an explosion.

"Tell your father about the museum program," Mrs. McKenzie suggested.

Taylor shrugged. "It's nothing."

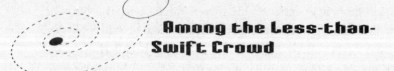

Among the Less-than-Swift Crowd

I'm gonna mess that kid up bad." Billy threw down his cigarette and ground the butt under the heel of his boot. Nobody talked to him like that. Not ever.

"Mess him up big time," agreed Jimmy as he paced in front of the bench.

Lance sat down on the back of the bench. "You know him?"

Billy shook his head. "Nope. But he's gonna know me." The image was burned in his mind. He'd mostly seen the kid from the back. But that was enough. There weren't a lot of kids with ponytails. *I'll find him,* Billy thought. He knew all the hangouts. He'd search around town this weekend as soon as he got out of detention. If he didn't find him in town, he'd find him in school. One thing was for sure—they'd meet.

"Wish we'd caught him," Lance said.

Billy reached up and gave Lance a push, toppling him over.

"Ow!" Lance hit the ground hard. "What'd you do that for?"

"For running so slow," Billy said. "You let him get away."

"Want to go to the Y?" Rick asked.

Billy didn't feel like moving. "Let's hang here for a while." He was still out of breath. And the kid might come back. Billy wanted to be there if that happened. He lit another cigarette and thought about catching him. Maybe he'd grab him by the hair and drag him around. Facedown on the sidewalk. That would be fun. Write his initials in blood.

After dinner, Taylor peeled one of the magnets from the refrigerator door and took it upstairs.

Ryan followed her into her room. "What are you doing?"

"Seeing if the disks are made of iron," she said. "Well, actually, iron, nickel, or cobalt—the basic ferromagnetic elements." She'd been thinking about the disks while she ate, and had come up with an intriguing assortment of possible tests, but this one was the quickest and simplest so it was a good place to start. At least until she could get her hands on some hydrochloric acid.

"I thought you didn't believe they're alien," Ryan said.

"I don't. But I'm still curious about their composition and function. Maybe that will help us determine their origin—which is definitely not extraterrestrial. I like searching for answers." She plucked a disk from the pile and touched the magnet to it. Instead of sticking, the disk went "*Zzzzzttt*," then disintegrated in her hand so quickly she didn't even have time to flinch.

"Nice going," Ryan said. "Want to pour acid on the rest of them? Or we could bake them in the oven. Wait—I know—let's put them on the train tracks."

Taylor didn't answer. She stared at the silvery powder that coated her fingertips and tried to think of a simple way to explain why the disk had disintegrated. Or even a complex explanation. But it was hard to think with Ryan chattering in her ear.

"How about a hacksaw?" he asked. "Or a drill. Too bad we don't live in Hawaii. We could toss a disk into a volcano. That would certainly help us determine its origin."

"Knock it off!" Taylor threw the magnet on her floor. "How was I supposed to know that would happen?"

"Aren't you supposed to know everything?" Ryan scooped up the rest of the disks. "I'll take them. They sure aren't safe with you."

Taylor dusted the powder from her hands. "Go right ahead. I'm finished, anyhow."

Ryan left, but came back a moment later. "Here. You helped find them. Take this." He held out a single disk.

Taylor wasn't sure she wanted it.

"Come on. Take one. It's only fair." He reached out further, as if offering a coin to a toll collector. "Please."

Taylor took the disk. It was easier than arguing with him. "Thanks."

"Just keep it away from magnets," he said.

"No problem. Unlike some people, I learn from my mistakes." Taylor studied the disk after Ryan left, half afraid it would explode in her hands, half eager to test it for zinc or chromium. She decided it would be best to hold off any more experiments until she gave the problem some thought.

Now she had to figure out where to put it. She didn't have a place for unidentified objects—extraterrestrial or earthbound. *Where does this belong?* she wondered. Finally, she opened her desk drawer and dropped the disk into the small wooden box where she kept her foreign coins. "Might not be foreign, might not be a coin," she said. "But it could be both." She closed the drawer and went downstairs.

Mr. McKenzie was waiting for her in the living room with a video. "Want to watch a movie?" he asked.

"What about Ryan?" Taylor asked. "Can he come down?" She felt bad about shouting at him.

"Do you think he deserves to?"

Taylor figured it wouldn't make any difference if Ryan stayed in his room. And it wouldn't make any difference if he joined them. Either way, it didn't seem to matter. Why punish him when punishment didn't work?

"What if instead of punishing him for what he's done, you reward him for what he might do?" Taylor suggested. The instant the words left her lips, she backed a step away from her dad.

He surprised her with a brief smile. "You're going to make a great lawyer some day. Very convincing. Okay, tell your brother he can join us."

"Chemical engineer," Taylor said, though she waited until she was far enough away so her dad wouldn't hear her. He seemed to think she was headed for law school. No reason to tell him otherwise right now. He didn't cope well when his dreams were frustrated. She went upstairs to Ryan's room.

Empty Space

Ryan scanned his room in search of a good hiding place. There weren't many choices. One by one, nearly everything he enjoyed had been removed as punishment. No computer, no video games, no posters, not much at all beyond a bed, a lamp, a desk, some books, and two dusty, unfinished model spaceships that Ryan suspected had been left in place to serve as proof of his failure to ever finish anything. Ellis called the room "The Fortress of Nothingtude." As far as Ryan knew, people living on death row had more in their cells.

He glanced at his closet. *No way I'm dressing up for anything in the next couple of months,* he thought. He slid the disks into the inside pocket of his sports coat, but kept one and took it to his bed.

Ryan stared at the disk, losing himself in a thousand dreams about the creatures that had made it. He wondered what their world looked like, what they ate for dinner. He wondered how they treated their kids.

He flipped the disk in the air. It gave off a high-pitched ping that warbled and echoed like a special effect from the movies. Definitely not an earthly sound. As the disk landed on his palm, he was surprised by its warmth.

"Weird." He touched the surface of the disk with his fingertip. It *was* warm. But maybe that was just the heat from his hand. He flipped the disk several more times, to see if it would grow even warmer, but it didn't seem to change.

Ryan decided to put it down and let it cool off for a while.

He sat staring at the disk, until his thoughts were broken by a light knock. "Just a minute." He stashed the disk with the others, then opened his door.

We're watching a movie," Taylor said. "You're invited."

"I'm busy."

"Yeah, right." She glanced past him into the empty room. "Come on. Do the family thing. Movie. Popcorn. Warmth and chuckles. Domestic harmony. It'll make Mom happy."

"I don't think so."

"I'm sorry I yelled at you," Taylor said.

"No big deal. I asked for it."

Taylor nodded. "Yeah. You did. Look, it's a good movie. Come on down with me. Please?"

She wasn't sure he was going to come, but he shrugged and followed her to the living room. Their mother joined them, too, though she brought a book. Mrs. McKenzie was a big fan of romance novels. Taylor was half embarrassed by the covers, which usually featured shirtless hunks with bulging muscles coming to the rescue of helpless females whose own clothes were as torn and flapping as the slashed dresses of punk rock divas.

But she was glad her mom liked to read. Sometimes the two of them would sit together for hours, each lost in her own book. Her dad read a lot, too. But he liked books that claimed to make the reader a better person. He'd even written his own book, about how to be successful. It was called *Failure Is Not an Option: A Guide to Success in Business and in Life.* There were still five thousand moldly copies stacked up in the garage.

Two minutes after the movie started, Ryan rolled off the couch and flopped onto one of the beanbag chairs. Three minutes after that, he started tapping his foot and looking around the room. Five minutes later, he stood and said, "I'm going upstairs."

"Don't you want to see what happens?" Taylor asked.

"Not really."

"That boy can't finish anything," Mr. McKenzie said after Ryan left. "Not even a movie."

Taylor opened her mouth, then sighed and sat back. The movie played on, against the slow, steady sound of pages turning in her mom's romance novel. As the credits rolled, Taylor glanced at the photographs her father had selected to decorate one wall. A pitcher who threw a perfect game in a World Series. A batter with an amazing hitting streak. A player who'd gone the longest without missing a game. They were icons of perfection. Once, in a scrapbook, she'd seen a photo of her father on his college baseball team. He was smiling.

The phone rang in the kitchen.

"I got it," Taylor said, eager to leave the tomblike mood of the living room. "Hello?"

"Hi," Ariel said. "So what was all that stuff about a spaceship?"

A Flicker of Recognition

Stupid, boring old movie, Ryan thought. He was more interested in the disks from the spaceship and the movies they held. He got one out of the closet and flipped it.

The disk flickered. He let it sit on his palm for a moment, trying to decide whether it felt warmer. He couldn't tell for sure.

He grabbed two more disks by the edges, and put one on each thumb. He flipped the disk in his right hand, but tossed the other one up in the air without spinning it. They both landed on his bed.

Ryan reached out and touched the two disks at the same time. "Cool," he said. Then he laughed. The disk he'd flipped was slightly warmer than the one he'd tossed. And that was cool.

He flipped one of the disks again and again, trying to spot any variations in the flicker. Ryan smiled when he realized this was the sort of thing Taylor would do. The smile quickly faded. *Poor Taylor,* Ryan thought. For all her talk of science, she was still chasing after the fantasy of a happy family life. She might as well have wished for a unicorn.

"Fairy tales," Ryan muttered as he flipped the disk.

Mingled with the ringing, warbling ping, he heard his father's words, those same words that had followed him since the summer he was six. *That boy never finishes anything. That boy never finishes anything. That boy never finishes anything.*

S paceship? Oh, right..." Taylor hunted for an answer that wouldn't be a lie. "We didn't find any ship. You know how much Ryan likes to make fun of my passion for science."

Ariel laughed. "That's what Kara said. She figured Ryan was playing a joke on you. Listen to this—she thinks he's hot. Weird, huh? I mean, I've known him so long, I can't think of him that way. He's not hot. He's Ryan. But I guess I can sort of see where she'd think Ryan is kinda nice. Of course, he'd be nicer if he didn't dress like such a disaster. He makes the average skater look preppy. A haircut would help, too. Don't you think?"

Taylor clutched the phone as her mind locked on Ariel's first sentence. "Kara? You told her?"

"Come on, it's no big deal. She wanted to know what we were talking about. I had to tell her. Otherwise she gets all bitchy. You don't really mind, do you?"

"I guess not," Taylor said, but she felt as if Ariel had betrayed a secret. What else had Ariel told Kara? That Taylor still slept with a ragged old stuffed cat named Kitty? That once in a while she liked to play with coloring books? That she'd had a crush on Josh Cavaletti last year and had written a whole bunch of poems about him? Taylor and Ariel had shared so many secrets. Were those secrets still safe, or had they been spilled? Maybe that's why Kara always seemed to smirk at her when they passed in the hallways.

They talked for a few more minutes, but Taylor didn't feel that she was really taking part in a conversation. It all seemed empty, like listening to a movie with her eyes closed.

"We're getting together tomorrow, right?" Ariel asked. "I won't be around Sunday. My parents are dragging me to a wedding in Newton. Some cousin I've never met."

"Sure."

"Great. I'll see you then."

As Taylor hung up the phone, she thought about something else Ariel had said. Kara liked Ryan. Taylor shuddered at the idea, which mingled in her mind with images of insects that ate their mates. Not that anything would ever come of it. Kara went through boys the way Ellis, with his frequent nosebleeds, went through Kleenex. The school was littered with Kara's castoffs, including some she'd dated and dropped repeatedly. She'd lose whatever interest she had in Ryan soon enough.

After Taylor settled into bed, rhythmic murmurs drifted through her window. Nighttime voices that were low, but not low enough, floated across the floor. Her parents did a lot of their serious talking in the living room. If the windows were open, the words found a path of no resistance. The topic was always the same.

"We have to do something about him," Mr. McKenzie said.

"I'm out of ideas," Mrs. McKenzie said. "I just don't know how to get through to him. He doesn't seem to care about anything. He's letting his whole life go to waste."

"All he ever thinks about is himself. Why can't he be more like his sister?"

"*Stop saying that,*" Taylor whispered. It wasn't fair to Ryan. And it wasn't fair to her. Every achievement was dampened by the knowledge that it would become part of the filter through which her parents viewed Ryan. Last year, after Ryan and her dad had been battling worse than usual for a whole week, Taylor almost flunked a math test on purpose, just to take some of the heat off him. She answered the first two questions wrong. But in the end, she couldn't bring herself to fail. Or even make a single intentional mistake. She'd fixed her errors, and scored a 98—which was almost good enough for her dad.

It would get tougher when school ended. She'd probably graduate first in her class, unless that loathsome creature Gilbert Spaldeen pulled off some sort of miracle. Then there'd be the summer softball league. She'd hit doubles and snag line drives while Ryan hung out in the park with Huey, Owen, and the other skaters—if he was allowed to leave the house at all. After that, she had the museum program, her volunteer work at the animal shelter, and regular trips to the library. Then on to high school, where she hoped she wouldn't have to work too hard to convince her teachers she wasn't like her brother. Sometimes, she wondered if life would be easier for both of them if he stayed back a year.

"He's throwing it all away." Her father's voice grew harsher. "He had so much talent. It's a crime."

Taylor closed her window. She was glad Ryan couldn't hear any of this from his room across the hall. But she knew he'd heard plenty of similar conversations. Her parents had long ago given up restricting discussion of their disenchantments to private moments. She wondered whether he even noticed anymore.

Fortunately, the hours she'd spent searching through the woods had tired her out enough that her thoughts soon faded, giving way to sleep.

The Game Room

Ryan wasn't sleepy. He sat on his bed, flipping a disk. But all it did was flicker a little. Finally, he stashed the disk in the jacket pocket and went to bed. With no school tomorrow, he planned to sleep a good long time.

It didn't work out that way.

The itching woke him up early the next morning. "Oh great," he groaned when he saw the angry blotches on his hands. After slathering himself in calamine lotion, he thought about going down to the living room to watch TV. But he didn't feel like dealing with anyone in his family, so he stayed in his room.

Ellis came by that afternoon, and the wardens allowed him upstairs. "You figure anything out with those disks?" he asked.

"Nope. I tried, but no luck." Ryan pulled a disk from the closet, showed Ellis how it flickered, then put it away. He didn't bother mentioning Taylor's stupid experiment with the magnet.

"Hey, it's still cool we found them. Maybe it's just as well they don't work. Who knows what could happen?" Ellis said. "So, what do you want to do?"

"I'm grounded."

"No problem." Ellis tapped his baggy pants pockets. "I'm a walking entertainment center. Ellis the Amusing." He pulled a deck of cards and a game player from his left pocket. Then an iPod from his right pocket, and a thin paperback of horror stories from his back pocket.

"No pinball machines or go-carts?" Ryan asked.

"Saving them for later," Ellis said. He spread the goodies across Ryan's bed. "Wish you could come over. I got new speakers. They're small, but they kick butt. I can make the whole place vibrate. I think I almost shook a filling loose last night."

"I wish I could come, too." Ryan picked up the deck of cards. "Crazy eights?" he asked.

"Sounds like a plan," Ellis said. "Sadly, that's about as crazy as my life gets."

Ryan shuffled the cards. "You think about aliens much?" he asked as he dealt.

Ellis nodded. "All the time. You know why?"

"Why?"

"Because we're aliens. Adults own the world. They run everything and make all the rules. Nothing on this planet fits us. It's like being a lefty, except it's your whole body and mind that's out of whack."

"Maybe so," Ryan said. "But we're pretty pathetic aliens. We don't have a spaceship, light sabers, or voice-activated robots."

"I'll bet alien teens don't get any of that cool stuff, either," Ellis said. "Alien dads get to play around with the matter transmitter while the kids have to take out the garbage."

"Yeah, some things are universal." Ryan settled down on the floor, happy to spend the day playing games and talking about aliens. He might have been grounded, and he might be in danger of failing a couple of classes, but other than that, he didn't have a care in the world.

ant to go to the Smith's Ferry?" Taylor asked Ariel when they got together on Saturday afternoon. The small town, just over the river, was one of Taylor's favorites. The older section had a pedestrian walkway lined with bargain shops and craft galleries.

"We *always* go there," Ariel said. "Don't you think it's kind of tacky? How about Bigelow Junction? It's way better."

"Too expensive," Taylor said. She'd made a couple of trips to the trendy new mall, built around an old train station, but the shops were real fancy. Everything seemed pretentious and fake.

"We don't have to buy anything," Ariel said. "We can just look."

Taylor shrugged. "Sure. Why not." The main thing was that they'd be doing something together.

They went downtown, then caught a bus to Bigelow Junction. As Taylor followed Ariel through the front entrance, she noticed a group of older boys watching them.

"They're checking us out," Ariel whispered. She ran a hand through her hair.

Taylor shook her head. "Not us. Just you." There was no denying Ariel was gorgeous. Boys had been looking at her since the fifth grade.

"Don't talk like that," Ariel said.

Taylor sped up, eager to get away from the group by the door. But wherever she and Ariel went, she was aware of the stares. And aware that they weren't aimed at her.

They ran into Lucy, Taylor's next door neighbor, and Lucy's

friend Sammi, and a couple of other kids from school. Before they left, Ariel bought a tiny tube of mascara that seemed, as far as Taylor was concerned, to be way overpriced. Especially when she calculated the cost per gallon. Taylor bought a soft pretzel. It seemed way overpriced, too. Even without working out the cost per pound.

"You sure you don't want to sign up for the summer program at the museum?" Taylor asked as they rode the bus back home.

"Ick." Ariel shook her head. "It doesn't sound like it would be much fun. Engineering?"

Taylor stared out the window at the passing traffic. "There's still time if you change your mind."

"The last thing I want to do this summer is take some silly class."

"It's not a class. It's more like experiments and stuff," Taylor said. "If you signed up, we could go together. My mom would drive us. It covers all kinds of engineering—mechanical, chemical—the works. Remember how much fun we had the year before last, when we went to see the geology exhibit?"

Ariel raised her arm and held the back of her hand near Taylor's face. "Do you like this color?"

"What?" Taylor asked.

"Kara said I should try something with a bit more beige in it. What do you think?"

"Sure. Try something with a bit more beige." Taylor settled in her seat and pretended to listen while Ariel talked about earth tones, French polish, and other mysteries.

Taylor spent most of Sunday morning studying, then hung out for a while next door with Lucy. After Lucy left for her piano lesson, Taylor went home and studied some more. Then, as she did every Sunday evening, she wrote down her goals for the week. Beside the usual academic list, she added a more challenging entry: *Keep Ryan from getting killed.*

Monday morning, after she'd finished her yogurt, she waited for Ryan to come down to breakfast. She hated to deviate from her schedule, but she was afraid of what would happen if he went to school by himself.

The Long Way Around

Ryan was surprised to see Taylor in the kitchen when he came down for breakfast. She was usually long gone before he even got out of bed. While he ate his cereal, her gaze flip-flopped between him and the clock. It made him feel like a player in a tennis match.

"Aren't you going to be late?" he asked after he'd slurped the last spoonful of sugary milk from the bottom of the bowl.

"Nobody's going to be late," she said. Her eyes flicked to the clock for the nine-thousandth time.

Ryan poured himself a second helping of cereal. Taylor groaned like she was going to explode. When he finished eating she dashed out of the kitchen. He found her fidgeting by the front door with her hand on the knob. The instant he got near her, she practically pushed him out onto the steps.

"Relax. It doesn't matter if you get there one second before the bell or ten minutes." Ryan couldn't understand why people would show up early for anything—especially school. That just meant they had to wait longer once they got there.

"How can you stand to be late?" Taylor asked. "Everybody stares at you."

"No they don't."

"And it's against the rules."

"Big deal. Everything's against some kind of rule." Ryan stopped to look at a dead squirrel.

Taylor let out a cry of frustration.

Ryan left the squirrel behind. "If you're in such a big rush, why are you hanging around?" he asked.

"To make sure you don't end up like that squirrel," Taylor said.

Ryan had no idea what she was talking about. When they reached the school, Taylor put a hand on his shoulder to stop him. Then she pointed ahead. Billy Snooks had planted himself in the middle of the front entrance, with his back pressed against the post that ran down the center of the double doors. Kids swung wide of him, brushing the hinges as they passed through the doorway.

"Let's go around the side," Taylor said.

"Why?" Ryan asked.

"I think he's waiting for someone special. Like maybe someone who mouthed off about his mother."

"You think?" Ryan had pretty much forgotten about that.

"Yeah, I think. Come on. He looks capable of harming mammals much larger than squirrels."

As Ryan followed Taylor to the side of the school, he pulled a disk from his pocket and flipped it in the air. Sunlight flashed off the polished surface. When it pinged, Taylor spun around.

"Why'd you bring that?" she asked.

"Just felt like it." He'd grabbed the disk on the way out of his bedroom. Even if he couldn't make it work, he liked the sound it made. And he enjoyed knowing he was the only person on Earth with an alien artifact in his pocket.

The first bell rang. "Come on. We'll be late." Taylor rushed toward the door, but still managed to toss back a final piece of advice. "Try to do something impressive in gym today. Okay? Let the teacher know you're giving it your best shot."

"Sure," Ryan said, "I'll dazzle him. No problem." His sister just didn't get it. It wouldn't matter if he ran a hundred meters in five seconds, or sank a dozen three-pointers while standing on one leg. Nothing he did would ever impress Coach Ballast. *I'd probably get a better grade if I wasn't even there*, he thought.

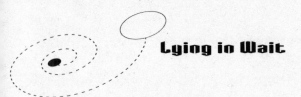

Lying in Wait

He has to be here, Billy thought as he scanned the crowd for any sign of a ponytail. As soon as he caught the little jerk—wherever he caught him—he was going to pound the weasel. It didn't matter if it was in school. Didn't even matter if it was right in front of the principal's office.

Billy realized a lot of scared-looking kids were swinging around to the side door. *This isn't working*, he thought. Maybe it would be better to search the halls between classes. And once the search was over, the fun would begin. Billy smiled at the thought of broken noses and snapped bones.

PART
TWO

Exploration

In form and feature, face and limb,
    I grew so like my brother,
That folks got taking me for him,
    And each for one another.
It puzzled all our kith and kin,
    It reached an awful pitch;
For one of us was born a twin,
    Yet not a soul knew which.

—Henry Sambrooke Leigh

The Answer Sinks In

The first time Ryan flipped the disk during social studies, kids were still filing in so the room was noisy enough to mask any sound. Even so, Ms. Gelman froze for an instant, as if she'd detected an alien presence in her universe.

Ryan grinned. Anything that annoyed her was worth repeating. He held his hand in his lap and flipped the disk low enough so Ms. Gelman couldn't see it. The problem was, a low flip didn't make much of a ping. It was more like a *plink*.

Near the end of the period, Ryan got an idea. He flipped the disk hard, just nicking the edge with his thumb. That gave the disk a whole lot of spin without sending it high in the air.

Ping! But this time a second tone, almost too deep to hear, pulsed through the air beneath the ping, like the *whumpf-whumpf-whumpf* of a large engine. Along the rim of the disk sparks flickered, far brighter than ever before. "Yes!" Ryan said. *That's the secret—keep it low with tons of spin.*

Ms. Gelman whipped her head around and skewered him with an icy glare. Ryan waited for her to look away, then tried another flip. This time, the flicker burst into a glow. As the disk hit his palm, the glow spread from the rim toward the center. It got halfway there before it faded. He tried again, spinning the disk so hard it became a blurred sphere. The glow nearly covered the whole surface.

The effect reminded Ryan of their junky old lawn mower. He'd pull the cord and the engine would sputter, almost start, then die. Finally, when his shoulder was aching so much he didn't think he could manage another tug, the engine would catch and roar to life. Ryan was positive he was close to making the disk come to life, too.

"What's going on here?" Ms. Gelman asked.

Ryan ignored her and flipped the disk again, letting it land on his open palm. This time the glow spread all the way to the center. *I did it,* he thought. There was a faint sizzle, like a steak hitting a pan, but the heat was no worse than a drop of candle wax. The disk sank into his palm a bit and the surrounding skin rolled over the outside edge of the disk—as if his hand were swallowing it.

"I will not tolerate disturbances in my classroom!" Ms. Gelman stormed down the aisle toward his desk.

Ryan froze.

"What is so fascinating down there?" Ms. Gelman asked. "I didn't think anything existed that could hold your attention for more than five seconds."

Ryan curled his fingers into a loose fist to hide the disk. "Nothing."

"Don't lie to me. What do you have in your hand?"

Ryan shrugged.

"Show me!" she demanded, slamming the desk with her own hand and grabbing his wrist.

Ryan uncurled his fingers.

"*Hmph,*" Ms. Gelman said. "I see your hand is as empty as your mind. Lucky for you."

Ryan stared at the unbroken skin of his palm. Except for a slight bump, there was no sign that an alien artifact had just become part of his body.

Ms. Gelman wasn't through with him. "You are going to start paying more attention in my class. Do you understand me?"

Ryan opened his mouth, but he didn't utter a word. Instead, he let loose the loudest, rudest burp that had ever burst from his gut. It caught him completely by surprise.

FLIP

As kids all around Ryan erupted in laughter, Ms. Gelman's face shifted from red to purple. "Get out of this classroom!"

"Whatever you say, darling," Ryan said.

"Out!" Ms. Gelman screamed. "Get out of my classroom!"

Darling? Where'd that come from? he wondered as he left his seat. And that burp. On a scale of one to ten, it was an eleven and a half.

With each step he took, his head felt more . . . crowded.

He stared at the disk-sized bump in his palm. *What's going on?* A childhood memory came to him. He'd hurt his hand. How? Ice. That was it. Putting a block of ice in the icebox. The heavy weight had pinched his fingers.

Icebox? Ryan shook his head. The memory was strong. Other memories washed over him. The sound of horse hooves on cobblestones. The smell of roasted peanuts at the stadium.

"I'm not myself," Ryan said. Not just himself. Something else was wrong. Suddenly his clothes felt tight. He loosened his belt a notch. And then a couple more. That was better.

Relax. Another thought. Not his. But his right now. Two sets of memories sloshed through his brain. His own grew dimmer as the other grew stronger.

A bell rang. Ryan wandered down the hall. *Where am I going?* "Spanish," the fading mind whispered. That would be a disaster. He'd better keep his mouth shut. Then English. Which wouldn't be any fun, either.

Fourth period, he had health. No. That wasn't right. He had gym. He rubbed his hands together in anticipation. Gym. Hot diggity. That was going to be a whole heap of fun.

Taylor was hoping to catch up with Ryan on the way to the locker room for fourth period gym. She figured it wouldn't hurt to give him one more tiny little reminder about the importance of trying his best.

The hall ended at a T intersection, with the girls' lockers off to the left and the boys' to the right. She and Ryan both had gym, alternating every other day with health class so it was on Monday, Wednesday, and Friday one week, then Tuesday and Thursday the next. Taylor had no problem following the schedule, but she knew it drove Ryan crazy. She'd tried to explain to him that if the first day of gym for any month was odd, all the gym days that month would be odd. It was a pretty interesting pattern, actually. But he'd just laughed and told her the only odd part was the way she found that sort of stuff so fascinating.

Probably cutting again, Taylor thought. Or taking his time because he hated gym so much. That's why she was startled when she walked onto the field and saw Ryan hanging around with the rest of the boys at the baseball diamond.

"Let's get warmed up," her teacher, Ms. Foster, called. Taylor slipped into her usual place between Deena and Susan. Ariel, unfortunately, had the other gym class on the opposite days.

As Taylor stretched, she watched the boys. They got right into their game. Ryan's team batted first.

"Everyone up. Let's get that blood pumping." Ms. Foster blew her whistle and started counting out jumping jacks.

Taylor jumped and watched the game.

"Jog in place," Ms. Foster called.

"How symbolic," Deena whispered. "We're going nowhere as quickly as we can."

"Like Alice," Susan gasped, already out of breath. "—*Through—the—Looking Glass—*"

Taylor jogged and watched. Ryan's team was doing well. When he came to bat, right after Huey, the bases were loaded.

"Sit-ups," Ms. Foster called.

"Easy out," the shortstop yelled. The fielders abandoned their deep positions and strolled toward the base lines. Obviously, they didn't expect much from Ryan.

Come on, Taylor thought, *just get a decent hit.* Even a single would drive in a run. That would be enough to make Ryan look good. Especially compared to all the times when Taylor had seen him stand there and take three strikes. It drove her crazy the way he didn't even try. She paused at the top of her next sit-up. Something wasn't right.

"Oh, that's just great," she said when she realized why the scene seemed strange.

"Problem?" Deena asked.

"Ryan's batting lefty," Taylor said. It was just like him to fool around and stand on the wrong side of the plate. Coach Ballast was going to be furious. And Ryan would flunk gym for sure.

"Lefty. How sinister," Deena said.

"Push-ups," Ms. Foster called.

Taylor rolled forward, put her palms on the grass, and waited for Ms. Foster to start counting. At least she was facing Ryan. Next to her, Susan groaned and said, "Just kill me now."

On the mound, the pitcher ripped a fast one toward the plate.

Ryan didn't seem ready. Taylor wished she could reach across the field and smack him on the head. The ball shot toward the waiting catcher's mitt. Finally, Ryan swung.

"Oh my God!" Taylor shouted.

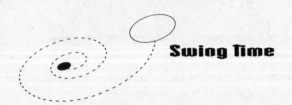

Swing Time

She's gone. He knew that right off.

The ball cleared the fence by a good ten feet. A beautiful sight he never grew tired of, no matter how many hundreds of times he'd seen it before. He dropped the bat and trotted toward first. That was the other beauty of a homer. No need to rush. Everyone in the stadium froze, admiring him. Especially the young ladies in the stands. As he rounded third he waved at them and shouted, "Hello, ladies. How ya doing?"

It felt great to connect like that. Strange, too. With a metal bat. Still, it was wonderful to take a solid swing and send the old horsehair for a ride.

"How'd you . . . ?" a red-headed kid asked after he crossed home plate. "That was . . ."

"It's what I do, sport," he said. "It's what I'm good at." He grinned and spat on the ground, then glanced at the manager. The man stared back. He looked like he'd just seen a magician make an elephant disappear. He bowed and reached up to pull his cap off, then realized he wasn't wearing one. He looked down at his legs. Sweat pants? What kind of outfit was that for a ball player?

"Nice hit," a teammate said, slapping him on the back.

"Awesome," another said.

It pleased him to be appreciated.

On his next turn at bat, the fielders hugged the fence and the manager moved to the corner of the back stop. He took a hard swing at the first pitch and completely whiffed it. He missed the second pitch, too.

From the corner of his eyes, he noticed the manager shake

his head. "I knew it was a fluke, McKenzie," the man muttered. "Once in a lifetime, everybody connects."

McKenzie? Who's McKenzie?

The third pitch never had a chance. He clobbered it. He waved at the ladies again on his tour around the bases, and smiled at the speechless manager. "Maybe twice in a lifetime?" he asked.

They didn't congratulate him this time. But he was no stranger to envy. You do good, people are happy. You do too good, they start to sulk. Especially if you do things they can't.

There was dead silence when he strolled to the plate on his last turn. *Time to have some fun.* "Right there," he said, pointing to the scoreboard beyond the fence. He took one strike, then blasted a cannon shot that nailed his target dead center.

He was rewarded with scattered gasps from both teams, and applause from the ladies.

On the way into the locker room after the game, everyone stared at him. He didn't mind. He was used to it. He loved crowds and attention.

"Pants getting tight," he joked as he struggled into his street clothes. He patted his stomach. There was a comforting full-ness to the way it bulged over his belt. Nothing worse than an empty stomach. "Takes a lot of weight to hit those long balls."

A kid hanging around his locker nodded. Nice kid. A bit too skinny, though. "That probably explains why I fail so misera-bly at this." The kid grinned. "Ellis the Under-weighted."

"So let's get some lunch," he said as he closed his gym locker. He thumped the kid on the back. "I'm sure hungry. Hope they have hot dogs. I have a hankering for hot dogs. Gonna eat me a bucketful."

s that your brother?" Ms. Foster asked as the class headed into the locker room. "You're twins, right?"

Taylor nodded. "Yeah, but we're not identical."

"He should try out for the baseball team," she said.

"I'll tell him." Taylor had to struggle to keep from laughing at the suggestion. The image of Ryan in a team uniform, sitting in a dugout with his ponytail sticking out the rear of his cap, was just too bizarre. But, amazingly, he'd listened to her and made an effort today. A huge effort. She never would have guessed he could hit so well. Maybe, with encouragement, he'd make more effort in other areas. She thought about how peaceful life would be if Ryan even managed to rise to the level of mediocrity in his classes.

Taylor got dressed, then headed toward the cafeteria with Deena and Susan. She joined Ariel at her regular spot at the end of the table. A moment later, Kara cruised by. Her hip brushed the corner of Taylor's tray, nearly knocking it to the floor. Taylor thought about shouting, "Watch where you're going!," but it didn't seem worth the effort.

Kara hadn't even looked at Ariel as she went past. *Snob*, Taylor thought as Kara completed her regal stroll and took her place of honor at the popular girls' table.

"You want to go join them?" Taylor asked, annoyed that Ariel was staring across the cafeteria with the expression of a puppy trying to get in out of the rain.

"No."

"They'll pretend you don't exist when I'm with you," Taylor said. "You're losing points just breathing the same air I breathe."

"I'm dragging you down, too," Susan said. "You want to be popular, you aren't supposed to have *big-boned* friends. That's why *popular* and *petite* both start with the letter *p*. As does *purge*."

"We are the rocks that bind the feet of social climbers," Deena said. "Hey, that's a keeper." She flipped open her ever-present notebook and started writing.

"They're not like that," Ariel said. "Kara didn't see me. That's all. Otherwise, she'd have said hi. If I went over, they'd let me join them."

"Is that what you want to do?" Taylor asked.

"I'm here, aren't I?" Ariel said.

Deena kept talking as she wrote. "There sat us . . . no status . . . stare at us . . ."

"Too fat, us," Susan added. "Well, just me, but that wouldn't rhyme."

"Maybe you should change your name," Taylor said. "Tara, Kara, and Ariel doesn't work. How about Sarah? That would fit."

"Stop it," Ariel said.

"Or Lara? I like that. Tara, Kara, and Lara. Sounds like a girl band."

"Do you want me to leave?" Ariel asked.

"No. Sorry. I didn't mean it." Taylor turned her attention to her lunch. As she ate, a pang of guilt grew in her chest, expanding until it pressed against her lungs. She tried to think of something nice to say to Ariel to make up for her comments. She couldn't seem to find the right words.

Halfway through her sandwich, she noticed a crowd had gathered around one of the skater tables near the corner of the cafeteria.

"I wonder what's going on?" Susan said

"Something silly," Taylor said. "Probably involving food."

"Yeah, like a gross-out contest," Deena said. "Remember when that kid sucked ketchup up his nose and spat it out his mouth? It was wonderfully symbolic. Sort of like performance art."

"Don't remind me." The memory, from way back at the start of the school year, still made Taylor queasy.

Across the room, the crowd started chanting, "Go! Go! Go! Go!"

Then everyone shouted, "Five!"

There were assorted whoops and cheers. A moment later the crowd picked up the first chant again. "Go! Go! Go! Go!" Kids stomped on the floor in rhythm to the cry.

"I have to check this out," Ariel said, springing from her seat.

"Six!" the crowd yelled.

That's where Ryan sits, Taylor thought. He and Ellis usually went to the table in the far corner by the windows.

"Seven!"

Ariel stood on tiptoe near the edge of the mob. At the same time, Taylor saw Gilbert scurry away from the crowd. He aimed a smirk in her direction on his way toward the hall.

What's that weasel up to? she wondered. It was no secret he'd hated her ever since she'd defeated him in the second-grade spelling bee. Subsequent staggering losses in third through seventh grades just added to his bitterness. *Psittacosis* had been his downfall last year. The fact that she was beating him out to graduate first in the class didn't help his attitude, either.

As Gilbert left the cafeteria, Ariel spun around and raced back to Taylor. "You'd better come see this," she said.

A shout of "Eight!" rose from the crowd.

Snapshots: Crowds

The crowd pressed around Ellis from all sides. He was used to seeing the tops of heads, not the middle of chests. He tried to shift his seat, but there wasn't any room. He glanced at all the faces above him. Nobody looked back. That, he was used to. But he wasn't used to having so many people not looking at him. The huge amount of inattention felt weird, especially when the attention was focused on someone sitting right next to him. It was almost as if the more people who didn't notice him, the less real he became.

Click

The crowd pulled at Kara. She was dying to find out what was going on. But there was no way she was going to show any sign of interest. She refused to play the role of spectator. Not unless there was a good chance of being noticed.

Click

The crowd was as natural to him as air and sky. On or off the field, they swarmed around him, eager to shake his hand or touch his arm. He loved the fans. Almost as much as he loved food. But not as much as he loved putting one over the fence.

Click

The crowd wasn't bad at the lunch truck down the block. It beat the cafeteria food. And it beat sitting in a room filled

with so many losers. Billy had needed to get out. He'd searched
the halls between periods, hunting for that kid. He'd been so
sure he'd find him that way. No luck. The school was too big.
Time to get more people in on the hunt. There were at least a
dozen guys he could count on. That would be plenty. They'd
cover the halls. And watch every exit when school let out. There
was no way that long-haired idiot would get away.

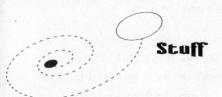

Stuff

Taylor circled the crowd until she found a spot with a clear view. She saw Ryan and Ellis at the table, along with Huey, Owen, and Stitcher. Ryan was eating a hot dog. Everyone else was watching him.

What's the big deal? Taylor wondered. It just looked like some guys having lunch. Ryan might be eating a little faster than usual, but that was nothing to stare at. She was used to seeing him stuff his face. Around her, the shouts of "Go! Go! Go! Go!" continued.

As Ryan finished the hot dog, the crowd yelled, "Nine!"

Ryan glanced up, smiled at Taylor, and said, "Hiya, kid."

Kid? What was he talking about? He was the kid. She was two minutes older. And at least two years more mature. Taylor squeezed closer, and noticed a pile of hot dogs stacked like building logs on Ryan's tray. He snatched one up. After he'd inhaled it, the crowd shouted, "Ten!" This was followed by applause and cheers.

Ryan smiled as if pleased by the attention, then reached out with his left hand and picked up his eleventh hot dog.

Midway through the destruction of wiener number twelve, the outer fringes of the crowd parted. The chanting died as Principal Guthrie waded toward the table, with Gilbert bobbing behind him like a fidgety cow tail.

Rat, Taylor thought as she glared at Gilbert.

"McKenzie," the principal said when he reached the table. "Why am I not surprised to find you in the middle of all this?"

Ryan spoke to him through a large amount of unswallowed food. "I'm just eating my lunch, sport."

"Come with me," he said.

Ryan shoved the other half of the hot dog in his mouth. With bulging cheeks he bellowed, "Must be he wants to introduce me to the mayor! Lead on!" He jumped up and followed the principal out of the cafeteria. His stomach hung over his belt, stretching his shirt to the point where it resembled a giant sausage skin. When they reached the door, Taylor heard the principal say, "Your parents are going to be notified about your behavior. I can assure you of that."

Ryan responded with a roar of laughter. "The whole world knows about my behavior, sport."

As the crowd wandered off, Taylor dropped into the empty seat next to Ellis. "What was that all about?" she asked. "Did you guys make some kind of bet?" She noticed that there was nothing on Ellis's tray except the remains of a grilled cheese sandwich, an open carton of milk, and a quivering mass of Jell-O that was almost the same color as Ellis's hair. No huge piles of anything. Obviously, it wasn't an eating competition.

Ellis shrugged. "I don't have a clue. Ryan loaded up on hot dogs when we went through the line. Said he was starving. Kept calling me 'kid,' too. Maybe he's having a growth spurt. We're adolescent males, after all. Our main directive is to eat. I'm usually Ellis the Ravenous. Even right after I've eaten."

Huey and Owen nodded in agreement.

"We burn fuel at a rapid rate," Stitcher said.

"We need to constantly replenish ourselves," Huey said. He reached over and snagged a hot dog from Ryan's tray. "No point letting these go to waste. He won't be back any time soon."

His actions inspired a mini feeding frenzy as the boys stripped the remaining food from the tray with the speed of undernourished piranhas.

"Nothing like a hot dog or two to get you through the day," Owen said. He sighed happily and took a large bite.

"But not a dozen," Taylor said.

"That does seem sort of extreme," Ellis agreed. "The scary part is that it's all got to come out eventually. You might want to invest some money in a couple of those bathroom air fresheners. I'd recommend autumn pine. It has a nice outdoorsy aroma. You know, if I ate that much, I'd look like I swallowed a cinder block. Ellis the Bloated. I'll bet Ryan won't even need to eat again until next week. Sort of like a snake." Ellis flicked out his tongue, then eyed his Jell-O.

"Snake it!" Huey cried.

As Ellis dove his head toward his tray, Taylor hurried back to her table. The thought of Ryan eating that much, combined with the image of Ellis attacking the Jell-O, made her stomach ripple. She didn't even feel like finishing her sandwich now.

Hey, I'm sorry about saying that stuff," Taylor told Ariel when the bell rang.

"Don't worry about it," Ariel said.

"See you in math?"

"Yeah, I'll see you there."

Relieved that Ariel wasn't angry, Taylor headed off to Spanish. On the way, she spotted Snooks near the front door, talking with another thug.

Taylor wanted to hurry past him. She was afraid Snooks would connect her to Ryan since they'd been together just moments before the incident in the park. But she slowed down when she heard the words, "Blond ponytail."

"I think I seen someone like that around," the other kid said. "But I don't know his name."

Taylor stopped and pretended to look through her Spanish textbook while she listened to the conversation.

"He's got a black shirt with that weird green face. Whatcha call it?" Snooks asked.

"Whatcha call what?"

"The face. You know. Like some kind of weirdo from Mars. Starts with an A."

"Astronaut?" the kid ask.

"No. That ain't it," Snooks said.

"Alien?"

"Yeah—a black shirt with a green alien on the back. That's about all I saw. His back. Freakin' coward. Said stuff about my mother and ran off. No guts. Won't do him no good. I'll kill him when I catch him. Then we'll see his guts. Nobody talks about my mother."

"I'll help," the other guy said.

"Can't be that many dorks with ponytails," Snooks said. "If I don't catch him now, I'll find him when he leaves. Only four ways out of here."

Taylor thought back to the scene in the cafeteria. Ryan was wearing a yellow shirt with a cartoon of a duck skating off a cliff. Nothing close to an alien. It didn't matter. Snooks would keep searching until he found Ryan. She needed to warn him as soon as possible. She definitely had to reach him before he left the building. Otherwise, he'd probably stroll right out the front door without checking to see whether it was safe, his ponytail waving at Snooks with all the maddening arrogance of a slap in the face.

Nap Time

The hot dogs had made him sleepy. The last thing he wanted was to talk with the mayor. But he guessed it was good publicity. Lucky for him, when they reached the office the mayor's assistant pointed to a chair and said, "Sit right there until I get to you. You're the least of my problems."

"Sure thing, kid," he said. Funny way to talk to a baseball legend, though. He knew what it was like with big shots. They loved to keep you waiting. Made them feel important. He didn't care. It had been a good day. Three home runs, a nice little lunch, a chance to meet some fans. Life didn't get much better than that. He settled down in the chair and dozed. Once in a while, a bell rang in the distance, followed by the sound of shuffling crowds.

He drifted pleasantly, dreaming of the Bronx, until a closer, louder bell jangled him awake. His eyes flew open and he leaped to his feet.

"What the hell?" Ryan shouted. His mind, like a tape in reverse, replayed the morning's events at high speed.

On the other side of the counter, the secretary glanced up from the phone and gave him a sour look. "Watch your language," she said. "And sit down."

He checked his hand. The disk was gone. So was the poison ivy. His pants hung loosely on his hips. He tightened his belt a few notches, then dropped into the chair.

Did I do all that? Ryan ran through the memories at a slower pace. Gym class. Lunch. The home runs. The hot dogs. The mother of all burps. Dream? No way. Everything definitely happened. *Cool!* It reminded him of a car trip. He'd been a passenger, but he'd seen everything the driver saw.

No. That wasn't quite right. He could have kept some control. But it was more fun to sit back and enjoy the ride. He probed his palm. There was no sign of the disk. But the experience had been awesome while it lasted. He glanced at the clock and realized he'd already missed most of his afternoon classes. No great loss.

The secretary's phone rang again. After a very short conversation, she hung up and said, "The principal wants to see you now."

Ryan walked into the familiar room and plopped into his usual seat. He wondered which lecture it would be this time. "How Dare You?" was one of Principal Guthrie's favorites. "Who Do You Think You Are?" was another of the top ten. And of course, there was the old classic, "We're Not Your Enemies," also known as "We're Just Trying to Help You."

"Do you have any ambition at all?" the principal asked. "Any plans? Any idea what you're going to do with your life?"

Ryan shrugged. He hadn't expected "What Are Your Plans for the Future?" Planning was Taylor's specialty, not his.

"Do you even care about anything?"

To his surprise, Ryan thought, *baseball*. But that was ridiculous. He avoided baseball as much as possible. Though this morning, briefly, he'd cared about the game.

The things he really cared about, the disks, skating, life on other planets—the cool and interesting stuff—wasn't what the principal would want to hear about. Ryan remained silent. He knew that anything he said would just prolong the lecture. Principals never asked a question if they thought they'd like the answer.

"Nothing to say? I figured as much. Now listen to me, and listen carefully. I am tired of having to waste so much time dealing with disruptive students. You are going to change, and change immediately. Do you understand?"

Ryan nodded and fought back a smile. *Change immediately.* He'd already done that today.

The principal lectured him for a few more minutes, handed him a letter to take home, then pointed to the door and said, "Get out of here."

Ryan passed through the empty halls to his ninth period art class.

hen her last class ended, Taylor raced to the art room, hoping to catch Ryan before he left. She found him at the sink, rinsing a paint brush. Her relief spilled out in a flood of tangled words. "Looks is Snooking for you. Alien gang with the blond shirttail."

"What the heck are you talking about?" Ryan asked. "You learning Russian or something?"

Taylor took a deep breath and tried again. "Snooks is looking for you. Not just him. His whole gang. They're looking for a kid with an alien shirt and a blond ponytail."

Ryan pointed at his shirt. "Relax. I gave the alien the day off."

"What about your hair? There aren't that many guys in school with ponytails."

"No problem." Ryan walked up to the art teacher's desk. "Can I borrow these for a second?"

"Sure," Ms. Alvarez said.

Taylor gasped as Ryan started hacking at his hair with a pair of scissors. A moment later, he was holding the scissors in one hand, and an unattached ponytail in the other. He shrugged and said the same words Taylor remembered from the woods when they'd first talked about a spaceship. "There's one less, now."

He offered the hair to his teacher. "Want this? Maybe you can make something with it."

Ms. Alvarez sprang out of her seat and backed away from Ryan.

"You want it?" Ryan asked, turning toward Taylor.

Taylor slowly shook her head. How could he do that? She remembered when she'd decided to get her own long hair cut for the first time, two years ago. It had been rough to sit in the chair and hear the scissors snipping away a part of her childhood. Ryan didn't seem to care at all. Maybe her parents were right. Maybe there was something wrong with him.

"You sure?" Ryan asked.

"I'm sure," Taylor said.

Ryan put the scissors back on the desk, then tossed the hair into the garbage can. "Guess Snooks can hunt for ponytails all he wants now."

He headed for the hall.

"Is that your brother?" Ms. Alvarez asked.

"Yes, ma'am." Taylor wondered what kind of trouble this was going to cause.

"Twin?"

"We're not identical."

"He needs to see the school psychologist," Ms. Alvarez said.

"You don't understand," Taylor said. *Or maybe I don't understand.*

"I'm sorry. We're legally bound to report any violent or self-destructive behavior."

"Oh great," Taylor muttered as she rushed after Ryan. He'd already had his share of meetings with school psychologists. Along with an assortment of other psychologists, counselors, and therapists that her folks had dragged him to. As far as Taylor was concerned, the whole family would be a lot happier if they'd stop spending money on specialists and buy the big-screen television her dad had been wanting for years.

But she had a more immediate concern. She caught up with Ryan before he reached the front door. "New hair style or not, I think we should go out the side exit."

"Why?" Ryan asked.

"Because Snooks is waiting for you out front."

"He won't recognize me now," Ryan said.

"I'd just feel better if we went that way. Okay? We can cut through the parking lot and swing up to the street."

"Sure. Anything to make you happy. That's my goal in life. See—I really do have ambitions."

Taylor noticed that Ryan wasn't calling her *kid* or *sport*, or using any strange phrases. And he'd held the scissors in his right hand. The weirdness seemed to be over. But it had left behind plenty of questions. "What was up with the hot dogs?" she asked.

"Nothing. I was just hungry," Ryan said. "I don't see what the big deal was."

Taylor didn't answer. She'd spotted one of Snooks's gang at the side door, checking out everyone who walked past. *Maybe I can distract him while Ryan slips by*, she thought. Another thought quickly followed. *Who am I kidding? I'm not Ariel.* Heads never turned when she walked down the hall. She had no clue about the skills it took to capture a boy's attention. Taylor tensed up as she went out. The thug's gaze lingered on Ryan's head for a moment, then he scowled and looked away.

We made it. Taylor never guessed a day of school could be that stressful.

As they reached the parking lot, a deep, rough voice called from behind, "Hold it! I've been looking for you."

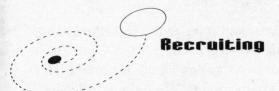

Recruiting

t first, Ryan didn't realize someone was calling him. He was too lost in his own thoughts to pay much attention to anything else. He kept checking the corners of his mind, expecting to discover that he wasn't alone. He finally stopped as the footsteps reached him.

"Hang on," Coach Ballast said.

"What'd I do this time?" Ryan asked.

The coach stared at Ryan as if he'd just discovered he'd chased after the wrong person. "You're in my fourth period class, right?"

As Ryan nodded, he realized his hair hung down the sides of his head at a weird slant, like he'd gotten it cut by a drunk barber in a dark room.

"McKenzie?"

Ryan nodded again.

"You really need to think about coming out for baseball," he said. "What position do you play?"

"I don't play team sports," Ryan said. He waited for the shouting to start. Teachers were like parents. They got angry when he didn't do what they wanted.

Not this time.

Coach Ballast smiled as if they were playing some sort of game and said, "Just think about it, slugger. Okay? There are lots of advantages. Baseball's pretty important around here. The players are treated very well. You might even find it helps your grades." He winked, then walked back into the building.

"Yeah, forget the hot dogs," Taylor said. "Where'd you learn to hit like that? Have you been going to the batting cages or something? You must have been practicing."

"Nope. No practice. I just swung hard," Ryan said. He dredged those moments from memory. The feel was still there. He might even be able to do it again—if he wanted to. "Yeah. That's all there is to it. Pick your pitch and swing hard."

"It's that easy?" Taylor asked. "Get real. I've been playing softball since I was little, and I hit maybe one or two home runs a season. You know I spend at least a half hour a day working on my batting all summer. Don't tell me it's easy."

"Hey, it was easy today. And you should talk. You're the one who's always telling me that algebra is easy." He thought again about the memories that had been left behind. "You know, baseball's actually not a bad sport."

"Yeah, right," Taylor said. "You won't even watch games on TV."

"I won't watch them with Dad," Ryan said. "He cares about it way too much." During the last World Series, the tension had grown so bad that Ryan had stayed out of the house whenever a game was on.

"Speaking of Dad, he's going to freak the moment he sees your hair," Taylor said as they reached the house.

"Dad hated my hair," Ryan said. "He kept threatening to cut it himself. Looks like I beat him to it."

"Mom won't like it," Taylor said.

"She won't even notice." To prove his point, he went right into the living room and said, "Hi, Mom."

"What did you do?" his mom shrieked.

"I needed a change," Ryan said. *Okay, she noticed.*

"It's terrible."

"Can you fix it?" Ryan asked. He figured he probably looked pretty weird right now. He didn't care at all about fashion, but he wasn't eager to have everyone on the planet stare at his head.

"I can't make it any worse." She led him to the kitchen and pointed at a chair. "Have a seat."

Ryan sat while his mom trimmed his hair. He almost felt like he was a little kid again, which was kind of nice.

"That wasn't so bad, was it?" she asked when she was done. She'd spent a long time making the two sides perfectly even.

"I guess not. Thanks." Ryan helped sweep up the clippings, then went to his room, where he lay on his bed and thought about hitting home runs.

After a long while, he got up to check his haircut in the bathroom mirror. His mom had actually done a decent job, which made sense, since she really paid attention to details. It was still him—just sort of different. In his mind, he saw another face. A famous face from old black and white photos and grainy newsreel films.

His dad had a whole shelf of baseball junk. Ryan went to his parent's bedroom and found a book called *The World's Greatest Ball Players*. He already knew who he'd been. But he needed to see if the memories were accurate.

He checked the index, then turned to the section on Babe Ruth and read the biography of the legendary left-handed home-run hitter. Everything matched. The childhood spent in Baltimore. The attitude. The appetite. Tons of details Ryan hadn't known about before he'd flipped the disk. They were all in the book. And all in his head. *It's real,* he thought. It wasn't his imagination.

"That's a good book. You can borrow it if you want."

Ryan snapped the book shut and looked up. His dad was standing in the doorway with this pathetically eager expression on his face. Ryan knew if he showed the tiniest interest in baseball, they'd become the best of pals. For at least five minutes. And every minute of closeness would create hours of anger when he screwed up. He'd learned a long time ago that there was no way he'd ever be good enough at anything to satisfy his dad.

"No, thanks. I was just checking something." He put the book back, then left his parents' bedroom before his dad could whip out a glove and suggest they play catch. *Babe Ruth,* Ryan thought, feeling a tingle dance down his spine. *I was Babe Ruth. One of the greatest legends in the history of baseball.*

The thrill faded. *And now I'm just Ryan again.*

He wanted to flip another disk right away. But they'd be eating soon. Whatever wonderful legend he became, he didn't want to waste it at the dinner table. Not stuck there with his parents and Taylor. Maybe after dinner. Though that wouldn't be much fun, either—not up in his room, alone. Better to wait for school. Or for the weekend. He and Ellis could each do one. Now *that* would be awesome.

Ryan's good mood lasted until dinner, when he handed over the two envelopes.

"What's this about a disturbance at lunch?" Mr. McKenzie asked after he'd read the first letter.

"Beats me," Ryan said. He glanced at the take-out cartons that sat unopened on the table. Twice cooked pork. General Tso's chicken. Beef lo mein. Egg rolls. Every second Monday. It was his favorite meal. Especially the chicken. "I didn't do anything wrong."

"You never do," his dad said. "And yet, somehow, you're always in trouble. You never ever do *anything.*" As he said the last word, he slammed his fist on the table hard enough to make the salt shaker jump. He yanked the pen from his pocket, signed the letter, flung it to the floor, then opened the second one.

"Well," he said, "I see you sure as hell didn't do *anything* in English class. Another incomplete assignment. I can't believe this. What's wrong with you? You don't make the slightest ef-fort. It's English, for god's sake. You've been speaking it all your life." He shoved the letter over to Mrs. McKenzie with such force that she flinched. "Look, our son is amazingly consistent."

That makes two of us, Ryan thought.

His mom took the letter, read it, and sighed. With her other hand, she adjusted the position of the salt shaker.

"What did you get on your last English paper?" his dad asked Taylor.

"I think it was an A," she said quietly.

"Just an A?" he asked.

"An A plus, I guess," she said.

Mr. McKenzie turned back to Ryan. "Maybe you need to spend more time studying," he said. "Maybe you need to go up to your room right now."

"But . . ." Ryan looked down at his empty plate.

"Go!" his father shouted.

hose idiots have got to go," Billy said. He'd come back to the park, hoping the kid with the ponytail would show up. It was an okay place to hang out. A nice change from the 7-Eleven, except for the noise. The scrape of wheels against concrete, and the clatter of boards tumbling out of control, was getting on his nerves. Billy knew the value of silence. Adam used to pound him when he made any noise. At least there wasn't a pack of screeching little kids on the playground. It was too broken down for that.

"No problem," Lance said. He headed for the tennis courts, where a half dozen skaters were disturbing Billy's peace. Rick tagged along with him.

Two of the kids took off before Lance and Rick even got close. Lance barked a couple words and all the others split, except for one kid who kept skating. *Bad move,* Billy thought.

Lance gave him a push. Billy smiled as the kid went down hard. "Tough break," he said. He laughed when he realized he'd made a joke. He repeated it for Jimmy, who laughed, too.

The kid got up, grabbed his skateboard, and limped away.

"That's better," Billy said when his troops returned.

"Yeah, much better," Rick said. "You know what? I kind of like this place."

Billy nodded. "Me, too. Might as well stay a while. Got no reason to go anywhere else."

Take-out Food

Go!"

As Ryan stomped off to his room, Taylor thought about how that same small word had sounded so different when it was chanted by the crowd in the cafeteria. In school it meant *we're on your side.* At home it said, *you don't belong.*

"Ryan did well in gym today," Taylor said.

Her father glared at her.

"He hit three home runs."

For an instant, his face softened. Then the scowl bounced back. "That's not very funny, Taylor. Not funny at all. You know as well as I do that he doesn't even try. I don't appreciate you making jokes about it." He dumped some chunks of chicken on his plate and muttered, "Home runs. That'll be the day."

Taylor gave up. He'd never believe her. She barely believed it herself. Her parents started eating. The silence in the room felt like ten school buses stacked on top of her chest. She picked at her egg roll, then ate a bit of lo mein. As she'd feared, the silence was soon replaced by something worse.

"I don't know what's gotten into that boy's head," her mother said. She carefully sliced a strip of pork into three equal pieces, then speared one of the pieces on her fork, along with a snow pea and a bamboo shoot.

"He's headed right for failure," her father said. "If we don't get him straightened out, he's going to end up living on the street and eating from garbage cans."

Taylor put her fork down. "May I be excused?"

Mrs. McKenzie looked over as if surprised to discover there was a third person in the room. "Aren't you hungry?"

"I've had enough," Taylor said. "May I please go?"

"Sure."

Taylor took her plate to the kitchen, where she grabbed a jar of peanut butter, a knife, and a loaf of bread. She brought the food upstairs.

"Go away," Ryan said when she knocked on his door.

She walked in and held up the bread. "I brought you a sandwich. I'll try to sneak you some Chinese food later. Dad'll kill the chicken, but there's always pork left over." She put everything down on the bed.

Ryan glared up at her from his seat on the floor by the closet. "I didn't ask for anything."

"Technically, it's not a sandwich yet. It's a kit," Taylor said, patting the loaf of bread. "The directions are on the back of the jar. Just give a shout if you need help."

Ryan didn't laugh at her joke.

"Want to tell me what's going on?" she asked.

"Why? So you can write a paper about it and get another wonderful grade?"

"Right, blame me. It's all my fault. It's everyone else's fault. You're just an innocent victim."

"I didn't say that. I just wish I wouldn't get in trouble for every single thing I do."

That makes two of us. Taylor tried again. "What's going on?"

"Nothing's going on," he said.

"Nothing?"

Ryan turned away from her and opened the peanut butter. Taylor waited until it was obvious he wasn't going to give her an answer. "You're right. Nothing's going on. Silly me. Everything is completely normal around here. We're just one big happy family. We're so happy, I could explode with joy. Kaboom." On the way out, she noticed Ryan's alien sweatshirt in a basket of clean laundry. "You'd better not wear that to school."

"Why not?"

"Snooks will kill you."

"So?"

"Don't talk like that, Ryan," Taylor said. *Another little word,* she thought as she left his room. *So.* A little word that said a lot. The memory of Ryan with the scissors passed through her mind again, followed by an image of him locked up somewhere so he wouldn't hurt himself. So . . .

She pushed that thought from her mind. Ryan might cause all kinds of problems, but he wasn't crazy.

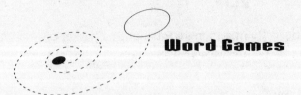

Word Games

I'm not crazy," Ryan said.

"Of course you aren't." Dr. Joyceman gave him a thin-lipped smile that didn't involve the rest of her face. "And, for your information, we don't use that word."

"So why am I here?" He'd been called to the office at the start of first period, before Ms. Gelman even had a chance to give him more than a couple of glares and scowls. He'd expected another lecture from the principal. Instead, they'd stuck him in a room with the school psychologist. If anyone was crazy, it was Snooks, who'd been waiting out front again before school started. Ryan got a kick out of walking right past him without being noticed. There was no way Snooks was ever going to recognize him.

Dr. Joyceman picked up a writing pad and clicked her ball-point pen. "We're just concerned about you."

Ryan knew that was a load of crap. They didn't care about him. They cared about trying to make each day as uninteresting as possible. They cared about budgets. They cared about lesson plans. They cared about avoiding disruptions. They didn't give a damn how he felt when a teacher told him he was a loser. Or yelled at him for no reason.

"Let's play a game," Dr. Joyceman said. "I'll say a word. You say the first thing that comes into your mind. All right?"

Ryan said the first thing that came into his mind.

"That's a very colorful expression," Dr. Joyceman said, "but why don't you wait for me to give you a word."

Ryan nodded and waited for her to give him a word.

"Here goes. Hot."

"Cold."

"Dog."

"Cat."

"Responsibility."

"Failure."

"School."

"Sucks."

"Homework."

"Sucks."

"Tests."

"Stupid."

"Hair."

"Shampoo."

"Scissors."

"Rock."

Dr. Joyceman paused and scrunched her eyebrows, obviously puzzled. "Rock?"

"Rock breaks scissors," Ryan explained. *It's a game, stupid.*
She nodded and continued. "Dreams."

"Sleep."

"Career."

"Burgers."

"Father."

"Failure."

"Son."

Ryan shook his head. "I'm tired of this."

"Fair enough. Let's move on."

She had Ryan take a test on a computer. It asked really stupid stuff like, "Is anybody putting poison in your food?" and "Do people follow you?" He zipped through the questions until he got to one that asked, "Do you hear voices in your head?"

He hesitated. But Babe Ruth hadn't been a voice in his head. Babe Ruth had been a reality in his head. Finally, he marked it, "No."

Ryan glanced up. Dr. Joyceman was watching him and taking notes. When he finished the test, they started another stupid word game.

And so it went for the rest of the day—tests, talking, games that weren't really games, more tests—while the disk he'd brought sat unused in his pocket. They even had lunch in the room, and kept going until the end of ninth period.

"Did I pass?" he asked as Dr. Joyceman put away her notebook.

"There's no pass or fail here," she said, speaking so openly he knew she was lying.

I wonder how I'd do if I'd used the disk, Ryan thought. Would Dr. Joyceman think Napoleon was crazy? Would she have fun playing word games with Shakespeare, or sharing lunch with Attila the Hun? *Would she like me better if I wasn't myself?*

Snapshots: Lunch

"You're not yourself today."

Taylor looked up from her sandwich. "I'm worried about Ryan," she said. *He's the one who's not himself,* she thought.

"That's nothing new," Ariel said. "You've been worrying about him for as long as I can remember."

"This is different. He's acting really weird." She checked across the cafeteria. There was no sign of him. Ellis was all alone at the table.

"If you aren't going to be yourself, can I be you?" Susan asked.

"That's deep," Deena said, flipping open her notebook. "I'm going to steal it."

Click

Kara stared past Ariel, making sure their eyes didn't meet. *You don't exist right now,* she thought. *You're invisible.* Kara knew that she herself, on the other hand, was very visible. All through lunch, she'd caught Ariel staring at her with an expression that said, "I want to be like you." If that's what Ariel really wanted, the first step was simple. She had to dump Taylor and those other losers. It was going to be fun to watch the little smarty pants suffer.

Click

Ellis sat alone, eating his lunch. Ryan had vanished. Stitcher was out for at least a couple of days. Apparently, he'd taken a bad crash on his skateboard in the park last night. Huey and Owen were probably in the band room, practicing some bizarre duet for clarinet and tuba. Ellis hated eating by himself.

He looked over at Taylor's table. She wouldn't mind if he joined her. But her friends were there. Deena was always saying stuff he didn't understand. She made him feel stupid. Susan seemed to dislike him because he was skinny. Ariel was nice to him, but she was so pretty that Ellis often couldn't talk when he was near her. Not without sounding like a complete idiot.

Taylor was pretty, too. Maybe even prettier than Ariel, he thought as he studied the two of them together. But she was so much like a sister, he had no trouble talking when she was around. *I wonder if she knows how pretty she is?* He figured she must. How could she not know?

free Pass

Billy had hit so many lockers his knuckles ached. It didn't help. He couldn't think of anything that would help except finding that kid and pounding him into a bloody pulp. Make him so ugly, even his own mother wouldn't be able to stand him. But he'd had no luck so far. As he walked down the hall after coming in from lunch, he hit another locker.

"What do you think you're doing?"

Billy glanced over his shoulder. Some ancient guy with watery eyes and a coffee-stained tie had decided to hassle him. Billy didn't know the teacher's name. It didn't matter. He punched the locker again, ignoring the pain in his hand.

"Young man, I'm talking to you."

Slowly, Billy turned around and shot two eyes full of attitude right through the teacher. He'd learned that dead-eye stare from Ace. *You can't do anything to me*, he thought. *And I could hurt you real bad. Wanna find out?* Death-row attitude. Nothing to lose.

The teacher slunk off down the hall.

Billy smiled. *They're scared of me, too.* He'd always worried that he'd get in trouble if he was violent in school. But maybe they'd just leave him alone. If they were scared enough, he could do anything he wanted. *Anything.* You don't screw around with a tiger. You stay out of its way.

H and them over," Mr. McKenzie said with a growl.

"There's nothing to hand over," Ryan told his father.

"No letters?" He seemed almost disappointed.

"Afraid not." Ryan didn't bother explaining. *I couldn't get in trouble today, Dad. I was too busy having my head examined.* He figured his parents would learn all about that sooner or later. The psychologist was probably writing up a report. It wasn't the sort of thing he'd be allowed to carry home. They'd send it in the mail. *Congratulations, Mr. and Mrs. McKenzie, you've won a prize!*

"That's wonderful," Mrs. McKenzie said.

His father shook his head. "One day doesn't mean anything. His teachers are probably tired of telling us about the small stuff. They're waiting for him to screw up in a big way."

"I think he's really trying," his mom said. She gave Ryan a hopeful look.

"Yeah, I'm trying," Ryan said. Right now, he was trying to keep from knocking the table over. *Look, Dad, nobody has to wait for me to screw up. I can do it right now.* But he was willing to put up with a large load of crap if it got him the one thing he wanted from his parents. "What if I stay out of trouble tomorrow, too?" he asked. "Can I have my skateboard back?" He really needed to get to the park.

"You expect to be rewarded for two days of good behavior?" his dad asked. "Two days?"

Why not? I get punished for five seconds of bad behavior. Ryan knew better than to share that thought.

"It's a start," his mom said.

Ryan's dad shrugged. "What the hell. It's not going to happen. Sure. Keep your nose clean for another day and you get your skateboard back."

"Great." Ryan lifted the bun off his burger and picked up the ketchup. Nothing came out. He smacked the bottom. It still wouldn't come out.

"Put the cap back on the bottle and shake it," Taylor said. "It's a thixotropic liquid. It flows great if you shake it up."

Ryan stared at the bottle for a second, then sighed and put it down. He really didn't need ketchup.

But there was one other thing he wanted. Halfway through the meal, he asked, "Can I go over to Ellis's after dinner?" All day, he'd been dying to show his friend how the disks worked.

"Not tonight," his father said.

"Can Ellis come here?" Ryan asked.

Mr. McKenzie threw down his fork. "Why do you always push? I said *no*. But that's not good enough for you. You're never satisfied. You never get enough."

Ryan slid his chair away from the table. His dad was wrong. Ryan had gotten more than enough. He grabbed the edge of the table and tried to fight down the anger. *Don't blow it.* He thought about his skateboard. "I'm done," he said. He headed out of the dining room.

"Clear your plate," his dad called.

"I'll do it," Taylor said.

Ryan went up to his room and closed the door, then opened his closet and reached for a disk. The memories of yesterday flooded over him—the cheers, the crowd, the admiration. Being good at something. Being really good. But it was risky. His dad was like Ms. Gelman, waiting to pounce on the smallest mistake. It probably wasn't safe to flip at home. If they found out, they'd take away the disks. Just like they'd taken everything else he cared about.

Ryan decided to wait. He really wanted his skateboard back. He grabbed a book and got in bed. A few minutes later, the doorbell rang downstairs. He didn't care. Someone else could get it.

Bearing Fruit

s Taylor finished clearing the table, the doorbell rang. "I got it," she called.

When she opened the door, she found herself face to face with a large basket of fruit. Even through the plastic wrapping, she could smell the aroma of ripe pineapple and peaches. The words *secret admirer* flashed through her mind. But she quickly dismissed that fantasy. Admirers sent flowers, not fruit. And they sent them to girls like Kara.

"Ryan McKenzie live here?" a muffled voice asked from behind a bunch of grapes.

"Yes," Taylor said.

The basket moved forward into her hands. Taylor thanked the delivery man, then staggered upstairs.

"You have a fan," she said as she put the fruit on Ryan's desk.

Ryan plucked the card from the wrapper, glanced at it, then dropped it next to the basket. "I guess he really wants me on his team."

Taylor read the message. *Great hitting, Slugger. Hope you'll think about joining us. Best wishes, Coach.* "Guess so. Nice-looking fruit, though."

"Help yourself," Ryan said.

"Thanks." She snaked her hand under the cellophane and grabbed a tangerine. She liked the way they peeled so neatly. "It's a weird world. If you can hit a ball, you get all kinds of breaks."

"It's a weird world even without sports," Ryan said.

"But it's the only one we have." Taylor smiled. That sounded like something Deena would write in one of her poems. "Where were you today?"

"School," Ryan said.

"I didn't see you at lunch," she said.

"What a coincidence. I didn't see you at lunch, either."

Of course not. You weren't there, Taylor thought. She let it go. Ryan already had two parents grilling him. He didn't need a third inquisitor. But something was going on. He'd been acting way stranger than usual these last couple days.

Taylor went to her room and got the disk Ryan had given her: *Is this doing something to him?* she wondered. It was just a little piece of metal. But a tiny piece of plutonium could make people sick. A tiny pill could change a person. Could one small disk affect Ryan? Maybe it sent out some kind of signals. She thought about the magnet. Obviously, the disk was more than just an ordinary sliver of metal. She decided she'd have to try another experiment. *I just hope this one doesn't destroy anything,* she thought.

The next morning, Taylor put the disk in her right front pocket as soon as she got dressed. She had no idea how quickly any effect might show up, but she figured she wouldn't have a long wait.

What if I can't control myself? She imagined running wild in the middle of a class. One bad incident could tarnish her forever, spreading from teacher to teacher as they sat in the lounge discussing their worst students. *You won't believe what Taylor McKenzie did in my class this morning . . .*

Taylor? She'd always seemed so nice.

Not anymore.

What a shame. We had such hopes for her.

I guess she turned out to be a lot like her brother.

No surprise. They're twins, after all.

Thank goodness we still have Gilbert.

Taylor reached halfway into her pocket. She didn't want to risk losing control. She balanced that fear against the image of Ryan spending the rest of his life in his room, or on the street. Which of those fears was more likely to come true? *I'll be fine,* she thought, pulling her hand back out.

It started to rain as she walked to school. That didn't stop Snooks from keeping his vigil by the front entrance. But he looked like he was just going through the motions. Taylor figured he'd give up soon.

Brilliant

Ryan hadn't planned to bring a disk to school. Not when he was so close to getting his skateboard back. But he'd grabbed one on his way out so he could show Ellis his discovery. It was too awesome not to share. He didn't get a chance until the end of second period.

"You have to see this," he said, hanging back by the side wall until the other students left. He pulled the disk from his pocket and flipped it perfectly the first time. The disk glowed brightly as it spun. He'd planned to let it drop to the floor, but at the last moment he stuck out his hand, worried that the disk would melt into the linoleum and be wasted.

Ellis yelped and jumped back when the metal sank into Ryan's palm.

"Relax," Ryan said.

"Nurse!" Ellis screamed. He reached toward Ryan's hand, then froze. "Oh my God. What do I do? I don't know first aid. Ellis the Unprepared." He ducked down and stared at the back of Ryan's hand. "Is it going to sink right through?"

"*Shh,*" Ryan said. "Relax. I'm okay." And he was okay. Because this time, he knew what to expect. He held on to a fragment of his own identity as a thousand thoughts flooded his mind. The universe unfolded, revealing itself in interwoven particles and forces that spread before him like strings of equations. Time and space danced their infinite and infinitely beautiful dance. His mind embraced a tidal wave of ideas, sorting through them in search of one that was ripe for contemplation.

A local force intruded among the universal forces. Someone was tugging at his arm.

"Can you make it to class?" Ellis asked.

"Certainly. Though the time of our arrival is relative to our reference frame, of course."

"You're really freaking me out," Ellis said. "You know that? Please tell me nothing is going to burst out of your stomach and slaughter everyone. I have enough stress in my life already. If I have to worry about dying, the pressure will kill me."

"You shouldn't think such terrible thoughts," Ryan said. He headed toward English. Next to him, the boy kept talking, but Ryan's mind was elsewhere, racing at the speed of light.

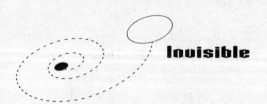

T hat worked fast," Kara said as she left her second period class. She pointed down the hall at Ryan, who was walking toward her with the geeky kid.

"What worked fast?" Tara asked.

"Are you blind?" Kara asked. Sometimes Tara just didn't pay attention to the important things. "Look."

Tara squinted, then spread her hands and meekly said, "I'm sorry. I don't know what—"

"Remember, Monday, I said he needed to lose the ponytail?" Tara nodded.

"Ariel must have told someone. The message got right back to him." Kara was pleased that Ryan had responded so quickly. And that Ariel was so predictable. What a wonderful little puppet she was going to be.

"Definitely an improvement," Tara said. "You were absolutely right. Good call."

"He wants me," Kara said. "I'll bet you he'll be sending me flowers and writing mushy poems before next week. Let's hope he has a decent allowance. I should let Ariel know I like roses." She leaned against the wall and waited for Ryan to come closer.

Every boy who went by checked her out. Some tried to hide it. But the flush on their cheeks told the truth. Kara loved having so much power. She could get any boy in the school to do whatever she wanted.

"Look at that," she said to Tara. "He's started to grow a mustache." They'd make a hot couple. Especially after she gave him some fashion tips. Those baggy sweatshirts just didn't cut it.

He'd almost reached her now.

"Watch this," she whispered. "I'll make him blush." Kara closed her eyes half way and pursed her lips as if kissing the air. *Irresistible,* she thought. She jutted her hip at an interesting angle. *Come and get it.*

Ryan walked past her as if she didn't exist.

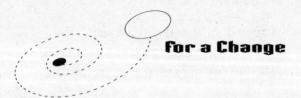

All morning, as she carried the disk in her pocket, Taylor tried to stay aware of her own actions. She quickly discovered that it was impossible to keep constant watch on herself. Her thoughts just seemed to have a mind of their own.

"Do I seem any different today?" she asked Ariel in homeroom.

"New eyeliner?" Ariel guessed.

"Am I acting strangely?" she asked Susan when they were changing for gym.

"Check with Deena," Susan said. "That's her specialty."

Deena responded to the question with, "*Strange* is merely an uptight term for *misunderstood*. Oooh—keeper alert!" She pulled her locker open and grabbed her notebook.

Taylor closed her own locker. Since she didn't have pockets in her gym shorts, she'd left the disk in her pants. She didn't like interrupting the experiment, but she was already pretty sure the disk had no effect on her.

The rain, harder now, forced the classes to stay indoors, where the boys and girls each got half the gym.

Taylor spotted Ryan just as Coach Ballast jogged over to him. From a distance, it looked like Ryan was trying to grow a mustache. Weird. She sure didn't understand male hormones.

"Hey, how ya doing?" Coach Ballast asked. "Ready for class?"

"Certainly," Ryan said. "Physical education is an essential component of a balanced existence."

Taylor was impressed. Ryan was definitely scoring points now.

"*Essential component?* Kind of an egghead thing to say, but

I like the way it sounds." Coach Ballast put his arm across Ryan's shoulder and led him toward the corner of the gym. "You know, Slugger, I don't think you've had a chance to be captain, have you?"

As Taylor got ready to play basketball, she watched Ryan pick his team. He chose Ellis first, then Huey and Owen, none of whom was known to have ball-handling skills. The games started, with pairs of teams using the baskets that swung down along both sides of the gym.

During the rest of the period, Taylor saw Ryan's team get mercilessly stomped. Ryan acted like he didn't even know what to do with the ball. Whenever he got his hands on it, he threw it straight up in the air. Taylor figured he was trying to make Coach Ballast lose interest in him. As usual, Ryan's plan backfired.

"Good one, McKenzie," Coach Ballast said at the end of the period, his loud voice booming across the gym. "I needed a laugh. These rainy days drive me crazy." He slapped Ryan on the back, nearly knocking him off his feet. "You really are a kidder. Can't wait to get you on my team. I'll bet you're a catcher. Right? Catchers are always the team joker. I guess you have to be kind of wild to spend all that time with your head so close to a swinging bat."

Taylor realized that nothing Ryan did would erase the memory of those home runs. After she changed and headed for the door she remembered the disk in her pocket, and felt a new appreciation for the story of the princess and the pea. But those thoughts were driven from her mind as she left the locker room. At the other end of the hall, by the boys' locker, she spotted a loud, laughing crowd.

She knew, without even looking, what that meant.

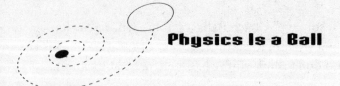

After English, Ryan enjoyed an amusing break for physical education. The instructor was kind enough to let him select a team. Though the game itself was perplexing, Ryan found a great deal of pleasure in imagining that the ball was a subatomic particle.

He introduced, in his mind, a second ball, and then a third. Then balls of other sizes, moving in different directions. He varied their density, both in proportion to their size and in inverse proportion. In a sense, he played basketball with the universe. He kept the experiment running even after the game ended. It was a wonderful mental exercise, filling all his thoughts as he left the locker room and stepped into the chilly corridor.

Casual Day

Taylor reached the intersection by the main hall just ahead of Ryan. She heard a dozen overlapping comments, from the clever to the crude, rising from the cluster of boys who surrounded him.

"Ryan's making a fashion statement."

"Hey, forget something?"

"What do you think this is, a Calvin Klein ad?"

"I guess Ryan's decided to hang out for a while."

"At least he remembered his shoes."

Taylor glanced at Ellis, who said, "I tried to tell him, but he wouldn't pay any attention to me."

Then from behind her, she heard more voices. Girls' voices. Taylor rushed toward Ryan and put a hand on his chest before he could reach the spot where the two groups converged. He seemed totally unaware of all the attention.

"Forget something?" Taylor asked him.

"I don't think so," Ryan said. "Though you have presented me with a paradox. If I've forgotten something, I couldn't be expected to remember that, could I?" He chuckled, and his eyes sparkled as if he were amused by the discussion.

"Think again." Taylor pointed at his legs. "I believe pants are part of the school's dress code."

Ryan glanced down. "Oh, pants. Of course. How forgetful of me."

Before Taylor could suggest that Ryan rethink his wardrobe, Coach Ballast came out of the locker room. He took one look at Ryan, who was standing there in his shirt, socks, shoes, and underwear, then tilted his head back and roared with laughter.

"I love this kid," he said. "What a joker." He held out a plastic-wrapped package that contained a stack of foil packets. "Here, Slugger. Take this. My treat. It's a protein powder. All the players use it. Helps build up muscle. Totally natural ingredients. A friend of mine's been trying to get me to sell it." The label had the words *Roaring Bull Protein Supplement*, along with a cartoonish picture of a bull blowing twin jets of steam from his nose and flexing one foreleg to show off a bulging biceps.

Sure makes me want to chug down a quart or two, Taylor thought.

"Thank you." Ryan took the package into the locker room.

"What a kidder," Coach Ballast said as he headed down the hall.

When Ryan came out, he was wearing pants, but he'd left his books behind. Taylor sent him back for them. When he emerged, he had his books, but he'd forgotten the protein powder. Taylor figured that was just as well. The last thing he needed was to bulk up like some cartoon bull.

"You're going to have to find a better way to discourage Coach Ballast," she told Ryan. "That's what's going on, right? You're acting weird to get him off your back."

"Weird?" Ryan asked. "What do you mean?"

"Never mind." Taylor went to lunch. When the period ended, she caught up with Ellis as he dumped his tray. "Does Ryan seem normal?" she asked.

"You're asking me? If I knew what normal was, I'd be the role model for it. I'd teach classes and run workshops. But I don't have a clue. You might as well ask me how to fly. Ellis the Earthbound. Of course, if I ate enough beans, I'll bet I could achieve lift-off. Ellis the Accelerated. Wow. I never thought of that before. If you were on some planet with really low gravity, and you farted, you'd end up in space. Assuming you weren't wearing a spacesuit. I guess if you were wearing a suit, you'd end up in deep doo doo."

Taylor got the feeling Ellis was hiding something. But she knew he was too loyal to Ryan to spill any secrets.

As she left the cafeteria, she walked past Kara, who was still at her table with a couple of friends. "Book girl," Kara said, sneering. Taylor thought about cutting her down with a clever comment, but figured it would be a pointless exercise. Anything sophisticated would go right over her head. Besides, in Taylor's world, *book girl* was a compliment. She hurried on, wondering why Kara had seemed so angry with her.

When her last class ended, Taylor pulled the disk from her pants and put it in the small front pocket of her backpack. She was positive it hadn't had any effect on her, but it still felt creepy carrying the thing so close to her body.

Obviously, the disk wasn't responsible for Ryan's weird behavior. There had to be another explanation. She wondered what kind of trouble he'd gotten into today. But much to her amazement, when she saw him at home he told her he hadn't had any problems.

"None at all?" she asked. As she spoke, she studied his upper lip. There was no sign of a mustache now.

"Nope. Looks like I'll get my skateboard back. You know what else? I think I did okay on my math test. As a matter of fact, I have a feeling I aced the sucker."

"That's great," Taylor said. "Be sure to tell Mom and Dad."

"They won't care," Ryan said.

"Of course they will."

"They only care when I do something they can yell about."

"That's not true. They'll be thrilled. You'll see."

Taylor was so sure she was right, she tried to get Ryan to talk at dinner. "Tell them about your math test," she said.

"It's not important."

"Come on. You think you did well, right?"

"Maybe. It wasn't as hard as usual."

While Taylor waited for her parents to react to this information, the doorbell rang. She ran down the hall, wondering whether they were about to get another fruit basket.

"Are your parents home?" the man on the porch asked.

"Sure. Come in." Taylor recognized him. It was Mr. Zorn, Ryan's algebra teacher. *This can't possibly be good,* she thought as she led him inside. Her hopes for a peaceful dinner faded away. "I'll get them."

She broke the news to her parents. Everyone followed her to the living room, where Mr. Zorn was pacing by the couch.

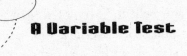

A Variable Test

Ryan wondered how anything he had done could possibly have brought the math teacher to his house. Nothing came to mind, but he had a feeling he wasn't getting his skateboard back tonight. If ever.

"I'm sorry to interrupt your evening," Mr. Zorn said. His face was pulled into a frown. "I need to talk with you about Ryan's algebra test."

"Let's hear the bad news," Mr. McKenzie said, as if he expected this all along.

Mr. Zorn held out a sheet of paper. "I just finished grading this exam at home. As you can see, your son achieved a perfect score."

Perfect? Ryan thought. His delight was erased by Mr. Zorn's scowl.

"He got a hundred!" Mrs. McKenzie asked. The glow of pride on her face was enough to light the room. "I knew he could succeed if he put his mind to it."

"Actually," corrected Mr. Zorn, "a hundred twenty, if you count the extra credit questions."

In the silence that followed, Ryan noticed that the news caused a variety of reactions. His mom was still smiling. His dad seemed suspicious. Taylor's expression puzzled him. It was so unexpected, he didn't recognize it at first. *She's jealous,* he realized. Nobody else in the family was supposed to break 100. Or 80, for that matter. She'd looked at him the same way when she'd asked about the home runs. He'd never seen her act like that before then. But he'd never done anything better than her before, either.

"Well, isn't that excellent," Mrs. McKenzie said.

"It *would* be wonderful," Mr. Zorn said, "except I can't quite figure out how a student with a sixty-three average suddenly managed to perform flawlessly." He stared at Ryan for a moment, then jabbed his finger midway down the page. "And I certainly can't figure out how he'd know enough to answer problem seven with an entirely different method than the one I taught in class. Either your son is a genius, or he's a very clever cheater."

"I didn't cheat," Ryan said. He waited for his parents to defend him. Neither of them spoke.

"Come on," Taylor said. "You know he's telling the truth. Has Ryan *ever* been accused of cheating? Even once?" She glanced at the test in Mr. Zorn's hand and frowned, as if she wasn't sure she believed her own argument.

"I guess not," Ryan's mom said.

"There's a first time for everything," Ryan's dad said. "Or maybe he's just never been caught before."

"It's easy enough to find out." Mr. Zorn held up another sheet of paper. "I took the liberty of preparing some new questions. All the boy has to do is answer them correctly, in my presence, using any method he wants, and I'll apologize for doubting him."

"Go ahead," Ryan's mom said. "Do the problems."

"No way. I already took the test. I'm not taking it again. School's over for the day." Ryan remembered how easy the test had seemed. But he didn't think the memory of that ability would be enough to help him now. He headed out of the room.

"Hold it!" Mr. McKenzie shouted. "You get right back here. Or else."

"Or else what?" Ryan asked, spinning around to face his dad. "What more can you do to me? Take away my air? Chain me to my bed?"

"Do it!" his father shouted.

Ryan snatched the paper from Mr. Zorn, grabbed a pencil from the coffee table, and knelt on the floor with the test. The great mind—the incredible genius, Albert Einstein—was gone. Ryan was on his own. He scribbled at the problems for a couple minutes, then dropped the pencil and stood up. It was hard to think with everyone staring at him. He wondered whether any of them knew that even Einstein had trouble with math when he was young.

Mr. Zorn studied the paper. "This looks more like your usual work," he said a moment later. "A little better than usual, perhaps, but far from perfect. You got the easy ones, except where you made careless errors. But you missed the hard one. It looks like you didn't really try. I'm going to let it go this time," he said, turning to Mr. McKenzie. "I can see you already have enough problems to deal with. But I hope you understand that there will be no second chance. If I catch your son cheating again, he'll be expelled."

"And I'd certainly support that decision," Ryan's dad said.

Ryan escaped to his room before anyone could yell at him again. "This sucks," he muttered as he sank down on his bed. The first time in his life that he did great on a test, he got in trouble for it. What was the point of trying?

His door swung open and Taylor walked in.

"I didn't cheat," Ryan said. "Honest to God, I didn't cheat."

"Hey, I'm the one who defended you down there," Taylor said. "Remember?"

"Right. But you still hated thinking I got a perfect score."

"No I didn't."

"Sure you did. I'm not blind, Taylor. I know what I saw."

"Well, maybe it bothered me a little," Taylor admitted. "But I was still on your side. Right?"

"I guess." Ryan couldn't argue with that. Taylor might be a pain in the butt, and she might be a smug-faced know-it-all who drove herself crazy trying to be the best at everything, but it was true—she'd stood up for him in front of two parents and a teacher. That was pretty brave.

"Something's going on," she said. "You've changed. Hitting home runs. Eating a dozen hot dogs. That stuff was crazy enough. But the math test proved it. I don't have a clue how you did some of those problems. No matter what anyone else thinks, I know you didn't cheat. There has to be another explanation." She reached out and touched his upper lip. "You had a mustache this morning. And now you don't. What's going on?"

Ryan was surprised she hadn't figured it out. But he realized Taylor found it hard to accept anything that didn't fit inside one of the neat little boxes into which she divided the world. The time had come to expand her universe. "If I tell you, you've got to promise to keep it a secret. Okay?" He didn't want her blabbing this to their parents. Ten seconds after his father learned about them, the disks would be history.

"There's no way I can make a promise like that."

"Look," Ryan said. "It's nothing illegal. It's not even against school rules. I can absolutely guarantee that nobody has ever told me not to do this. So, do you promise?"

"Sure. Okay. I promise."

"It's the disks."

Taylor shook her head. "Ryan, it's not the disks. I carried one with me all day. Am I stuffing my face with hot dogs or walking around without my pants?"

"You can't just carry them. You have to activate them."

"How?" Taylor asked.

Ryan closed his door, then reached into his closet. "I'll show you." Why not? He was in the mood to change his mind.

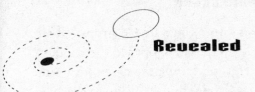

Revealed

I'm not falling for that Alkazar the Space Conqueror routine again," Taylor said. Eager as she was to learn the truth, she wasn't planning to play along with one of Ryan's stunts.

"This is for real," he said. "Watch what happens. It's so cool. Just try not to scream." Ryan flipped the disk.

"Oh my God!" Taylor gasped as the glowing disk sank into her brother's hand. The sight drew something far worse than a scream from her. It drew everything she'd eaten that day. Fighting the nausea, she fled to the bathroom, where she knelt by the toilet and threw up. Even after her stomach was empty, it spasmed each time the image ripped through her mind. She felt like she'd just witnessed some barbaric form of body modification.

Finally, when she felt she had everything under control, she climbed to her feet and rinsed her mouth. The next wave that hit her wasn't nausea, but panic. "Ryan!" she cried, realizing that she'd left him alone in his room with that awful thing melting through his hand. She dashed down the hall and through the door. "Are you—" The words hung in her throat. Ryan was perched atop the back of his chair.

"An audience," he said, rising up on his toes. "How marvelous."

"Get down from there," Taylor said.

"It would be a pleasure." He did a flip, landing with catlike grace between the desk and bed. "Come along, you must see this." He grabbed Taylor's hand and dragged her toward the window.

"Wait," she said. "What are you doing?"

"You're right. What was I thinking? I need props." Ryan dropped her hand, snatched up the chair, opened the window, and climbed onto the porch roof, taking the chair with him. Taylor rushed over just in time to see him swing up to the main roof.

"This is ridiculous," she muttered, climbing out after him.

Ryan scampered along the peak of the roof. When he reached the edge, he set the chair on one leg. Then he sat in the chair. "Fetch my bicycle," he called to Taylor.

Taylor couldn't even think of a response.

Ryan rose to a hand stand on the back of the chair and waved his legs in the air.

"Come inside," Taylor said. "Right now."

"Not until you applaud." He lifted one hand from the chair. "As you can see, I'm currently unable to do so myself."

"Just come in. *Please.*"

He shook his head. "I demand recognition. And admiration."

Taylor clapped.

"For this, I risk my neck?" Ryan said. "Show some enthusiasm."

Taylor clapped louder.

"Is that the best you can offer? It sounds like one horse taking a stroll."

Taylor clapped so hard her hands stung.

"I guess that will have to do." Ryan got to his feet, bowed, and carried the chair down from the roof with the ease of someone who performed daring stunts every day.

"What are you doing?" Taylor asked when they'd gone back inside. She grabbed his wrist and looked at his palm, afraid of what she might see. There was a disk shaped bump under his skin. But it was smaller than the disk he'd flipped. As she watched, it shrank even further. *It's dissolving,* she realized.

"You don't like feats of daring?" he asked, pulling his hand free. "Everyone likes feats of daring. Wait, I know! We must perform for the parents." He raced out the door.

"Stop," Taylor shouted, chasing after Ryan. If he started balancing on the furniture, their folks would have him locked up for sure.

Ryan performed cartwheels down the hall toward the stairs, then leaped onto the banister. He stuck out one leg and balanced on the toe of his other foot. Taylor heard her dad shout, "What's going on up there?"

"Nothing," Taylor called.

As she reached for Ryan, his face changed. The look of concentration softened, then vanished. "Uh-oh . . ." He waved his arms for balance, then toppled, landing right on top of her.

"Oof," Taylor grunted as they tumbled to the ground.

"Will you kids knock off that roughhousing!" Mr. McKenzie called from below.

Taylor pulled herself free and sat up.

"Whoa, that one wore off fast." Ryan held his hand out. "Look. All gone."

She stared at his palm. "It's real . . ."

"Yup," Ryan said. "Pretty cool, huh?"

"Cool?" Taylor sprang to her feet. "Did you see that thing melt into your hand? Not cool, Ryan. Not cool at all. Look what it made you do." She shuddered when she realized how close he'd come to giving a circus performance for their parents. Or falling off the roof.

"It didn't *make* me do anything. It *let* me. You'll change your mind when you try one," he said.

"No way." Taylor fought down another wave of nausea at the idea of a disk sinking into her skin. It would be like getting branded. That wasn't even the worst part. Ryan had obviously lost control of his actions when he'd used the disk. She would never put herself in that situation. Why would anyone want to go running around a roof? "Who were you?" she asked.

"Let me think," Ryan said.

"You don't even know who you were?" Taylor asked. "How could you not know?"

"Do you go around thinking 'I'm Taylor McKenzie'? On second thought, maybe you do. But whoever I was, I didn't. I mean, he didn't. So shut up for a second and let me think."

Taylor bit back a response. A couple seconds later, Ryan said, "I was The Great Blondin."

"Who?"

"The Great Blondin. The most famous high-wire artist in the world." He sounded surprised that she didn't recognize the name.

"I never heard of him," Taylor said. "You're making it up." She couldn't imagine Ryan would know something she didn't.

"Nope. It's true. I . . . he . . . was the first person to walk across Niagara Falls on a high wire," Ryan said. "I don't care whether you believe me." He headed back to his room.

Taylor went to her computer and got online. Within seconds, she found out there really was a Great Blondin.

"Did you check it out?" Ryan asked when Taylor came back to his room.

"Yup. He walked across Niagara Falls on a wire. Dangerous, risky, and pointless. Sounds like something you'd do."

"It's not pointless. It's amazing. Talk about someone who finished everything he started. I guess he didn't have much choice. He was an unbelievable guy. I learned tons of stuff about him from the disk. It's a lot of fun. Come on. You've got to try one."

"Absolutely not. And you shouldn't, either." This was totally unnatural. People weren't meant to absorb knowledge through their skin. Nothing came that easily. At least, nothing worthwhile. "Who knows what it's doing to your body. Or to your head."

"It's not doing anything. At least nothing bad. It cured my poison ivy. And look how I did on my algebra test."

"Yeah. And look at the trouble it caused," Taylor said.

"So I'll be more careful next time. It's none of your business, anyhow. Just remember, you promised not to tell."

"I remember." Taylor already regretted making that promise. She was sure Ryan was going to get into big trouble with the disks. Eventually, all of this would come tumbling down on his head.

PART THREE

Users

A child should always say what's true
And speak when he is spoken to,
And behave mannerly at table;
At least as far as he is able.

—Robert Louis Stevenson

Ryan's Rules

Ryan came up with some rules to keep himself out of trouble. Rule number one was obvious: *Never flip until after first period.* Ms. Gelman watched him too closely. All his teachers expected him to mess up, but the others didn't seem to take such a huge amount of pleasure in being proved right.

Rule number two: *Don't flip before a big test.* He'd already discovered there was nothing that would draw attention quicker than succeeding when everyone assumed he'd fail. They'd either think he was cheating, or ask him to join some stupid team. Since there was no way to know how long a disk would last, he wouldn't risk a flip in the morning even if the test was hours away.

Finally, rule number three: *Don't screw up your fun with too many rules.* He had no desire to live like Taylor, who seemed to have a rule for everything from how to behave to how to store her pencils. She kept her green pencils separate from her yellow ones, for God's sake. What was the difference? They both had gray lead.

Ryan discovered that the school day could be reasonably enjoyable when he wasn't himself. Thursday morning he became a Strong Heart warrior, one of the bravest of the Sioux. He let those around him chatter away, not joining in their endless conversations and constant boasting. There was strength in silence. Though he got yelled at for taking off his shoes.

That disk wore off before lunch, so he flipped again and spent the afternoon as an ancient Greek scientist. Unfortunately, science had changed a great deal over the years, so he had a bit of trouble when the teacher asked him a question about atomic bonds. And more trouble when he leaped to his feet during class and shouted, "I found it!" He couldn't help himself. He'd finally solved a difficult problem involving a gold crown.

Friday, things got a little weird. It was the first time he became a woman.

Snapshots: More Rules

There are some simple fashion rules," Kara told Ariel as they walked down the hall. "They make all the difference." It amazed her that so many girls just didn't get the most basic concepts. Even the sorriest loser could improve her appearance with a bit of effort.

Ariel nodded.

"You've got to lose that thrift-shop look," Kara said.

"I didn't get this at a thrift shop."

"Hey, I'm taking the trouble to help you. Don't argue with me," Kara said.

"Sorry."

"Do you want help or not?"

"Sure."

"Good. It's not like you're hopeless." Kara smiled at Ariel. "You could be pretty if you knew what to wear. You don't want anyone to mistake you for one of those losers."

Click

Rules are for whimps, Billy thought as he sat on the fence and dangled his legs over the "KEEP OFF THE FENCE" sign.

The park was the perfect spot to hang out now that the skaters realized how dangerous their sport was. People sometimes still walked along the paths, but not often, especially after dark. Cops came by each evening on foot. Billy knew their schedule and made it a rule to leave before they showed up. He just didn't seem to get along with them.

* * *

Click
    Ellis had one rule he lived by: *Avoid trouble.* Whether that meant trouble with teachers who could hurt his chances of maintaining his solid C average or trouble with sub-human thugs who could hurt him in much more painful ways, it was a rule that guided his every thought and action. The latest version of this rule was: *Don't go anywhere near the park.* The potential danger level had risen dramatically now that Snooks had turned the place into his own personal kingdom.

On the other hand, he figured there was no harm in taking up Ryan's offer to try a disk. He just wouldn't do it in school. That way, there'd be no chance of trouble.

Regal Bearing

yan held off flipping until after Spanish since they had a test every Friday. He was pretty sure he'd blown this one, as usual, but that was less likely to cause trouble than if he'd aced it by becoming some famous Spanish-speaking legend like El Cid, Picasso, or Old El Paso.

The instant he slipped into his seat in English, he flipped. Up front, Ms. Yancy started chirping about the joys of haiku. Around him, kids groaned.

A moment after the disk melted into Ryan's palm, Ellis poked him on the shoulder and whispered, "Haiku? Hi, cuckoo. Hichoo!" Ellis wiped his nose and sniffled like he'd sneezed, then shook his hand as if trying to fling something off his fingers.

Ryan studied him for a moment. "We are not amused."

Ellis gulped. "You just used another disk, didn't you. Wasn't yesterday enough? You went all morning without saying a word. Then you spent the whole lunch period floating stuff in your milk and muttering about gold crowns. You keep this up, they're going to carry you away."

Why was this horrid commoner questioning him? Ryan turned away from the rude boy and gave his attention to the delightful woman who was offering a most fascinating lecture on Japanese poetry. Such a wonderful country, Ryan thought. The ceramics and fabrics imported from there were among the loveliest in the world. As the bell rang, the teacher said, "Don't forget, your short stories are due on Monday."

Ryan went to the physical education session. As he stood by his locker, he nearly shrieked. But queens do not shriek. They may gasp, but they never shriek. Still, it was quite appalling to realize he was surrounded by boys. Noisy, boisterous, naked boys.

"I say," he commanded. "What's the meaning of this? I demand you all desist from disrobing immediately!"

The kids looked at Ryan and burst out laughing, as if his words were a joke.

"My word!" He scurried out of the locker room, fanning his face with his hand. This was thoroughly scandalous.

"Hold on there," someone called.

Who dared give him orders? Had everyone forgotten the proper protocol? A large peasant had approached. Most likely a woodcutter, based on the size of his arms and the massive blotches of sweat on his shirt. Was all of civilization falling apart?

"If my players cut gym once in a while, I don't have a problem." The man winked. "The team works really hard, so they deserve a break now and then."

Ryan had no idea what to do. He certainly wasn't going to wink back.

The man kept talking. "I'm looking forward to seeing you at tryouts. Oh boy—I gotta go. If I leave them alone too long, they'll stuff Izbecki in the supply closet." With that, he left.

Ryan remained in the hall. He had no desire to encounter anyone else. These former colonists were quite ill mannered.

"Are you alone in there?" Ellis asked the moment he came out of the locker room. He tapped Ryan's head.

"Yup. It's only me." The disk had worn off right before the end of the period.

"Who were you?"

Ryan thought back. This was the strongest disk he'd used so far. He realized he hadn't even recognized Coach Ballast. But there was no doubt what legend he'd been. "Queen Victoria."

"Oh gross," Ellis said. He shuddered like he'd just been tossed in a snow bank. "You ever seen a picture of her?"

Ryan nodded. Then he shuddered, too.

"Did you have 'em?" Ellis asked.

"Have what?"

"You know . . ." Ellis grabbed his own chest with two hands.

"Shut up."

"Why couldn't you have been someone hot? I mean, Marilyn Monroe is a legend, right? Wouldn't it be cool to share your head with someone like her? Whoa! Even better—wouldn't it be awesome to share your body with her?"

"I don't know," Ryan said. He really didn't want to think about it. But he wanted to share the thrill of the disks with Ellis. "You going to flip today?"

"Not here. It's too easy to get in trouble. I've already had enough of that for one day. And it wasn't even my fault. I mean, I didn't ask to get stuffed in the supply closet. Let's wait. I'll do it after school," Ellis said. "I think."

"Stop worrying," Ryan said as they headed down the hall toward the cafeteria. "It'll be great."

Even though a week had passed Billy still couldn't walk the halls without constantly scanning the crowds for a ponytail or a stupid alien face.

"Give it up," Lance said. "You're never going to find him."

Billy glared at Lance. *Better just keep your mouth shut.* But Lance didn't keep his mouth shut. "I'll bet he's told all his friends what he did. Bet he's told the whole town."

The rest was pure reflex. Billy swung hard, catching Lance on the side of his jaw with a right hook and knocking him clear across the hall. Lance hit the wall and dropped. For a moment, Billy worried that he'd killed him. That would be a real pain. His mother had already spent a bunch of money on lawyers the last time Adam got in trouble. For all the good it did. Billy was relieved to see Lance's hand twitch. A moment later, he opened his eyes.

"What's going on here?"

It was another stupid teacher, coming out of his classroom to snoop around. A young guy, this time.

Billy shrugged but didn't bother to say anything.

The teacher walked over to Lance, whose cheek was already starting to swell. "Are you all right? What happened?"

"Nothing." Lance pointed at his untied laces. "I tripped."

"Well, try to be more careful," the teacher said. He gave Billy an uneasy glance, then vanished back inside his classroom.

Billy kicked Lance. Not real hard. Just enough to make him grunt. He'd never kicked anyone in school before.

It felt nice.

"Come on, get up," he said. He realized if he didn't say something, Lance would stay right there all day. These guys were totally lost without him. He pretty much had to do their thinking for them. "You gotta get off the floor. You want to get in trouble?" It was a good thing he was there to watch out for his friends.

Billy realized he was hungry. He hadn't eaten much yesterday. His stomach had been too messed up. Probably that protein powder. He'd found a whole bunch of it in the locker room the other day, so he'd guzzled down four packs after school. But it tasted like crap and gave him the runs. He'd thrown the rest out. But he was feeling better now.

"Let's go to the truck," Billy said as Lance staggered to his feet. "I'll let you buy me lunch." He rubbed his right hand. It hurt, but not too badly. Lance's jaw wasn't all that much harder than a locker door.

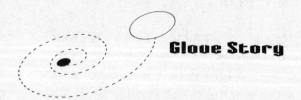

Glove Story

Want to go to the movies tonight?" Taylor asked Ariel at lunch.

Ariel shook her head. "I can't. I need to buy some clothes."

"That's fun, too," Taylor said. As much as she enjoyed window shopping, it was even better to go out with someone who actually planned to make a purchase. "There's a sale at that outlet store over in Smith's Ferry."

Ariel made a face. "No way. I need to go to Junie's Casuals."

It was Taylor's turn to make a face. The store was horribly expensive. "How're you going to afford that?"

"I've still got some of my birthday money," Ariel said.

"I thought you were getting a new glove."

"My old one's fine." Ariel picked up her milk carton and opened it. "Besides, I'm not even sure I'm playing softball this year."

"What a coincidence. I'm not playing softball this year, either," Susan said. "Or last year. Or the year before that. Or next year, for that matter."

"Not playing?" Taylor asked. She tried to catch Ariel's eye, but her friend wouldn't look at her. "We play every year."

"There's this cheerleading camp I heard about." Ariel pushed a straw into the open top of the carton. "It sounds like a lot of fun."

Taylor dropped the discussion. *What's next?* she wondered. One by one, the solid blocks that formed her world had started to crumble. The summer league wouldn't be the same without Ariel.

The mention of softball reminded Taylor that she hadn't seen Ryan on the field that morning. *It's not my problem,* she thought. She held off as long as she could. But, hard as she tried, she couldn't suppress her need to know. Near the end of the lunch period she went over to his table. "Did you cut gym?" she asked.

"I had permission," he told her.

"Permission?"

Ryan nodded. "I think it was some sort of free sample. Coach Ballast wanted me to see what it was like to be a member of his team."

"The guys on the team get all the breaks," Huey said.

"I wish they'd treat the band that way," Owen said.

"Think he'd let me do that?" Ellis asked.

"Sure—right after you overcome your fear of balls, bats, cleats, and sliding into base," Stitcher told him.

Huey grabbed Ryan's arm. "You gotta join the team!"

"No way," Ryan said. "Are you out of your mind?"

"Not at all. Just think about it—if you're on the team, that means we have a friend who's at the top of the popularity food chain."

"Yeah," Owen said. "Instant upgrade. This is too good an opportunity to miss."

Taylor knew what he meant. Every popular kid was like the center of a small solar system, with friends who shined from reflected light. Star athletes were among the brightest objects in the school universe. Ryan and his friends, right now, were distant comets, moving through the dark, empty places between suns. *So am I,* she realized.

"Do it for the good of the gang," Huey said. "Take the bullet for us."

"Not a chance," Ryan said.

The other boys headed out. But Ryan stayed in his seat and reached into his pocket.

Taylor heard the ping of a disk. "Will you please stop that? You're going to get into so much trouble."

Ryan gave her a kindly smile and stroked his chin. "Perhaps not," he said as he left the table. "You can fool some of the people all of the time."

"But you can't fool all of the people all of the time," Taylor called after him.

Presents of Mind

yan had powerful memories of the struggle to heal the nation after the war. Unfortunately, he had no memories of the concept of binary numbers. Math class didn't go well. Science was even more of a mystery than usual. He managed to survive wood shop without a mishap, which was actually an improvement. His teachers seemed to assume that anyone who did poorly in regular classes would be a genius with power tools. Based on his grades, they apparently expected Ryan to build whole castles out of scrap lumber. Instead, he'd made a candleholder that exploded on the lathe, a clock that fell apart when he tried to take it home, and a bookcase with more strange angles than a flight of fun-house stairs.

Art went okay, though Ms. Alvarez still wouldn't look him in the eye. He noticed that there weren't any scissors, chisels, or knives in sight. Midway through art, the disk wore off.

After school, Ellis came home with him. Ryan was all set to flip. But Ellis wasn't. He kept listing reasons why he should wait until tomorrow, or the weekend, or maybe next month. Or after graduation, at the very latest. Or right after college.

Ryan waited patiently. But as it got closer to five-thirty, he realized they were running out of time. His father would be home soon. They needed to flip right away, and then get out of the house.

"No more excuses. No stalling. You have to flip," Ryan said. He grabbed a disk from his closet. "It's awesome."

"I don't know," Ellis said. "You've been getting into a lot of trouble with them."

"Hey, I get in trouble without them," Ryan said. "Come on.

Just think—we'll be the only two people on Earth who've ever experienced alien technology."

Ellis sighed. "What do I do?"

"Just flip it."

Ellis took the disk and flipped it up in the air with the exaggerated motion of a ref making a Super Bowl coin toss. He caught it on his palm. "Didn't work. It figures I'd get a dud disk."

"Flip it hard," Ryan said. "You've got to give it a ton of spin."

"Like this?" Ellis flipped the disk again. It shot across the room, ricocheted off the wall, and flew back toward Ellis's head. He screamed and ducked.

"Not quite," Ryan said as the high-pitched cry stabbed at his ear drums. He picked up the disk. "Here. Hold out your hand." It would be easier to flip for Ellis than to try to teach him how.

"You sure it won't hurt?" Ellis asked. "I have a very low tolerance for pain."

"It won't hurt at all." Ryan spun the disk in an arc toward Ellis's palm.

At the last instant, Ellis jerked his hand back. "Sorry," he said as the disk fell to the floor and lost its glow. "I got nervous. Ellis the Apprehensive."

"Relax." Ryan picked up the disk, relieved to see it hadn't melted into the floor.

Ellis held out his hand again and closed his eyes. He whimpered when the disk hit his palm, but kept his arm still. "Can I look now?"

"Not yet." Ryan was afraid Ellis would panic if he saw the disk melting into his flesh. Some people just seemed freaked out by that. Like Taylor. Though Ellis wasn't the sort to puke. "I hope you get someone cool." He figured it wouldn't hurt Ellis to spend time as a great leader or champion athlete. It might even give him some confidence.

A moment later, Ellis's eyes shot open. He gasped and backed away from Ryan.

"What's wrong?" Ryan asked.

Ellis scanned the room as if he'd suddenly found himself in a chamber of horrors. He edged toward the door. "So many dangers. So many traps. So many ways to die."

"Chill out," Ryan said. "Just hang here until you get it under control. Okay?"

"Here?" Ellis asked. "Not in this house. No. Not here. The walls could fall and crush us both. Or bury us alive. I must find a safe haven." His gaze shot to the floor and all color drained from his face. "Do you hear that? The heart! It's still beating! It won't die!"

"Wait," Ryan called as Ellis fled. Ryan chased after him. Before he reached the bottom of the stairs, he heard the front door slam. He hurried to catch up.

"Where do you think you're going?" Mr. McKenzie shouted from the hallway where he was hanging his coat.

Ryan froze. Thank goodness his father hadn't caught them flipping.

"I'm sure you've got plenty of school work to keep you busy," Mr. McKenzie said. "If you spent less time running around, you might actually make something of yourself."

Ryan swung by the kitchen to grab the portable phone. At least he could call Ellis and find out what was going on. Ellis had a cell phone in his bedroom. Ryan knew that's where it would be. Ellis never took it anywhere because he was afraid someone would steal it.

"Poor guy," Ryan said. He went upstairs and waited for Ellis to get home. "I guess you didn't become Marilyn Monroe."

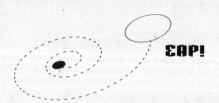

1843

Ellis shrank against the far wall of his brain as fears flooded through him like angry snakes. These weren't his fears. Not his alone. The man had brought them when he'd burst into Ellis's mind.

Death lay everywhere. Shadows hid dark creatures who waited to pounce and sink their claws into his flesh. The animals in the street could devour him at any moment. Even the small ones were a danger. A squirrel bite could spread an incurable disease through his bloodstream, leaving him frothing at the mouth as insanity overwhelmed his mind. A tree, its inner rot concealed from the eye, might topple at the merest breeze, pinning him to the earth as he slowly died of asphyxiation.

His heart fluttered like a moth beating itself to death against a window. He ran home, hurrying toward the only act that could drown out the fears, the only way to remove the demons.

In his room, he grabbed a pencil and paper.

Title? "The Death of a Boy." Setting? An ancient town near the coast of Britain. No, make it more exotic. Portugal. Yes, that was perfect. A seaport town amidst winding streets paved with ancient stones.

Write! He poured his fears into words that could freeze the strongest heart. It was a story of loss and sorrow. Darker than his tale about the pit and the pendulum. Crueler than the story of the black cat. Bleaker than his poem about the raven. Hopeless. Lost. Forlorn.

Nearby, the bells rang. Bells. Constant bells. He shut his mind against the sound. *Tintinnabulation.* The bells rang on.

He wrote for hours, then collapsed into a deathlike sleep.

Ryan didn't see Ellis until Saturday afternoon. "You okay?" he asked when Ellis came into his room. "I tried calling you all night." He stared at the heavy circles under his friend's eyes. "The phone kept ringing, but you didn't answer it."

"Never more," Ellis said.

"What?"

"I mean, never again."

"Was it that bad?" Ryan asked.

"Bad? Do you have any idea who I was?"

Ryan shook his head. He didn't have a clue.

"I was Edgar Allan Poe," Ellis said. "He was so terrified of everything, he makes me look fearless. I still can't get some of his nightmares out of my mind." Ellis whacked himself on the forehead with his palm. "I don't know if I'll ever be able to go into an old house again."

"Sorry," Ryan said. He hadn't thought it was possible to have a bad experience with a disk. "I wasn't trying to freak you out."

Ellis plopped down on a chair. "That's okay. At least I got my story written for English."

"Don't let one bad experience turn you off. You need to try another disk," Ryan said. "You could get someone really cool."

"No way."

"It'll be great this time. I promise. You could be King Arthur. Wouldn't that be awesome? Or Julius Caesar."

"Caesar got stabbed about a zillion times," Ellis said. "By his friends. Not my idea of a wonderful memory. Ellis the Pin Cushion."

"Okay, bad example," Ryan said. "But it's been great for me every time. Even the queen was kind of cool. Did you know she could draw real well?"

"Ryan, I don't care if she could fly through the air and fart quarters. I am never ever touching another of those disks."

"You sure?"

Ellis nodded.

That was too bad. Ryan had hoped they could do some disks together. It looked like he'd just have to use them all himself.

Life was good for Billy. He had his own place to hang out. And nobody mentioned the kid with the ponytail. Everything was under control. "I'm like one of those warlords," he said to Lance as they sat in the park after school.

"Whatcha mean?" Lance asked.

Sometimes, Billy just wanted to choke Lance for being so stupid. "I got this for us. Right?"

"Right," Lance said. "You got this for us."

Billy imagined himself in armor, leading an army and riding a giant horse through a field of enemies, slaying them with a sword so heavy no other man could lift it, and then claiming the land for his own.

Click
Ellis missed Ryan. The old Ryan, that is. The one he could depend on. *I'm Ellis the Overstressed*, he thought. It was horrible not knowing from moment to moment who his friend would become. The possibilities were endless. Ryan was channel surfing through history with an unmarked remote control and no program guide. The potential for disaster was infinite. Sooner or later, it would all have to end badly.

Click
Kara had never met a boy she couldn't completely control. Until now. Ryan acted like he lived in his own little world. Maybe he was playing hard to get. It wouldn't work. She wasn't

going to waste time chasing him. She didn't chase boys. They chased her. That's the way it was. No boy was worth that kind of effort. *He's just not my type, anyhow,* she thought. It was his loss. Besides, she'd never really been interested in him.

Click
     Taylor realized any attempt to control Ryan was destined to fail. He'd do what he wanted, no matter what she said. That didn't keep her from trying. She couldn't seem to stop herself. At least he'd eventually run out of the disks. Then everything would get back to normal. Assuming he didn't do something disastrous while he was sharing his head. He had no idea how lucky he'd been to make it this far. Taylor hoped his luck would hold a while longer.

Getting Hip

Life was great for nearly a week and a half as Ryan flipped out with an awesome assortment of legends. One morning, he conquered the world, then wept because there were no worlds left to conquer. He flew on wings of feathers and wax from a tower prison, soaring over the labyrinth he'd built on the island of Crete. He planted the seeds of a thousand apples, and shot another off the head of his son. He went to the Olympics in 1935 and showed the world that an American athlete could leave arrogant racists in the dust. He searched Florida for the Fountain of Youth, repelled the Saxons from Britain with the help of a wizard, danced the role of the prince in *Swan Lake* at the Bolshoi Ballet, traveled the Underground Railroad, and survived the sinking of the *Titanic*.

The bigger the legend, the harder it was to keep control, but so far, none of them had caused any real problems. He still got into trouble, but no more than before the disks. Not at first. Then, Wednesday morning after social studies, Ryan flipped himself a whole lot of heartbreak.

The moment the disk sank into his palm, Ryan felt his lip twitch. He felt his hip jerk. He slicked back his hair, then stepped into the crowded hallway.

Something was wrong. They weren't mobbing him. They weren't swarming over him, screaming, fainting, throwing themselves at him.

"I'll just have to give them a show," he said. "Remind them who I am." He strode through the open doors of the auditorium. This was where he belonged. A couple of kids followed him. That was better. He was already feeling more like himself.

He grabbed the mic stand from behind the curtain and dragged it to center stage. No guitar. No backup band. He'd have to do without. That was okay. He knew how to take care of business. He hadn't even opened his mouth yet, and they'd started to come, pulled by the power of his personality. But he was just warming up. He wouldn't be satisfied until every seat was filled.

Leaning close to the mic, he let fly. Man, it felt good. It felt right. It made him feel so alive.

More Games

Life."

"Cereal."

"Death."

"Inconvenient."

"Fiction."

"Heat."

"Heat?"

"Yeah. Heat. You know, friction causes heat."

"I said *fiction.*"

"Oh. Sorry. Look, is this necessary?" Ellis asked. He'd been with the woman all morning and was getting tired. Though the attention was nice.

"We're just worried about you," Dr. Joyceman said. "Your English teacher thought your story was a little bit . . ."

"Morbid?" Ellis asked.

"Disturbing," Dr. Joyceman said.

"Dark?"

She nodded. "Forbidding."

"Ominous?"

"Threatening."

"Brooding?"

"Introspective."

"Hamburger?"

Dr. Joyceman stared at him.

"Oops," Ellis said. "I thought we were playing that word game again. Figured it was my turn to go first." He sighed and went back to trying to convince her that he wasn't depressed, suicidal, or insane.

Dr. Joyceman held up an abstract painting. "Tell me what you see."

"A lack of talent?"

"No. That's not what I mean. Tell me what images you see in the painting."

Ellis saw a man attacking a hamster with a samurai sword, but he figured it would be best to leave out the sword part and just mention the hamster. They moved on to the next picture, which clearly showed two witches setting each other on fire, followed by one featuring a whole room full of coffins. Ellis didn't mention any of that. In the middle of the test, he paused and glanced at the door.

"What's wrong?" Dr. Joyceman asked.

"Do you hear singing?"

"Do *you* hear singing?" she asked, grabbing a pen from the desk.

"No," Ellis said. He didn't like the way she'd perked up. She reminded him of a cat who'd just spotted an injured bird. "I don't hear anything. I never hear anything. It was just a question. You know, like *Do you think it's going to rain?*"

"Let's try not to get distracted," Dr. Joyceman said, putting her pen back down.

"Sorry."

"Have you ever had a ringing in your ears?" she asked.

"No!" Ellis screamed. "My ears are just fine. Can I go? Are we finished?"

"Good for you—screaming is a sign of progress. Let it out. I think you're repressing too many of your feelings. That's not healthy. I'd like to get together with you on a regular basis. I truly believe it could help." She opened an appointment book and leafed through the pages, then shuffled through Ellis's file.

"That really isn't necessary," Ellis said. "It was just a story. Honest. I'm the happiest guy on the planet. Ellis the Adjusted. I'm famous throughout the school for my optimistic outlook. Life is grand. It's a wonderful adventure."

"Fourth period would be good," she said. "Maybe two or three times a week. Of course, you'd have to miss gym and health."

"I guess there's a lot to talk about," Ellis said. "I'm feeling sort of repressed. This could take the rest of the year." He looked toward the door again. "You sure you don't hear singing?"

I'm with the Band

The shortest path from science to English involved a narrow, crowded flight of stairs. During the first two weeks of school, after timing several routes, Taylor discovered it was quicker to go around to the front hall and cut through the auditorium. Usually, the auditorium was empty second period. Today, a cluster of kids jammed the doors. Singing—loud, wild singing—echoed off the walls. *Please let me be wrong*, Taylor thought as she pushed through the crowd. She hoped she'd find someone other than Ryan at the center of the disturbance. Anyone else.

No such luck.

"This is insane," Taylor said. Ryan couldn't carry a tune. Whenever he sang along with the radio in the car, she had to hum real loud to drown him out. But right now, he was doing a lot more than carrying the tune. He was singing the heck out of it.

And dancing. No, it wasn't dancing. It was something else. His feet stayed where they were, but his hips kept moving. The only word Taylor knew that came close was *gyrating*. Ryan finished the song, drawing loud applause from the crowd.

Oh lord, Taylor thought when she recognized the next song from late-night ads for oldies music. It was "Jailhouse Rock." Ryan was singing and moving like Elvis.

More kids crowded through the door. A couple of girls were dancing in the aisles. Taylor spotted Kara and her friends in the front row.

The last thing Ryan needs is attention, Taylor thought. She scanned the auditorium to make sure Billy Snooks wasn't around. She was still worried that, one way or another, the bully and her brother would eventually come face to face. At the moment, there was no sign of Snooks. But there were other signs of trouble.

Like a salmon fighting the current, Gilbert pushed his way out the door. On stage, Ryan kept singing, and playing an imaginary guitar.

All too soon, Gilbert returned, along with the principal. "Up there," Gilbert said, unnecessarily pointing toward the stage.

"Come on folks, let's get on to your classes," Principal Guthrie shouted. "You all have somewhere you're supposed to be." He climbed the steps to the stage and grabbed Ryan. A moment later, the two of them disappeared out the side exit.

As Taylor sat through the rest of her classes, she imagined the explosions this would cause. At the end of the day, she was almost afraid to go home. When she got there, she found Ryan up in his room.

"I told you something would happen," she said.

"Congratulations. Give yourself an A. No, make that an A plus. It must be rough being so smart."

"Does Mom know yet?"

Ryan nodded. "Oh yeah. She knows. They called her to come get me."

"Great. She must have been furious."

"She wasn't too happy."

"You weren't still Elvis when she came for you?" Taylor asked. She could just picture that encounter. *Good to see you, Momma. Let's go for a spin.*

"Nope. It wore off. I wish it hadn't. You have no idea how awesome it feels to capture a whole crowd with a song."

"Sure I do," Taylor said. "I'm in the chorus. We did that holiday show. Remember?"

Ryan snorted and shook his head. "I'm not talking about putting a bunch of parents to sleep with 'Oh Tannenbaum.'"

"Hey, we sounded real good," Taylor said. "We even got our picture in the paper. And it was my own voice. Not some trick that didn't last."

Ryan's smirk faded. "Yeah. I guess you're right."

"Well, it could have been worse. Imagine if they'd called Dad at the bank. Then you'd really be in trouble." Mr. McKenzie was a loan officer. From what Taylor knew, he spent a good part of his day explaining to people why they couldn't borrow money, and then sitting there while they yelled and told him how rotten the bank was. He'd wanted to leave all that for a career as a management consultant—whatever that was—but the complete failure of his book had put an end to those plans.

"Mom called him as soon as we got to the car." Ryan sighed, then started humming a random collection of notes that bore a slight resemblance to "Blue Suede Shoes."

Taylor decided to leave the room before he started singing. She thought about leaving the house, too. She probably would have if there wasn't so much homework waiting for her. She wasn't looking forward to being around when her father got home. He was edgy enough most of the time, without receiving any phone calls about Ryan.

Around five-thirty, as she sat in her room double checking her algebra worksheet, she heard a car pull into the driveway. Then she heard the car door slam. Hard.

His Cup Runneth Over

Ryan's bedroom door swung open so hard it slammed into the wall. He looked up at his father, who was standing in the doorway clutching a white paper bag.

"It stops right now," Mr. McKenzie said.

He knows! Ryan thought. Guilt and panic surged through him. But that was ridiculous. Nobody knew, except for Ellis and Taylor. Ellis would never tell. Had Taylor broken her promise? Ryan glanced at his palm. There was no sign of the disk. But right now, with his father glaring at him, Ryan wished he wasn't alone in his head.

"Come here," Mr. McKenzie said. He jammed his hand in the bag and yanked out a clear plastic container with a green lid. "Fill this."

"What?" Ryan asked.

"Take the damn cup into the bathroom and fill it. Do I have to draw you a diagram?"

"You want me to pee in the cup?" Ryan asked.

His father nodded.

"You've got to be kidding," Ryan said.

"Now!"

Ryan snatched the cup from him and walked to the bathroom. Through the closed door, he heard Taylor rush into the hallway.

"Dad, you don't really think he's on drugs, do you?" she asked. "He couldn't be. There's no way."

"Thanks," Ryan whispered.

"I don't know what to think anymore," Mr. McKenzie said.

"Stop looking at me like I'm the bad guy. All right? I'm not the enemy. I'm his father and I'm trying to do what's best for him."

Leave me alone. That's what's best for me. Ryan returned to the hallway and handed the cup to his dad.

"I'll have the results Friday afternoon. Until then, when you aren't in school, you stay in your room. You eat up here. You study up here. You live up here. Understand."

"Yeah, sure," Ryan said. He didn't mind missing the family dinners. He had plenty of company waiting for him in his jacket pocket.

Prescription Plan

Taylor was afraid Ryan would activate another disk and run wild through the house. But when she peeked into his room that evening, he was lying in bed with his back toward her. She stepped inside and called his name, but he didn't answer, so she shut the door softly and went back to her room.

As bad as things were, she realized there was a glimmer of hope. Ryan would pass the drug test. She smirked at the irony of him finally acing an exam. She needed to think of some way to use that knowledge as a bargaining tool with her dad. The thought of her dad drew Taylor's eyes to her window. *Better close it before the show begins,* she thought.

As she grabbed the bottom of the window, the first words drifted up.

"You read the letter," Mr. McKenzie said.

I'm not going to listen. Taylor started to close the window.

"I know it seems drastic, but the school psychologist recommends it."

Taylor froze when she heard those words. She didn't want to eavesdrop. But she couldn't bring herself to shut the window.

"You read her letter. It's not just that he doesn't pay attention. The problems go way deeper. He's self-destructive. He's also delusional. She suspects he might even have some form of multi-personality disorder."

"He's our son," Mrs. McKenzie said.

"Look, we can't help him if we hide from the truth. I think we should follow her suggestion and get an appointment with this Dr. Mehan. Apparently, he's had a lot of luck with Zembutrol.

It's new. Not even on the market yet. He's doing some kind of test studies."

Drugs? Taylor thought.

She couldn't hear what her mother said next. But then her father started talking again. "Bob Sylveri at work swears it's the best thing that's ever happened to his kid. It's like a miracle. He's a different boy."

When she heard the name *Sylveri*, Taylor felt a weird ripple crawl across her flesh. There was a kid in her English class. She thought his name might be Sylveri, but she wasn't sure. He sat in the back and was real quiet. She couldn't remember him ever speaking. She wondered whether that was the kid her father was talking about.

The Dark of Night

It seemed a shame to waste a disk up in his room. But right now, Ryan didn't want to be himself. *Make it a good one,* he thought as he reached into the coat pocket and ran his fingers through his stash. He grabbed a disk and brought it to his bed. He'd become so good at flipping, he could do one without looking at it.

"Take me out of here," Ryan whispered as heat penetrated his palm.

He got his wish.

The world disappeared with a swiftness that staggered Ryan. Not just sight. Sound vanished, too, with deafening suddenness. For a moment, he was overwhelmed by the fear that he'd be lost in darkness forever. Then, as the memories filled his mind, he relaxed. He, no . . . she . . . knew this world. Not everything had gone away. There was touch. Vibrations, warmth and chills, air currents. There was smell. It was a rich world. She remembered the first teacher, the one who'd rescued her from isolation.

She explored the bedroom. It offered the senses so many rewards. In the closet, each of the three types of coat hanger— metal, plastic, wood—had a different feel. The metal hanger left its bitter scent on her fingertips.

An apple on the desk rewarded her with a flood of tart and sweet flavors. The hard stem clung to the dimpled top, making a wonderful contrast to the waxy peel.

The walls were rough. They'd been painted with a brush, not a roller. The painter had grown careless near the corners and worked too quickly. Something had once hung near the window.

The nail was gone, but the hole remained, along with a small depression where the hammer had struck too hard.

She made her way around the rest of the room and, finally, lay down in bed. The sheets had been laundered recently.

Airflow and vibrations. Behind her, the door opened. Someone stepped inside. The visitor left quickly.

Sleep came easily.

In the morning, Ryan was surprised to find he could see and hear.

Argument

On Thursday in English, Taylor checked the back of the room. The kid was there, quietly staring ahead as if he saw a different world than the rest of the class.

She tapped Susan on the arm, then pointed. "What's his name?"

"Ben Sylveri." Susan wrinkled her nose. "He used to be totally out of control. Spent a ton of time in the principal's office."

"He's pretty quiet now," Taylor said.

"Yeah. I think his folks got him stoned out on something."

During the period, Taylor kept sneaking glances at Ben. When she looked in his eyes, it felt like there was nobody home. At one point, a thin line of spit drooled from the corner of his mouth onto his desk. He didn't seem to notice. Taylor shuddered, turned away, and avoided looking back again.

Instead, she thought back to the beginning of the year, hunting for memories of a different Ben Sylveri. As she sorted through a thousand crowded images, she found him. A wild, noisy kid. One memory, stronger than the others, returned with a jolt. He was the one who'd sucked the ketchup up his nose the first week of school.

Whatever he'd been before the medicine, he was a zombie now, spaced out on Zembutrol. She could still hear her dad's voice. *Bob Sylveri at work swears it's the best thing that's ever happened to his kid. It's like a miracle.*

"More like a nightmare," Taylor whispered.

After school, she went right up to Ryan's room. She didn't want to tell him about the plans to drug him. Not if she could avoid it. The house was already enough of a battleground. If he knew, he'd probably start screaming at their father, or do something really crazy, and then he'd definitely be hauled off to see Dr. Mehan. Maybe, if she could figure out some way to get him to stop using the disks and stay out of trouble, there'd be a chance.

"You ever think about taking a break from the disks?" she asked.

"No way. They're great. You should be happy—I'm learning all sorts of stuff."

"That's not how people learn," Taylor said.

"It's how I learn. Hey, that reminds me. I've been thinking about something."

"What?"

"I'd bet you'd like physics. It's your kind of thing."

"Physics is okay. But I like chemistry," Taylor said. "And you have no idea what *my thing* is."

"You'd like physics even more," he said. "I'm not talking about the baby stuff you've done in science class. You know, pulleys and ropes and all that crap. I'm talking about the really deep stuff. The fabric of the universe. It's perfect for you. Have you ever read about Einstein?"

"I know all about Einstein," Taylor said. "More than you." She couldn't believe he was trying tell her what to study.

"If you're so smart," Ryan said, "tell me what Einstein won the Nobel Prize for."

"That's easy," Taylor said. "The theory of relativity. Everyone knows that."

Ryan shook his head. "Then everyone's wrong."

"No they aren't," Taylor said.

"Yes they are. Look it up."

"I wouldn't waste my time," Taylor said as she walked out of Ryan's room. "I know when I'm right."

"Nineteen twenty-one," he called after her.

"This is stupid." Taylor was sure she was right. She went on-line to find proof. She wanted to rub the information in Ryan's face and wipe away that smug expression.

But there it was. Albert Einstein had been awarded the Nobel Prize in Physics for his work on the photoelectric effect. In 1921. His theory of relativity came later, he didn't get a Nobel Prize for that.

"I was wrong," Taylor said. She kicked the leg of her desk. This wasn't fair. She'd earned every scrap of knowledge she'd ever learned, and here was Ryan getting tons of facts dumped into his head without turning a page or taking a single note. If everyone did that, there'd be no reason to study. No reward for effort.

She realized her attempt to stop him from using the disks had totally failed. She needed time to come up with a better plan. It was useless to try to talk with him right now, anyhow. All he'd want to do is gloat about being right.

For the moment, she decided to read the article on the photoelectric effect. It looked interesting. Not that she'd ever admit it to Ryan.

When Taylor answered the phone after dinner, a voice she didn't recognized said, "Mr. McKenzie, please."

Her father hated to be disturbed in the evening. "Who's calling?" she asked.

"Dr. Mehan."

Taylor clutched the phone and thought about Ben Sylveri. She wanted to tell the doctor he had a wrong number. Or that the McKenzies had moved. Or offer any of a dozen other lies.

"Hello? Are you there?" he asked.

"Yeah. Hold on. I'll get him."

Taylor watched her father's eyes when she said, "It's a Dr. Mehan."

"I'll take it in the bedroom," he said. Something flickered across his face, but he turned away too quickly for her to tell whether it was guilt or relief.

Later, he came downstairs and wrote Dr. Mehan's name on the calendar. As Taylor had feared, her brother had an appointment a week from Monday.

The knowledge kept her awake that night. *Should I tell Dad about the disks? Would it help?* She saw a thousand ways that any attempt to save Ryan could go wrong. Her dad would ask her how long she'd known and why she hadn't spoken sooner. He'd use the disks as proof that Ryan was out of control. Worst of all, if she broke her word, Ryan would never trust her again.

Taylor didn't know what to do. But she knew she had to do something. She found her father in the living room, watching one of his favorite old movies, *The Natural*, about a baseball player.

"Can I talk with you?" she asked him.

"Sure," he said, pausing the movie. "Need an advance on your allowance? I have the power to approve loans, you know."

Taylor couldn't think of any way to slide gently into the subject. "You can't put Ryan on Zembutrol."

His face hardened. "How do you know about that?"

"I heard you and Mom talking about it."

"You're listening to our conversations? That's something I'd expect from your brother. Not from you. I'm very disappointed." He turned the remote control over and over in his hands as he spoke.

Taylor shook her head. "I wasn't trying to. I heard you from my room."

"It's none of your business," he said. "This isn't about you."

"It is my business! You want to turn my brother into a zombie. First you go crazy because you think he's on drugs, and then you decide to put him on drugs. That makes sense."

Mr. Mckenzie got off the couch. "You have no idea what you're talking about. This is for his own good. The boy needs to learn to deal with reality."

"Reality?" Taylor shouted. "Nobody in this family wants to deal with reality. Look at us! Mom spends every minute she can with her nose buried in those romance books. I spend half my life studying for tests and the other half memorizing spelling words so I can beat some pathetic little toad whose existence is even emptier than mine."

She waved in the direction of the television. "You spend all your free time watching old movies and baseball games. The first thing you do after work is have a drink. Too much reality following you home from the bank?"

"Stop it, Taylor," her father warned.

She couldn't stop. "Ryan's the only one who ever even tried to deal with reality. He's the only real person in this whole stupid family."

"You are way out of line."

"Don't do this to him," Taylor begged.

"Go to bed." His voice was barely under control. "Go!"

Taylor sped away from him before her mouth could get her into more trouble. She ran upstairs and slammed her door. "Damn it all!" she yelled as she threw herself down on her bed. The whole world felt out of control. She'd never shouted at her father before. Not like this.

Bored, and deprived of the company of his best friend, Ellis cranked the volume on his stereo and spent Thursday night studying the drawings of the disks. For fun, he made a list of the characters. There were forty-three, all together. Thirty-five appeared on the top half.

Ellis figured they were some sort of alphabet. The other eight only showed up at the bottom.

"Why eight?" he asked himself. He tapped his fingers on his leg. Then he looked down at his hand and said, "Why not?"

He couldn't wait to tell Ryan what he'd figured out.

Click

Kara couldn't get Ryan out of her mind. Not that she wanted to. He'd been amazing in the auditorium. They'd look unbelievably hot together at the graduation dance, too. He might not know it yet, but he was taking her. She couldn't believe she'd almost decided he wasn't her type.

Click

Billy had managed to push the bad thing from his mind during the day. But it ran through his thoughts every night. At first, he'd focused on the instant when the freak had shouted that insult. As he lived through the moment over and over, the scene stretched back. He'd been walking with Lance, Rick, and Jimmy. Lance told him Johnny's number. He'd needed a pencil, so he'd grabbed a backpack. He couldn't remember anything special about it. Couldn't even remember who it had belonged to. Just another faceless girl. There'd been a scream, too. A weird one. Like a little dog getting flattened. It echoed in his memories. Pure fear. He'd know it if he ever heard it again. He was an expert on all the flavors of fear.

A Bit of Hope

Taylor was nervous about going down to breakfast. She spent a few extra minutes in her room cramming for her social studies test, hoping her father would leave early. It was a big test. She'd studied all week, but it never hurt to put in some extra time. Finally, she knew she couldn't hold off any longer.

"Good morning," Mrs. McKenzie said when Taylor reached the kitchen.

Her father grunted a greeting from behind his newspaper, not even looking at her. Taylor gulped down her yogurt, eager to get on her way. As she headed for the door, he finally spoke. "We need to talk."

"I'm sorry about last night," Taylor said. Across the kitchen, her mother was taking all of the spice jars out of the cabinet.

"We both probably could have been calmer," her father said. "I understand you really care about your brother. That's good. Don't ever get the idea I don't care. I've been thinking about it all night."

She noticed dark shadows under his eyes, like the ones she'd seen in the mirror this morning. She'd drifted in and out of sleep, haunted by images of Ryan becoming Ben Sylveri. That would almost be like he'd died.

"It's so tempting," her father said. "So easy. Nothing else works. A little pill. What's the harm?"

He seemed to be thinking out loud as much as talking to her. *He really doesn't know what to do.* That scared her. Parents were supposed to have all the answers. But it also gave her hope.

"Maybe it just looks easy," Taylor said. "I've heard some of those drugs have bad side effects."

"The last thing I want to do is take any risks with either of you. But I don't know what else to try. I just can't get through to him."

"What if you gave him another chance?"

"That's all he's had. Years of chances. It's not that way in the real world. Nobody gives you a second chance. You get one shot. You either make the team, or you fail."

"He's doing better in gym," Taylor said, grasping for anything positive. "Coach Ballast loves him. I know he's going to pull up his other grades, too. I can help him study." It would be tough, but she'd find the time.

Her father shook his head. "Taylor, he's not getting better. Just the opposite. Did you see any of the stunts he pulled during the last couple of weeks? He's causing more trouble than ever. He's totally out of control. It just gets worse and worse. Maybe the drug test will explain all of this."

Taylor seized the opening. "If his drug test comes back okay, can you just let him have a couple of days to prove himself? He can do better. I know he can. I'll talk to him."

"What's the point?" her father asked.

"What's the harm?" she asked back. "What's the worst thing he's ever done? He's never hurt anyone. He's never gotten in a fight or destroyed anything. There are kids at school who beat people up. How'd you like to have a son like that?"

Her father's face had grown cold again, and his eyes shifted away from hers. "He's hurt his parents plenty of times."

"Please, just give him another chance."

"Not without a good reason. It's pointless."

Defeated, Taylor left the house. She didn't get far.

Ryan waited upstairs until he heard his father drive off. No point offering him another chance to deliver a lecture. His mother, who seemed pretty wrapped up in reorganizing the spice cabinet, kept giving him funny looks, but she didn't say anything. When he left, he was surprised to find Taylor sitting on the curb just one block past the house. "You okay?" he asked.

She turned toward him, her eyes streaked with tears. Ryan clenched his fists and scanned the street, ready to chase down whoever had hurt his sister. Someone was going to pay.

"What happened?" he asked.

As he stepped closer, she leaped up and started screaming at him. "Damn you, Ryan. Damn you!"

Ryan froze. Taylor kept screaming. Kids on their way to school stared at them, then hurried past. When Taylor stopped yelling and started sobbing again, Ryan said, "What did I do?"

She didn't even seem to hear the question. "I can't take it anymore," she said. "I just can't. Every day. Every minute. All I do is keep you out of trouble. I've got my own problems. Do you know how hard I've been working in school? One slip, and it's all for nothing. I'm so stressed out, I feel like I could rip in half. I can't handle any more of this. . . ."

"Look, you don't have to worry about me," Ryan said. He'd never realized she paid that much attention to him. "I'm fine."

Taylor screamed and buried her face in her hands.

"Okay, maybe I'm not fine. But I'll be all right. It's not your job to take care of me." He struggled to think of something to say. "Look, there's nothing to worry about. If I get held back, that works out perfectly for you. You can have the high school all to yourself. That would be better for both of us, anyhow. I wouldn't have to live up to your reputation, and you wouldn't have to live down mine."

Taylor dropped her hands. Ryan saw something disturbing in her eyes. Despair. A deep sadness. "What is it?" he asked.

"Dad wants to put you on drugs."

"No." A numbing sense of disbelief swept through Ryan. "You're wrong."

"Not this time. I wish I was. But it's true."

"What kind of drugs?"

"The same stuff that's got Ben Sylveri spaced out."

Fear chased away the numbness. Ryan knew Ben Sylveri. The kid walked around like he was already dead. "I'll run away," he said.

"You're thirteen," Taylor said. "You can't run away. You've got to deal with it."

"How?"

"I don't know."

"Yes you do. You have to." Ryan stopped when he realized what he was doing. She'd told him she couldn't handle his problems. And here he was, pushing her to help him. "Never mind. I'll figure it out."

"You shouldn't have to do it on your own," Taylor said.

"I'll be fine. I'd better get going. Someone once told me it's not good to be late."

"Wait." Taylor held out her hand. "First off, you can't bring disks to school. It might be too late to make a difference, but you've got to stay out of trouble."

Ryan's heart raced at the thought of going through a day without disks. He couldn't imagine sitting in his classes for those long hours, facing the glares of teachers who knew what a screwup he was. "I can control myself," he said. "I can handle it."

"No you can't," Taylor said.

"Yes I can."

"Please, Ryan. Don't lie to yourself. Whatever else you are, you're not a fool."

He sighed and pulled a disk from his pocket. Most of the time, he could control things. But maybe once in a while he let the disk take over for a bit. Not because he had to, but because he wanted to. "Here, hang on to this for me."

Taylor stared at him until he reached back into his pocket and pulled out a second one. "Go on ahead," she said, taking both disks from him. "I'll put these in my room." She looked down at the disks with a strange expression.

"What is it?" Ryan asked.

Taylor shook her head. "I spent hours trying to think of a way to get you to stop using these. I finally decided it was impossible. I gave up."

"So the one time you quit trying, you still succeed?"

"I guess." Taylor shook her head again and went back into the house.

Three times on the way to school, Ryan checked his pocket, even though he knew it was empty.

Taylor rushed back to her bedroom, stashed the disks in her foreign coin box, then hurried to school. It was the closest she'd ever come to being late. But she made it. Her head hurt from crying. Her eyes felt like they'd been rubbed with sandpaper. Her nose somehow managed to be stuffed and drippy at the same time. She couldn't believe she'd broken down right on the street. And then been thrust back into taking charge. The crisis was far from over. Ryan had given up the disks, at least for the day, but that didn't mean he'd stay out of trouble.

"You look awful," Ariel said when Taylor reached homeroom. "What's wrong?"

Dad wants to put Ryan on drugs. The words lined up in her mind, but wouldn't go any further. Taylor needed to tell someone. But Ariel was friends with Kara and her gang now. This was one secret Taylor didn't want spread through the school. It was the sort of rumor that could haunt her brother for years. Haunt her, too, since people refused to accept that twins could be different, no matter how much proof they saw to the contrary.

"Nothing's wrong," Taylor said.

"You've been acting strange for weeks. But I've never seen you look this bad. You sure there's nothing wrong?"

"I'm fine." Taylor turned her attention to her notebook so she wouldn't have to answer any more questions from Ariel. As she sat there, pretending to look at her social studies notes, she thought about how the two of them had always shared everything. Both the good and the bad. She and Ariel were the real twins. Or had been, once.

It's all changing. The day drifted by like a sad dream. Taylor's thoughts moved through memories of better days while her mind wrestled with fears of what the future held for Ryan.

yan couldn't keep the bad news to himself. "Drugs, huh?" Ellis asked. "Wow. My mom won't even give me an aspirin unless I've got a gaping wound. Ellis the Unmedicated."

"Yeah, drugs," Ryan said. At least he had a friend to share stuff with. That helped some. "I don't want to be walking around all spaced out."

"Your folks wouldn't really go through with it," Ellis said.

"Sure they would." Ryan told Ellis about the puppy he and Taylor got for their fifth birthday. "The dog had one small accident. All it did was pee on the carpet. Dad took it back to the pound."

"That's pretty cold," Ellis said.

"Yeah. If there was a pound for kids, they'd have dumped me years ago. I guess, since there isn't, they'll have to settle for drugging me."

"Then you've got no choice. You know what you have to do."

"I don't have a clue," Ryan said.

"You have to talk with your dad," Ellis said. "Guilt is a wonderful weapon. My mom uses it all the time. Why do you think you never hear people talk about *front stabbers?* It's so much easier to stab people when they aren't watching. You bring it up face to face, maybe he'll back off. You keep quiet, you're doomed."

"I guess." Ryan pictured how that conversation would go. A good old heart-to-heart chat with Dad. There was no way it wouldn't end up in a shouting match.

"Hey, look on the bright side," Ellis said.

"What's that?"

"You won't be alone. You've shared your head with all those legends. They must have left something behind. I mean, don't go in there like Elvis, but hit your dad with a touch of Lincoln."

"I'll try," Ryan said. Maybe there was some hope.

"Hey, not to change the subject or anything, but I figured out what's written on the bottom line of the disks. It's numbers."

"Like the running time on a movie?" Ryan asked.

"Yeah. Except we use ten digits." He wiggled his fingers at Ryan. "And they use eight." He tucked in his thumbs and wiggled the rest of his fingers. "Anyhow, most of the disks have two or three numbers. A couple have just one. Those must be real short."

Ellis kept talking about the numbers, but Ryan didn't pay much attention. It didn't seem very important right now.

After school, Ryan waited for his father to get home from work. Then he waited a while longer for his dad to suck down his after-work scotch and soda. Anything that made him more mellow couldn't hurt. Finally, Ryan went into the living room, where his dad was watching the news.

"Did you get the test results?" Ryan asked.

"You're clean," his dad said, not even bothering to look at Ryan. "No drugs."

He sounds disappointed. Ryan realized his dad had been hoping for proof. All the arguments he'd prepared suddenly seemed pointless.

"What are you waiting for?" his father asked, glancing away from the television. "Some kind of reward?"

"Aren't you glad I'm not using drugs?" Ryan asked.

"That's like asking if I'm glad you're not a murderer."

Ryan knew there was no way his dad was going to say anything positive. But he could at least get him to admit his plans. Maybe Ellis was right about guilt. "I heard you're going to drug me yourself."

Mr. McKenzie opened his mouth, as if to deny everything, then sighed and said, "Not drugs. Medication. There's a big difference. And it's for your own good."

It's for your own convenience, Ryan thought. "What if I can prove I'm not a total screwup?" he asked. "Will you change your mind?"

"I never said you were a total screwup."

"Sure you did. Every day. Every time you look at me." Ryan felt his face grow hot.

"That's not true," his father said.

"You know how many times I've heard you tell your friends that I quit the team when I was six?"

"You had so much potential," his father said. "And you threw it all away. Most people would trade anything for the gifts you were born with. Do you know how far I could have gotten if I had your talent? I'd be in the majors right now instead of behind some lousy desk. And if you had any heart, that's where you'd be headed. You quit before you ever really started. You just gave up."

Even now, years later, Ryan didn't want to relive those memories. That had been the worst summer of his life. The moment he'd shown the slightest ability to hit a baseball, his father had signed him up for a team. Ryan didn't have a clue about the rules. Especially base running. Everyone expected him to know what to do, as if there was some sort of baseball gene. They all shouted at him every time he made a mistake. The other kids. The coach. Even the parents. All that misery because his father wanted a ballplayer for a son.

The heck with this, Ryan thought. He spun away from his

father. But before he'd even taken two steps, the image of Ben Sylveri washed over him. "Damn it," he muttered. That wasn't going to happen to him. He turned back toward his father. "What if I stay out of trouble for a whole week? All the way until next Friday. Will you cancel the appointment?"

Mr. McKenzie snorted. "That's never going to happen. You've barely ever managed to go two days without messing up."

"If you don't believe I can do it," Ryan said, fighting to keep the tremble from his voice, "you've got nothing to lose. Is it a deal?"

"Sure, it's a deal," his father said. "Not that it will happen."

"Thanks for believing in me, Dad," Ryan said as he left the room.

Solo

aylor wandered into town after drifting through a schoolday that had passed in a hazy flow of half-remembered classes. Even now, everything seemed unreal. *I need a break*, she realized. *I've done enough for a while. The world can take care of itself.* Right now, she just wanted to pamper herself.

But how?

She thought about going to Smith's Ferry. It wouldn't be as much fun alone. Who could she call? The list wasn't very long. Lucy was more a neighbor than a friend. And Lucy always wanted to hang out with Sammi. But Sammi was too bossy. Deena and Susan never wanted to do anything. Deena liked to sit in her room and write depressing poems. Susan would go to a movie once in a while, as long as it was a comedy or an action film, but she never wanted to shop. Taylor had to admit that Ariel was pretty much her only real friend.

"I'm pathetic," she said. She walked to the south side of town, where a row of small shops with names like "The Ceramic Artichoke" and "Whimsical Knickknacks" ran along a wide alley down the street from the parking garage. Taylor decided to find a gift for Ariel.

You can't buy friends, she thought.

I'm not. She's already my friend. I just want to get her something nice.

It's a bribe.

No, it's a gift from a friend.

Taylor bypassed a basket shop and a fabric store, then went into a pottery shop that sold all kinds of miniature figures. As she browsed a shelf of glossy cats in the rear of the store, she heard a squeal of truck brakes from the delivery area, followed by the rattle of someone fumbling with the knob on the back door. She could see the driver through the small glass panel. From the way he stood, it looked like he was carrying a heavy package.

"Should I get the door?" Taylor asked the shop owner, who was busy with a customer.

The man shrugged. "He'll be okay. It's his job."

Taylor didn't like the idea of watching him struggle. She headed toward the door. Halfway there, she remembered her plan to take a break from helping everyone.

I can't even stick to a simple promise. No wonder I'm such a mess.

But this didn't count. It was too small an act to matter either way. "Hold on," she called. She turned the knob and swung the door open.

The delivery man maneuvered past Taylor and put a large box down by the side of the door. He grunted, "Thanks," grabbed his clipboard from the top of the box, then went to get a signature from the shop owner. Taylor liked the ring on his left index finger—a silver cobra with two tiny red gems for eyes.

Out of curiosity, she tried to nudge the box with her foot. It might as well have been glued to the floor. The man must have been incredibly strong. He glanced at her when he went back out, as if he wanted to say something. But when she smiled at him, he turned away. Still, she was glad she'd helped him. *Last time for today,* she promised herself. Someone else could get the next door. The next hundred doors, for that matter.

Taylor bought a small ceramic Siamese cat for Ariel, then spent another hour in town. She knew she was staying away from home on purpose, but she didn't care. Ryan would just have to avoid trouble on his own for a while. She needed the break.

Trying

Ryan almost got in trouble five seconds after he left the living room. In the hallway, his eyes locked on a tall vase his father had given his mother last year. It would have felt so good to smash the vase. He wanted to slam it to the floor and then stomp on the pieces until there was nothing left but powder. He really needed to break something.

Instead, he went out to the backyard, where an old tire hung from a branch of an apple tree. Ryan hit and kicked the tire until he was exhausted.

The weekend passed. *Five days,* Ryan thought on Monday morning as he got ready for school. He planned to keep his mouth shut in class and pay attention.

It wasn't easy. Right off, when he slipped quietly into his seat in social studies, Ms. Gelman gave him a suspicious look. The better he behaved, the more she seemed to think he was hiding something. It took all his self control not to stand up and walk out of her stupid class.

His other classes weren't much better. His teachers seemed disappointed that he wasn't performing his expected role. He wondered whether they'd gotten their training from his father. All around him, kids coped with school. Most of them managed to go for days, or even years, without getting into any trouble. His sister looked like she could go a whole lifetime. *What's wrong with me?* Ryan wondered as he shuffled from class to class.

"I'm exhausted," he said to Ellis at the end of the day. "My mind is totally fried. Paying attention is hard work."

"Tell me about it," Ellis said. "I leave here every day of my life feeling like my brain's been microwaved. School is turning me into a vegetable. Ellis the Eggplant."

"A whole week," Ryan said. "It's going to be brutal. One slip and I'm doomed." He was dying to flip. But his father would be waiting to pounce on the smallest act of misbehavior. Ryan knew he'd have to be crazy to do a disk at home. He also knew, despite the risks, that he'd give in to the urge before the day was over. His only hope was to remove the temptation.

"I need a favor," he told Ellis.

"Anything," Ellis said. "As long as it doesn't involve pain, bloodshed, or liver and onions."

"Take the disks. Just until next week. Okay?"

"No problem."

When he got home, Ryan put the disks in a paper bag. "Make sure you hide them," he said as he walked with Ellis to the front door.

"Don't worry. I've got the perfect place. Just call me Ellis the Obscure. Or should that be Obscurer? Want to know where?"

"You'd better not tell me," Ryan said. "Otherwise I might break into your room."

Ellis grinned. "In that case, they'll be at the bottom of the litter box." He headed down the porch steps, then glanced back and said, "Just kidding."

Ryan wanted to race after him and grab a couple of disks. Even one would be nice, to help get through the rest of the day. Just a short one. Ellis had said they were marked.

It took all of Ryan's strength to go back to his room.

He sat on his bed and tried to think of some way to pass the empty hours. He even took a shot at studying, but his mind kept wandering, wishing for a chance to escape into a more exciting life.

I'm nothing again, he thought. Not a hero. Not a legend. Not a great person. Not even close. Just a kid who has one chance in a million of staying out of trouble for a whole week.

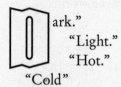

"Dark."
   "Light."
   "Hot."
"Cold"
"Brother."

"Wait. Was that right? *Light* is the opposite of *dark*. But you never said anything about opposites. I could have given a synonym, like *dim*. Or *unlit*. Would that be better? I'm not trying to be contradictory."

"Taylor, there is no right answer," Dr. Joyceman said. "Just say whatever comes into your mind. Okay?"

"This isn't going in my permanent record, is it?" Taylor glanced down at the notepad on the desk, trying to decipher the upside-down squiggles of cramped handwriting.

Dr. Joyceman shook her head. "I'm just hoping to understand your brother better. Since you're his sibling, and a twin, I thought it might help me to spend some time with you."

"We're not identical twins. You realize that, right? When you consider how little we have in common, we could just as easily have been born a year or two apart."

"I'm aware of that," Dr. Joyceman said. "And even if you were physically identical, I wouldn't expect you to have identical personalities. Is it all right with you if we get back to our words?"

"Certainly," Taylor said.

"Candle."
"Flame."
"Brother."
"Sister."

"Friend."

"Lonely."

"Life."

"No, I should have said *wax* instead of *flame.* Flames are destructive. That's negative thinking. Can I change my answer to *wax*?"

Dr. Joyceman nodded.

"Wait. Wax is pliable. That's not good. How about *wick*? That's my answer. A wick is an essential part of a candle. Are you sure this isn't going in my record?" Taylor asked.

Dr. Joyceman sighed and nodded again.

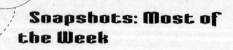

Ellis saw himself as a secret service agent, ready to leap out and take a bullet for Ryan if necessary. As much as he feared trouble, he promised himself that at the first sign a teacher was going after Ryan, he'd act up and draw the attention to himself. The decision felt good, except in his stomach, which ached nonstop from the first bell of the school day to the last, and his throat, which burned with a sour, acid taste, and his back muscles, which throbbed from the constant tension. And maybe his jaw, which hurt from clenching so much.

Click

Between Monday and Thursday, Billy streamlined his operation. At first, he'd used a whole sentence. "If you give me your lunch money, I won't hit you." Eventually, he discovered all he had to do was hold out his hand and say, "Money." It was nice having a steady job. He'd already made enough to get the part he needed for the dirt bike.

Click

Monday, Kara wore her hottest outfit. Ryan acted like she didn't even exist. Tuesday, she fumed. Wednesday, she cooled down and came to her senses. She really didn't like guys who sang and danced. Especially if they attracted all the attention.

"There's Ryan," Tara said to her Thursday morning as they hung out by their lockers.

"So?" Kara asked.

"You like him, right?"

Kara glared at her. "What ever gave you that idea?"

"Didn't you say so?"

Kara sighed. "Can't you even tell when someone's kidding? I mean, get real. You aren't that stupid, are you? Me and Ryan? No way. He's too much of a show off. Besides, I like guys with a little more muscle."

"Hey, I was kidding, too," Tara said. "You knew that, right?"

Kara smiled at her. "Of course."

Three *down, two to go,* Taylor thought as she took her seat in homeroom on Thursday morning. She'd gone through those days with her breath held, waiting for disaster. Each afternoon at lunch, she expected to find Ryan missing. Every time the loudspeaker crackled, she expected to hear the secretary say, "Ryan McKenzie, please report to the office." Each evening at dinner, she expected Ryan to hand over the envelope that sealed his fate.

"You need a system," she'd told him last evening. Organization was the key to success. That's why her notebooks were color-coded to the subjects, and why she was careful to keep an up-to-date list of her goals for the week, the month, and the year.

"I've got a sister," he'd said. "That's close enough."

But this sister was tired. She was glad there wasn't much longer to go.

"You look stressed out," Ariel said.

"I'm fine," Taylor said.

"I don't think so. You need immediate treatment. So how about we treat ourselves to a trip over to Smith's Ferry right after school? That's a perfect cure for all sorts of problems."

"You really want to?" Taylor asked. This was great. She'd been so sure they'd never go there again.

Ariel nodded. "Absolutely. Dr. Ariel's orders. I'll meet you out front. We can swing into town and catch the bus."

"Great." The promise of a trip delighted Taylor. Ariel had been almost like her old self since Taylor had given her the cat on Monday. It was as if the present had reminded her what good friends they were. Tuesday morning, Ariel had given Taylor a tiny ceramic otter.

The day seemed to weigh less heavily on her now. But the world crashed down during ninth period when she got her social studies test back.

"Seventy-three?" Taylor stared numbly at the alien markings. She rarely got a B. Never got a C. This was a C minus. Cold fingers gripped her spine as she tried to calculate the effect it would have on her average. Her mind was too dazed to perform the math. She scanned the test. A sea of red circles captured her mistakes. Stupid mistakes. Careless answers. How? She thought back. Last Friday. When she'd been so upset.

A gleeful cackle struck her. "Wow, you really blew it," Gilbert said.

Taylor jammed the test into her notebook. There had to be something she could do. When the bell rang, she rushed up to the teacher's desk. "Can I talk to you?"

"Of course," Ms. Exeter said. "Just let me take these folders to the office, first."

Taylor waited, rehearsing in her mind the words that would save her from disaster. Finally, Ms. Exeter returned.

"It's about my test," Taylor said.

Ms. Gelman stuck her head in the room. "Do you have a minute? We need to finalize the textbook order."

"Certainly," Ms. Exeter said. She glanced at Taylor. "Back in a sec."

It took forever.

"I don't know how I messed up so badly," Taylor said when she finally had Ms. Exeter's attention.

The room phone rang. "Excuse me one moment," Ms. Exeter said.

Taylor stood by the teacher's desk while the *one moment*

stretched out toward eternity. Finally, Ms. Exeter hung up the phone. "Now, what were we talking about?"

"This," Taylor said, pulling the test from her notebook and smoothing it out on the desk.

"A seventy-three isn't so awful," Ms. Exeter said. "A lot of students would be happy with that. It was a difficult test."

"But I never do this badly," Taylor said. "Can you give me some kind of extra credit work?"

"Would that be fair to the others?" the teacher asked.

"But I need—"

"I'm sorry. There's nothing I can do about it," Ms. Exeter said.

Taylor gathered her books and left the school. She got all the way to the sidewalk before she remembered her plans for Smith's Ferry. There was no sign of Ariel out front. Taylor checked her watch. School had ended more than half an hour ago.

She must think I changed my mind. Taylor hurried home and dialed Ariel's number.

"I'm sorry. She's not here," Ariel's mother said.

"Do you know where she is?" Taylor asked.

"She called me a couple of minutes ago. She went to someone's house. Give me a second . . . Kara. That's the name. Do you want to leave a message?"

"Yeah. No, never mind. Thanks." Taylor hung up. She couldn't believe Ariel had gone off with Kara. It wasn't right. If it had been her, she would have called Ariel, or gone to her house. She sure wouldn't have dumped her for someone else.

"Who needs her?" Taylor muttered. She walked next door to see if Lucy was around, but she'd gone out.

More time for my schoolwork, Taylor thought. She did her homework, then studied until dinner. But the disaster of her test grade hung over her. She wondered whether all the studying in the world could help her recover.

At the table, she barely listened as her dad asked Ryan the usual question, "Did you bring anything home from school?"

"No," Ryan said.

"That reminds me, Taylor," her mom said. "You got a letter today. It's on the counter."

Taylor's heart raced when she saw that the envelope was from the Huntington Museum. *I could use some good news.* A summer science program would help when she applied to colleges. It showed that she had goals and ambition. She hesitated, remembering the old saying that bad things happened in threes. First, the test. Then having Ariel ditch her.

"Don't be silly," Taylor whispered. This news would be good. Her science teacher assured her she'd have no trouble getting into the program. She'd never been turned down for anything involving school or education.

She tore open the envelope and pulled out the letter. The first sentence thanked her for applying to the summer program. The bad news came in the next sentence. *Unfortunately, it appears that you failed to fill out side two of the application. Since our enrollment is now complete, we urge you to try again next year.*

"What? Side two?" Her application was stapled behind the letter. Taylor stared at the page, all filled out in her neatest printing. Then she turned it over. There was a whole section she'd missed.

How could she have made such a huge mistake? Taylor thought back. It was the day they'd found the disks. She'd filled out the form while waiting for Ryan. He'd appeared just as she reached the bottom. That's when she'd put it away. Then there'd been all that stuff with Snooks and the backpack. She'd never even realized she had more questions to answer.

"So," Mrs. McKenzie said, "tell us the good news."

"I didn't get in," Taylor said. "They're full. Maybe next year."

"That figures," Mr. McKenzie said. "They probably take all

kinds of unqualified students, then don't have room for a high achiever like you. Maybe I can make a couple of phone calls."

"No, that's all right," Taylor said. She folded the application and stuffed it back in the envelope.

"You'd be perfect for the program," her father said. "I can't imagine why they'd turn you down. Those idiots. They made some kind of mistake. How typical. Haven't I warned you to watch out for that? The world is full of screw-ups." He held out his hand. "Let me see the letter. There has to be a way we can fix this."

"Really, Dad, it's all right." Taylor sat at the table and picked up her fork, but the food might as well have been ashes and straw. Her senses were dead.

After dinner, she went upstairs, closed her door, and sat on the floor. She squeezed her hands tight, but they wouldn't stop trembling. Her mind swirled with memories of every disappointment she'd ever known, each one catalogued and stored like all her old notebooks and reports. The worst parts of her life passed before her eyes, as if she were drowning in slow motion. For a while, she sat still, paralyzed by waves of bitterness dredged from her past.

Finally, she got up, fumbled through her desk drawer for the foreign coin box, and grabbed one of the disks she'd taken from Ryan.

Why not? she thought. For a couple of hours, she could be someone else. Maybe someone who didn't have to struggle so hard to get things right. Someone popular. Someone pretty. It would be so nice.

Taylor knew exactly what to do. She'd seen Ryan flip often enough. Spin it fast and low. She'd do that. As soon as her hands stopped shaking so much.

Sister Act

"Can Ellis come over?" Ryan asked his parents after dinner.

His father scowled. Ryan looked at his mother. "Sure. But just for a while. It's a school night."

Ryan called Ellis, then waited outside for him. They were on their way to Ryan's room when he heard the shout through Taylor's closed door.

"Avast!" she cried. "This brig won't hold me. I'll be free of it in a trice."

"Oh crap," Ryan said. He rushed down the hall and flung open Taylor's door just in time to see her leap between the curtains. He ran to the window.

Taylor had obviously landed unharmed, because she was already racing around the side of the house, shouting, "The Quedagh Merchant sails with the next tide!"

"Oh boy," Ellis said. "I think she flipped."

"No fooling." Ryan remembered his first disk. He hadn't even tried to control his actions. Luckily, the worst thing he'd done was burp at Ms. Gelman. He realized not everyone reacted the same. Ellis had gone completely crazy when he'd flipped. It looked like Taylor had flipped into a powerful legend. "We have to find her," Ryan said.

He ran downstairs. *Got to stay calm,* he thought. *Calm enough to fool the gatekeepers.* "Okay if we go for a walk?" he asked his mother.

"Sure. But not for too long. Your father and I are driving over to the Kerchner's later for coffee and cake. We want you home before we leave."

"We won't be long," Ryan said.

Ellis nodded. "I'm not a long-range kind of guy."

"We'd better split up," Ryan said when they reached the sidewalk. He figured Taylor was so noisy, she wouldn't be hard to find. "I'll cut toward town. You check by the school."

Ryan raced down the street. He was worried about Taylor. He had no idea how she'd handle taking second place inside her own head. But he was also thrilled. She'd finally get to see for herself just how awesome an experience flipping was. It was about time.

Closing Time

Billy was ready to go home. It was getting close to the time when the cops made their first patrol. He rose from the bench and headed out of his park. Lance and the others followed.

He really didn't want to go home. His mom was all flipped out about Adam getting in trouble again. It looked like he'd be spending at least six months in a jail in Oklahoma. Stealing a sandwich from some fancy supermarket. How stupid was that? His mom just kept going on and on about how people didn't understand her boys.

Just as Billy reached the street, he heard shouts from across the park, near the playground. It sounded like a girl having a wild time. Might as well see if she wanted some company. Maybe they could have a party.

"Let's check this out," Billy said, scanning the street. No sign of the cops yet. It looked like the night wasn't over.

The wind whipped through Taylor's hair as she ran. She felt so free, so alive. All that was missing was the salt spray in her face and the screech of gulls in the air. But that would be hers soon enough. The moment the lads arrived, they'd hoist anchor and leave this wretched land with its dismal prisons.

There it was. Her ship. She let out a whoop of pure joy at the sight, then ran up the netting and crossed the deck, nimbly avoiding a rotted section of planking. It was sad that the worthy vessel had fallen into disrepair. But they'd have her shipshape soon enough.

This is where I belong. She swayed with the gentle rocking of the surf. There was no pleasure greater than sailing deep waters, looting the hapless merchants who wandered in her path. "We'll set a speedy course for Comoro Island," she called.

As the ship rolled beneath her feet, Taylor was dimly aware that she hadn't always been a pirate. But her real self, caught up in the power of the legend, could only hold on, like a child clinging to a log in a raging river.

That was fine. She didn't want to be herself right now. Not when she could be free and alive. She cast her eyes to the horizon, scanning the land for friend or foe. She spotted both. Invaders, far off, slinking in from the starboard. A scurvy lot of 'em, with the look of trouble. A single lad stood off the aft side. An able-bodied crewman, no doubt. But what was holding him back?

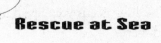

Rescue at Sea

Ellis figured his best bet was the old playground. That was the closest thing to a ship anywhere around.

When he got to the edge of the park, he spotted Taylor standing on the deck. He stopped for a moment, both from shortness of breath and an excess of caution. While he waited for his wheeze to drop from a rasp to a whistle, he gave a nervous glance toward the benches. They were empty. It was safe. Now all he had to do was get her to come with him.

"Hi," Ellis said. He walked carefully toward the ship, afraid of stepping on a rusty nail. "Taylor?"

She stared down at him but didn't answer.

"Captain?" Ellis said.

"What is it, lad?" Taylor asked.

"The crew are in trouble back at the brig," Ellis said. "We've got to hurry."

"Come aboard," she said. "I'll not shout 'tween ship and shore like some squeaking harbor rat."

The only way up was a stupid net rope. To Ellis, it was as welcoming as a spiderweb. He grabbed hold with both hands, set a foot on one of the cross pieces, and started to climb. Much to his amazement, he made it.

That wasn't so bad, he thought as he stepped on deck. Two steps later, his foot broke through the wood and he sank to one knee.

"Aye, you're a short one," Taylor said. "What was that message?"

"We must go back to the brig," Ellis said as he struggled to pull his leg out. "The crew needs you. Speaking of which, could you give me a hand, here?"

"Fear not. I'll rescue them." She pointed past Ellis into the shadows. "You stand fast and repel the boarders."

"Boarders?" Ellis asked. "What boarders?" He managed to twist around far enough to see a cluster of hulking figures crossing the park. His stomach lurched as he recognized Billy Snooks. Every other organ in his body lurched as he realized he was trapped. He turned back to Taylor, but she'd already leaped from the ship and sprinted away.

"Wait for me," he called, struggling to free himself. A heavy hand fell on his shoulder and he let out a yelp. As the sound echoed through the air, Ellis turned his head and saw something terrifying in Billy Snooks's eyes. Recognition.

He knows, Ellis thought.

More hands grabbed him and dragged him from the ship.

Back at the Brig

Ryan didn't see any sign of Taylor in town so he headed home to check if Ellis had found her yet. He got there just in time to spot Taylor running up the porch steps. "Wait. Don't go in," he called. If Taylor spent even five seconds with their parents right now, she'd be the next family member given the honor of peeing in a cup.

She flung open the door. Ryan raced after her, hoping his parents had already left.

"We'll empty the brig," Taylor cried.

Ryan slid to a stop next to her in the hallway. He saw his father standing frozen in place with one arm in his jacket. His mother stood by the coat rack with her mouth half open and her purse clutched in both hands.

Taylor slashed the air as if waving a sword. "A watery death for anyone who tries to stop us!"

"Right, Taylor, thanks," Ryan said. "That's the line I was trying to remember." He turned toward at his parents. "We're reading *Treasure Island* in English class. Big test tomorrow. Taylor's helping me study. I love the part where they"—Ryan struggled to mention a scene from a book he'd never read—"where they find the treasure."

"If any ship gives chase, we'll take 'em broadside, and feed the wretches all the hot lead they can swallow," Taylor shouted. "They've never grappled with the likes of me. I've sent many a man to the depths."

"She could be an actor," Ryan said. "Really impressive, huh? Once she starts, it's hard to get her to stop. She'll be talking like this all night. Well, don't let us hold you up."

"It's nice to see you studying," his mother said.

His father scowled and finished putting on his coat.

Ryan held his breath until they'd left. "You okay?" he asked.

"Good as can be expected on dry land," Taylor said. "I heard there was trouble at the brig. Have you a spare cutlass? Or a pistol? I've lost my weapons. Though I'll fight with fists and teeth if that's what it takes to free my men."

"Give me your hand," Ryan said.

"Aye, I'll trade hearty clasps with you, lad." Taylor held her hand out.

Ryan checked her palm. "Not a whole lot longer," he said. The disk had shrunk to about a third of its original size already. "I think we'd better hide out in the kitchen—I mean, the galley." He wanted to get her to stay in one place until the disk wore off. "We need to wait until the guards change watch. Then we can free the men." He couldn't help smiling. After all these years, and all the times Taylor had rescued him, here he was, keeping her from getting into trouble with their parents.

"Good thinking, lad," Taylor said.

They sat in the kitchen, where Ryan listened to Taylor tell tales of plunder and glory. Finally, she blinked, looked around, and said, "Oh my."

"You back?" Ryan asked. That was good. He was worried about Ellis, but he couldn't leave the house until Taylor's disk wore off.

She blinked again. "That was. . . . I was . . ."

"Some kind of pirate, I'd guess," Ryan said.

Taylor nodded. "William Kidd. You know, Captain Kidd."

"Fun, wasn't it?"

"No." Taylor shook her head. "Well, maybe a little. But I don't like being out of control." She closed her fist and put her hand in her lap, as if hiding away her weakness. "And I sure don't like my reasons for doing the disk."

"Stop being so hard on yourself," Ryan said. "You're always beating yourself up. You realize that? You hammer yourself worse than the folks hammer me. You're like your own mini version of Dad. But nonstop. At least I can get away from Dad. This is the first time you've ever been able to get away from yourself. So what if you tried a disk because you weren't happy? Big deal. Sometimes, you just have to do stuff without worrying about your reasons."

"Not me," Taylor said. "That's not how I am."

"Nobody's perfect," Ryan said. "If everyone was perfect, Dad would have a whole wall full of pictures downstairs instead of a couple of photos of guys who managed to avoid screwing up for longer than most of us."

To Ryan's surprise, Taylor didn't argue. Instead, she said, "And nobody's a total failure, either."

"What do you mean?"

"I mean, you can try to ruin your whole life. You can try to blow everything you do, but sooner or later you're going to do something right and discover that it's more satisfying than screwing up."

"I have no idea what you're talking about," Ryan said. If she thought he screwed up on purpose, she was crazy. Before he could say more, he heard someone stumble onto the front porch. He went down the hall and opened the door.

"Hey, what took you so long?"

Ellis staggered inside without answering. "Taylor, help!" Ryan shouted when he noticed all the blood.

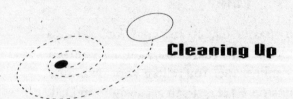

Cleaning Up

"Oh my God," Taylor gasped.

Ellis was slumped against the wall. Blood ran from one nostril, covering the left side of his chin and spotting his jacket. This wasn't one of his little nosebleeds. His cheek was swollen and his glasses sat at a strange angle. His left pants leg was ripped at the knee.

"What happened?" she asked.

"Snooks," he said. He touched his lip and winced.

"Ryan, get some wet paper towels." Taylor stepped closer to Ellis. "Let me see." She studied his face. The bleeding seemed to have slowed, though his lip was puffed up on the left side. "Your teeth look okay," she said.

Ryan handed Taylor the towels and she gently wiped the blood from Ellis's face. She remembered now—he'd come to the ship. "It's my fault," she said. He'd gotten hurt trying to help her. "I'm so sorry. I feel awful about this." The one time in her life she loses control, someone else pays the price.

Ellis lowered his head. He looked like he was about to cry.

"Hey, it's okay. Nothing's broken. Snooks could have done a lot more damage." She gave him a gentle pat on the shoulder. "I guess you're tougher than you look."

Ellis let out a wet cough that ended in a sob, then mumbled something, speaking too softly for Taylor to understand his words.

"You're safe," she said. "It's over."

"I told him . . . ," Ellis said, his voice barely above a whisper.

"Told him what?" Taylor asked.

"He made me. I shouldn't have . . ."

"Whatever you told him, it's okay," Taylor said.

"No it's not," Ellis shouted. A fresh trickle of blood dripped from his nose. "He recognized me from the day he took your backpack. I told him Ryan's name. I told him all about Ryan. I told him Ryan's locker number. I even told him Ryan got a haircut. I'm a rotten friend." He stomped his foot. "I stink."

Ryan put a hand on Ellis's arm. "It's no big deal. Come on. We'll walk you home."

During the five-block trip, Taylor's mind flitted between fear of tomorrow and memories of her time as a daring and carefree pirate.

"Are you going to be all right?" Ryan asked when they reached the house.

"Yeah. I'll be fine. But I'm worried about you," Ellis said.

"It'll be okay," Ryan said.

"I didn't tell you the worst part," Ellis said. "When he dragged me off the ship . . . you're gonna hate me . . ."

"What?" Ryan asked.

Ellis pointed to his bruised face. "This happened after I opened my big mouth. I didn't take a beating for you. The second he grabbed me, I crumpled like a little baby and told him everything. I thought that would save me. But he hit me just for the fun of it."

"Nobody blames you," Taylor said. "You wouldn't even have been out there if you weren't trying to save me. So it's really my fault."

Ellis cringed as he continued. "He knocked me down and then he started to kick me. There were other guys with him, too. I thought I was dead. Then, all of a sudden, they ran off. When I got up, I saw cops on the path at the other side of the park. If I'd just held out for a couple minutes, just kept my mouth shut, everything would be all right. I shouldn't have told him anything. I'm such a coward."

"You're not a coward," Ryan said. "A guy couldn't ask for a better friend."

"Thanks for saying that, even if it isn't true." Ellis started up the path to his porch.

"Hey," Taylor called after him, "what are your folks going to say?" As much as they'd cleaned him up, it was pretty obvious he'd been in a fight.

"My dad will be thrilled," Ellis said. "He's always wanted a tough son. Ellis the Brawler. I'll just tell him the other guy looks even worse. In a way, that's actually true."

After Ellis was safely inside, Taylor and Ryan headed home. "I can't believe I'm saying this, but maybe you should cut school tomorrow," she said. "Or get sick."

"Yeah." His lip twitched into a half smile. "I think I could be talked into that." He put his fist to his mouth and let out a convincing cough.

"Good. That'll at least give us some time to figure out what to do," Taylor said. Snatches of her evening were still coming back to her. "*Treasure Island*? That was pretty smart thinking."

"I've had some experience dreaming up explanations."

"I guess so. Thanks for keeping me out of trouble with the folks."

"No big deal," Ryan said. "Eight-hundred and thirty-five more times and we'll be even."

"Eight-hundred thirty-six," Taylor said. "But who's counting?"

Back inside, she made a phone call that had been on her mind since Ellis staggered into the house. Ryan wasn't the only one who had a good friend.

"Hi," Taylor said when Ariel picked up the phone.

"Hi," Ariel said.

There was a silence on both ends. Finally, fearing that Ariel would hang up, Taylor said, "I'm sorry I wasn't out front after school."

"I thought you'd forgotten," Ariel said. "I felt so stupid standing there. Like some kind of big loser. Then Kara came along and invited me over. I wouldn't have gone if I thought you'd show up."

Taylor explained about her social studies test. "Maybe we can do something tomorrow after school." She waited for Ariel to turn her down. *Sorry, I already have plans.*

"That would be nice," Ariel said. "I'll see you in homeroom."

"Great. See you tomorrow," Taylor said. *If I'm not visiting Ryan in the hospital,* she thought as she hung up.

I'm going to die tomorrow," Ryan said aloud as he paced the floor in his room. Taylor was right. He'd have to get sick. But that wouldn't be the end of it. Not now that Snooks knew who he was. It would never end until Snooks caught up with him and ripped his head off. Or until he got rid of Snooks. But that didn't seem possible.

"I'm such a screwup," Ryan said. There was no way to deny he'd caused a ton of problems. And not just for himself. His friends couldn't skate in the park now, thanks to him. Stitcher had gotten hurt. Huey hadn't bought lunch all week. He said he wasn't hungry, but Ryan knew better. Nobody was safe in school. All of it, every bit, was his fault.

There was one hope. It would probably blow his deal with his father, because it would almost certainly get him in some kind of trouble, but he had no other choice.

Ryan set his clock to wake him early. For once, he couldn't depend on Taylor to wake him. If he wanted any chance at all of surviving, he had to be up before her.

PART
FOUR
Battle

"You're sick of the game!" Well, now, that's a shame.
    You're young and you're brave and you're bright.
"You've had a raw deal!" I know—but don't squeal,
    Buck up, do your damnedest, and fight.
- - -
And though you come out of each gruelling bout,
    All broken and beaten and scarred,
Just have one more try—it's dead easy to die,
    It's the keeping-on-living that's hard.

—Robert Service

Alarm

The ping of a disk broke Taylor's sleep. The instant she recognized the sound, she raced over to Ryan, who was standing by her desk.

"I'm glad you keep everything so organized. Makes it easy to find stuff," Ryan said. He glanced down at his palm. "If Ellis is right, this is going to be a long one."

"Why'd you do it?" Taylor asked. There couldn't have been a worse time. Snooks was waiting to kill him. And he still had one day to get through on his deal with their dad.

Ryan curled his fingers into a fist. "We who are about to die salute you."

"What?"

"Nothing. Let's eat. I'm starved." Ryan turned toward the door.

"Wait. We need to figure out how you're going to skip school. You can't go downstairs without a plan. Besides, you don't look sick." Taylor grabbed his arm, gave a tug, and found herself sailing through the air. She landed on her bed, sending pillows and her stuffed kitty flying from the impact.

Ryan strode away as if nothing had happened.

Taylor lay stunned on the bed for a moment. The fall hadn't hurt her. But the fact that Ryan had tossed her, that was crazy enough to hold her there as she tried to sort things out. Who had he become?

She found him at the kitchen table, eating his way through a tower of pancakes. "Your face is kind of flushed," Taylor said. "Mom, doesn't Ryan look like he has a fever? I think he's getting sick. There's something going around. I could hear him coughing all night."

"I feel fine," Ryan said.

"Your brother looks perfectly healthy to me," her mother said.

"Nobody is missing school," her father said.

After he finished his breakfast, Ryan went upstairs. When he came back down, Taylor stared at him in disbelief. "You can't wear that sweatshirt," she said.

"Why not?" Ryan asked. "It's clean."

"But . . ." Taylor looked at the green alien face on the front of his shirt—the same face that was on the back. He might as well have worn a sign that said *Here I am.*

"Are you trying to get yourself killed?" she asked when they left the house.

Ryan shook his head.

"I can't believe you're planning to walk into school like there's nothing wrong."

"The matter must be settled," Ryan said.

"Who are you?" she asked.

"A man. Nobody special."

Taylor studied him. He'd definitely changed. People moved out of his way on the sidewalk—not as if they were afraid of him, but as if they respected him. The weirdest part was that he seemed a bit taller. Taylor checked his feet and saw the same sneakers he always wore.

Ryan paused for a moment by the park. "They have no right to take this from us," he said.

Taylor had no idea what he was talking about. She tried to convince him to go home, but he wouldn't listen. She begged. She argued. She pleaded. She reasoned. She did everything but grab him by the arm and drag him. She already knew how that would turn out.

FLIP

As she'd feared, Billy Snooks waited by the front door. "Let's go around to the side," she said.

Ryan glanced at her with calm eyes. "I'm not afraid. There's no reason to delay this contest."

Taylor took a step back. There was a power beneath the calmness, a strength unlike anything she'd ever seen.

"You!" Snooks snarled, pointing a huge, blunt finger at Ryan. "I'm gonna kill you."

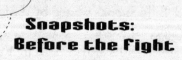

Snapshots:
Before the Fight

Ryan felt calm, but eager and alert—the perfect balance for a man-to-man contest. "We're all mortal. Remember that," he told Taylor. He turned his attention to the arena, and to the opponent who awaited him.

The crowd was alive. Ryan knew they sensed blood. They probably expected the blood to be his. But they'd quickly switch loyalties. With luck, he could draw them to his side. He'd done it before.

Click

Billy couldn't believe he was finally going to get his chance to pound the kid into dust. Better yet, he'd destroy him in front of the whole school. They were in for a show. He'd flatten the kid with one punch. And then start stomping. When the fight was over, they'd worship him.

"Come on, dead meat." Snooks slammed his right fist into his left palm. A circle formed around him as kids drew closer.

Click

"Good," Kara said. "It looks like Ryan's about to get his face broken." She skirted the crowd and headed toward the door.

"Want to watch?" Tara asked.

"Not interested," Kara said. Fights were only fun when the boys were fighting over her. Besides, anyone could see that Billy Snooks was going to end the whole thing pretty quickly.

FLIP

Click
    Ellis had almost skipped school. But he needed to know how much his cowardice would cost his friend. Before he left home, he took the back off one of his new speakers to check the disks. The bag was still there, jammed into the small space on top of the huge magnet that drove the speaker cone. *Ryan would kill me if anything happened to them,* he thought.

    When he got near the school, he spotted a mob gathered out front. Even from a distance, he could hear a slow, steady smack as Snooks punched his own palm. It sounded like thirty pounds of meat hitting a concrete floor. Wheezing and panting, Ellis ran the last half block.

Ringside Seats

hat's he doing?"

Taylor recognized Ellis's voice, but she didn't turn her eyes away from Ryan. "I don't know. But it's not just him."

"He used another disk?" Ellis asked. "I thought he gave me all of them."

"He got it from my drawer. It's someone powerful." Taylor was torn. She wanted to stop Ryan. But a small part of her believed he could handle Snooks. And a large part of her hoped that the small part was right. She thought about the day he'd hit three home runs, and how he'd balanced himself on a chair at the edge of the roof. The change, whatever it was, didn't just happen in his mind.

"This is terrible," Ellis said. "He'll get shredded."

"Maybe not." Taylor glanced at Ellis, whose face was bruised and swollen. "You look awful."

"True. But my dad's happy. He thinks he finally has the tough son he's always wanted. Parents get so grateful when you fulfill their dreams. He went out last night and bought me boxing gloves. We're going to the gym this weekend. Yippee. Boy is he in for a big disappointment. Ellis the Undefendable." He sniffled, tilted his head back, and added, "Like I don't have enough problems with nosebleeds already."

As Ellis pulled a wad of tissues from his pocket, Taylor turned her attention back to Ryan. The circle parted to let him enter. He stood straight, not slouching with the defeated posture of a kid who was about to get pounded into mush or ripped in half like a wet newspaper.

FLIP

When they were about five feet apart, Snooks roared a war cry and charged at Ryan, throwing a punch with enough force to turn a human face into a shattered mess of bone splinters, snapped cartilage, and torn flesh.

Taylor gasped and forgot all her fantasies of victory. Ryan was about to collide with a human freight train. When that punch landed, he'd be spitting teeth. Her hand flew to her mouth and she clamped her eyes shut.

Ryan slid smoothly under the punch and grabbed Snooks around the arm with one hand and around the waist with the other. As the fist sailed harmlessly past his head, he bent his body lower. For an instant, the weight of his opponent rolled across his hip and over his back. It was a move he'd practiced thousands of times. Snooks went flying, propelled by the force of his own punch.

He thunked down in the grass ten feet from Ryan.

Ellis's voice floated over the gasps of the crowd. "Whoa! Something that size should have a landing strip."

Ryan sensed that authorities were approaching. This was no longer the right time for the fight. And it wasn't the right place. "After school," he said. "Meet me in the park." It felt fitting to end this war on the same battlefield where it had begun.

Snooks rose halfway to his feet, then froze. "I'll be there," he said, staring at Ryan with eyes narrowed by rage.

"As will I," Ryan said.

Taylor opened her eyes just in time to see Billy Snooks hit the ground. He looked like he wanted to charge at Ryan and keep fighting, but Mr. Bulchner, the shop teacher, appeared on the front steps. A six-foot-five rock of a man who'd spent twenty years in the marines, he was probably the only person in the school who was tougher than Snooks.

As kids scattered, Mr. Bulchner strode over to Ryan and clamped a hand on his shoulder. "What's this all about?"

Taylor expected to see a flying teacher. Then Ryan would be doomed for sure. He'd be kicked out of school. Drugged. Maybe even sent away. But Ryan just looked up and said, "Nothing, sir." His voice was calm and polite.

"Well, get going. You don't want to be late," Mr. Bulchner said.

"Yes. As you wish." Ryan went inside.

Taylor tried to put the clues together. Maybe he'd become a legendary fighter. But there was definitely more going on. He seemed to have developed a respect for authority. No, it wasn't respect. It was something craftier, as if he knew how to obey the rules, but only when he had to.

"Snooks is going to want to hurt someone right away," Ellis said. "I'm not planning to volunteer for the role. I already had my turn. If he saw my all-too-familiar face, he'd pound me again. Ellis the Punching Bag. This time, I don't think he'd stop no matter how many cops came by. Let's go around." He wiped at his nose with the tissue, which came away unbloodied.

"Good idea." Taylor realized Ellis was right. Snooks would be in a real nasty mood, especially after half the school had seen

Ryan toss him across the lawn. A beaten bully loses his power. But Snooks was far from beaten. She thought about all those classic horror movies where the hero pulls out one weapon after another and blows away the monster, but the monster keeps getting up and coming back for more. *It would be nice, just once, if it was the good guy who couldn't be stopped,* she thought.

Taylor hurried around the building to the side door and went upstairs to her homeroom. The moment she took her seat, amid a sea of excited conversations, she realized a new legend had been born.

Victory March

They stared at him as he went past. That meant nothing. He didn't want their awe. He wanted their support. This had merely been a skirmish. The real battle lay ahead.

He studied the horde, reading their faces with the instincts that had helped him survive where so many others had died. He searched for those who could be trusted at his side when the fighting grew fierce.

"Awesome, man," a boy said to him. "You like whooped his butt." He threw an awkward punch in the air.

Not that one. He was weak. His courage was all in his tongue. Ryan spotted another boy watching him. This one had a serious face.

"Are you with me?" Ryan asked.

The boy nodded.

"That was amazing," Ellis said from the edge of the crowd.

"Thank you." Ryan looked into his eyes. Would he fight? It was difficult to tell. There was so much fear at the surface, it masked whatever lay beneath. Sometimes, the bravest heart hid under a blanket of terror.

Ryan picked three more companions from the group. Others trailed along. That was to be expected. There were always stragglers and glory seekers.

But this was a place of strict rules—just as rigorous as the school he'd escaped from, though far less deadly. "We must not be late," Ryan said. There was no advantage in displeasing the rulers.

Trailing a growing mob of supporters, Ryan headed for his homeroom. As he walked, he spoke to his soldiers, raising their spirits and preparing them for battle.

The Morning News

To Taylor's right, Mike Drucker and Tommy Snell chattered away. She usually ignored their conversations, which tended to be about pro wrestling, race cars, or the latest hot super model.

"I heard he punched him out," Mike said.

"Nah, he picked him up and body slammed him on the sidewalk. They said he broke Snooks's back." Tommy's voice dripped with delight. "He'll never walk again."

"No way. If that happened, there'd be an ambulance or something. Besides, Snooks must weigh at least two-twenty. The other guy's a lot smaller. What's his name?" Mike asked.

"Brian?" Tommy said. "No, that's not right. It's something else."

"He's her brother."

"Ask her."

"No, you ask her."

Taylor felt a tap on her arm.

"What's your brother's name?" Tommy asked.

"Ryan," Taylor told him.

"Yeah, right. Ryan," Tommy said. "I wish I'd seen the fight. I heard he smashed Snooks up real good. Punched his lights out. It's about time."

They had Taylor's attention, now. "There wasn't any fistfight," she said.

Nobody listened to her.

Debby Chomsky, who sat behind Tommy, leaned forward to join the discussion. "I was there. He picked Snooks up over his head and walked around with him. He looked just like those drawings of the guy holding up the world. Then he threw him down and started stomping on him with both feet. He woulda killed him if Mr. Bulchner hadn't come out and dragged him away. He took a swing at Mr. Bulchner, too. I saw the whole thing."

Taylor knew her brother would never stomp anyone. But there was no point trying to reason with this group. Throughout the room, conversations bubbled among clusters of students. Certain words surfaced over and over: *Ryan . . . Snooks . . . tossed him . . . beat up . . . the park . . . after school . . .*

Taylor realized someone was talking to her.

"Hey," Ariel said, "I heard Ryan punched out Billy Snooks. That's so cool."

Taylor shook her head. "It wasn't like that." She didn't want Ariel to believe the exaggerated stories. "Maybe Ryan pushed him or tossed him. I'm not sure. It all happened so fast. But it isn't over. Ryan told Snooks to meet him in the park after school."

"Oh, good. At least I didn't miss everything."

"It's not good," Taylor said. Her voice rose as her frustrations boiled over. "How can you talk like that? It's not good at all. That sounds like something Kara would say."

"Hey, you don't have to be all touchy, just because your brother's getting some attention," Ariel said. "You've been acting weird for weeks. I'd think you'd be happy for him. He's kind of like a hero."

Taylor knew Ryan didn't want to be anyone's hero. And all this talk wasn't helping. "Don't make a big deal out of it. Ryan doesn't need the attention."

"Oh my gosh, you're jealous," Ariel said. "That explains everything. That's why you're keeping secrets. And why you make fun of my friends. You don't want anyone else to be as important as you. Miss Smarty Pants. Teacher's pet. Oh so perfect. It drove you crazy at Bigelow Junction when the boys were looking at me."

"That's not true," Taylor said.

"And that's why you're always fighting with Gilbert. You hate him because he's just as smart as you. Maybe even smarter."

"You are so wrong." Taylor felt like she'd just been punched in the head. Or stabbed in the heart.

Ariel started to mock her. "Look at me—I won the spelling bee. Look at me—I got a hundred on the math test. No, silly me, I got two hundred. Look at me, look at me, look at me. That's all you care about. You've just been so stuck up lately, it makes me sick." She sneered and turned away.

The unexpected words stunned Taylor. Ariel was wrong about everything. Taylor didn't know how to answer the attack. She wasn't even sure if she wanted to bother. If that's the way Ariel felt, what was the point in trying to change her mind? *Stuck up?* she thought. *I'm not the one who's stuck up. It's you and Kara and all your other stupid new friends.*

Taylor glared at the back of Ariel's head. Beyond Ariel, outside the door, a noisy mob passed by in the hallway. Taylor caught sight of Ryan, speaking from the center of the crowd. As he moved down the hall, he raised a clenched fist and shouted something. Everyone cheered.

"I can't believe this," Taylor muttered. Ryan wasn't a leader. That was one of the few things they had in common. The disk had changed him. And it had changed the way others acted toward him.

Another cheer echoed down the hallway from the receding mob. Legend or not, Taylor hoped her brother stayed out of trouble. If there were any problems at all today, her father would carry out his threats.

Social Situations

This one was trouble. Ryan could read the threat in her eyes, and in the way she moved. But she was not an opponent he could defeat with fighting skills. She had the backing of authority. Still, hers wasn't real strength. She made a show of strength to hide her weaknesses, roaring like an ancient, toothless lion.

He sat at his desk and flexed his arms. His muscles bulged, tearing the right sleeve of his garment with a loud rip.

Ms. Gelman turned and glared at him. She carried her anger like a sword. Ryan shifted his gaze to the floor, avoiding her eyes. He hated tyrants.

While she spoke to the class, he kept his head lowered. He knew how to be humble. But even this irritated her.

"You haven't been paying attention," she said, storming over to him midway through the lesson.

"I've listened," he said.

"Don't lie. You haven't heard a thing I've said today. For that matter, you haven't learned a thing all year."

He could see she was determined to fight. He raised his gaze and met hers, showing no fear. She stepped back a pace. Good. Whether she knew it or not, he'd just taken control. Beyond her, on the board, he saw familiar words. *Centurion. Praetorian.* Her pride was her weakness. She was sure of her superiority, and sure of his flaws.

"Test me," he said. "If I fail, I'll accept any punishment you wish."

"You'll fail," she said. "It's all you know how to do."

"But if I prove myself . . ." Here was the tricky part. There was no reason for her to offer him anything. But he knew she expected him to fail. And he knew that the larger the reward, the more she'd enjoy watching him lose it. The chance to disappoint him would appeal to her cruel nature.

"Yes?" she asked.

"You'll give me an A for the rest of the year."

He watched her face. Saw the rush of surprise, followed by anticipation. "I could promise you the moon if you passed. It wouldn't matter."

"Then we have an agreement?" he asked.

She nodded. "Centurion," she said.

He defined it.

Her cruel smile vanished. "Cohort," she said.

Ellis turned around in his seat and waved his hand for her attention. His other hand was clamped over his nose.

"This test isn't for you, Mr. Izbecki," she said.

"*Mmnpphhh,*" Ellis said. He lifted his hand slightly, releasing a stream of blood.

"Oh not that again," she said. "Go on. Go clean yourself up. One would think you were made of glass. It's a miracle you have any blood left in you at all."

Ellis rushed from the room. Ms. Gelman turned back to Ryan and fired another word at him. He defined it. She gave him more questions about ancient Rome. Ryan answered each one. His only fear was that she would ask for history beyond his time. But frustration seemed to drive her in the other direction. She tried to stump him by moving further and further back, through the wars and the rulers of the past, and outward across the lands conquered by the empire, lands he knew well through long marches, savage battles, and tales told around the fire by fellow soldiers.

Finally, the bell rang. As he rose from behind his desk, he stared at her and said, "I trust you will keep your word." Then he turned and strode into the hallway, in search of more recruits for his army.

Taylor knew she was missing some obvious clue. She paused in the hallway after first period and scanned through the events of the morning, starting with the moment when Ryan flipped the disk. The way he'd acted seemed so familiar.

It'll come to me, she told herself. She was startled out of her thoughts when someone bumped into her arm. "Hey, watch where you're going," Taylor called, but the kid scooted away without a word of apology. A few more kids dashed by. Taylor glanced toward her English classroom and discovered why the hall in front of her had emptied. Up ahead, she saw living anger in the form of Billy Snooks. He stomped along, glaring at the world. Every few steps, he lashed out and punched whatever was next to him. *Bam!* He smashed a locker. *Thwump!* He smacked a wall.

He recognized Ellis, she thought. *Will he recognize me, too?* She backed up against the wall. Unexpectedly, it moved, throwing her off balance. She realized there was a door behind her. Unsure whether she'd been spotted, Taylor panicked and stumbled backward, out of the hallway. As the door closed and strange odors washed over her, she looked at the writing on the frosted glass. Backwards, in black letters, it read "SYOB."

"Ulp," Taylor gasped when she realized she'd just barged into the boys' room.

Kabap!

Someone kicked the bottom of the door.

Taylor held her breath—not a hard thing to do at the

moment—and waited as the bulky shadow passed by on the other side. If he came in, she was dead.

The thumps and crashes moved on down the hall.

An instant later, a hand tapped her shoulder.

Taylor jumped and screamed.

Behind her, Ellis screamed.

"You scared me," he said. "Why'd you scream? And what are you doing here? Do you know where you are? What if they caught you? What if they caught me here with you? They'd throw me in jail. Oh God, I'd probably end up in a cell with someone like Snooks—only bigger and meaner. Hurry. Get out." He waved a wadded handful of blood-soaked paper towels as he spoke—evidence of his own reason for being there.

"Don't worry, I'm going," Taylor said, eager to flee back into the fresh air of the hallway. She slipped out the door—just in time to bump into Kara. *Oh great,* Taylor thought. *Now the whole school will know.*

Kara's expression quickly shifted from surprised to amused. "I see you finally found a place where you belong." She snickered and moved on. But she didn't leave soon enough to miss the sight of Ellis ducking out of the boys' room behind Taylor.

Kara's snicker turned into a laugh. "This is great," she said as she left.

"Doomed," Taylor groaned. "I am totally destroyed. I might as well call my parents and tell them we have to move."

"Hey, I know the feeling," Ellis said. "I get it about once an hour. Ellis the Outcast."

As he spoke, Taylor remembered that Ellis was in her brother's first period class. "Did Ryan get to social studies?" she asked.

"Yeah," Ellis said. "It was amazing. He had this mob with him. I'd never seen anything like it. They were acting like he was some kind of football hero or something. What's that called when everyone admires you?"

"Charisma," Taylor said.

"Yeah, that's the word," Ellis said. "He was dripping with it. Wish I had some. And he said the weirdest thing ever. Though it was sort of cool, too."

"What?"

Ellis thrust his hand into the air like a warrior raising a sword. "We who are about to die salute you." As he spoke the last word, he struck his right shoulder with his left fist.

"Ohmygod," Taylor gasped, feeling as if she'd just been struck with Ellis's imaginary sword. Hearing those words again—the same words Ryan had spoken that morning—and seeing the unmistakable salute, the pieces she'd been struggling to sort through finally fell together. "This is bad. Really bad."

"Bad?" Ellis sniffed, then pinched his nostrils together with the paper towel. "Id's nod so bad. Id's jus' a liddle blood."

"I gotta go," Taylor said. "Right now." She sprinted down the hall. If her fears were correct, there was a good chance more than just a little blood would get spilled that afternoon.

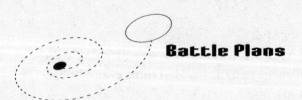

Battle Plans

illy kicked the bottom of the bathroom door. He thought about punching the glass, but he knew that wouldn't be smart. People who put up with all sorts of other stuff got weird when it came to a little broken glass. He wasn't going to take any chance of missing the fight.

He didn't go to his next class. He couldn't stand being in the building. Couldn't stand knowing that kids were talking behind his back. No way he was going to spend any time in a classroom until he set things right. But once it was over, he'd rule the place. They might as well change the name to Billy Snooks Middle School.

"I'm getting out of here," he told Lance. "Gonna find Ace. We'll need him in the park."

"Yeah," Lance said. "Time to settle this."

Things Are Looking Up

Taylor checked her watch. It was set to exactly match the school clocks. In one minute and thirty-eight seconds, she'd be late for class. Did it matter?

She realized it mattered a lot. She couldn't ruin her perfect record. But she wouldn't if she hurried. And she absolutely had to find out as much as she could right away. She dashed through the door of the library. The reference section was on the left wall, just past the entrance. Taylor scanned the dark brown spines of the encyclopedia volumes, looking for the letter G. There, *France* through *Gilgamesh*. No, next one. *Gillespie* through *Heraclitus*. There wasn't time to read anything now. She pulled the book from the shelf and hurried to the circulation desk.

"Can I take this out, just for one period?" she asked Mr. Castlemayer, the librarian. Taylor realized she may as well have asked if she could bring in a boom box and play heavy metal at full volume.

"That's a reference book," he said.

"Please?" she asked, trying to sound as needy as she felt.

"Oh go ahead, Taylor." Mr. Castlemayer said. "Nobody uses encyclopedias anymore. Not with all these computers. It's a shame if you ask me. A real shame. They're missing out on a wonderful experience. An encyclopedia is a date with serendipity. Take it. Just don't tell anyone I let you. Okay?" He gave her a wink.

"Deal," Taylor said, winking back. She dashed for the door, sped down the hall, and slid into her English class just as the late bell rang.

"Ms. Duly," Gilbert called out, "Taylor's late. She wasn't in her seat when the bell rang. That's the rule. It's on page thirty-five of the student handbook. She was standing. So that counts as late."

"Never mind, Gilbert," Ms. Duly said. "It's not your concern."

Taylor caught her breath, then noticed that Gilbert's eyes had locked on the book in her hands. She could imagine the thrill he must have felt as his tiny weasel brain recognized the chance to expose a crime far worse than mere tardiness.

"And she's got a reference—"

"Gilbert, let's get on with the lesson," Ms. Duly said.

Taylor took her seat, put the encyclopedia in her lap, and flipped through the slick pages toward entries beginning with "GLA . . ." She turned past *GLACIER, GLACKENS, GLAD-BECK,* and then she found the target of her search.

Ryan's words had pointed the way. *We who are about to die salute you.* One group had made that phrase famous. Gladiators. Fighting to the death in the Colosseum for the amusement of ancient Rome. Ryan had become a gladiator.

But which one? Which legend?

As Taylor skimmed the article, a name in bold-face type leaped at her from the bottom of the third paragraph.

"I'm such an idiot!" she cried, slamming her fist on her desk. She couldn't believe it had taken her this long to figure everything out. The answer seemed so obvious now. She also couldn't believe she'd just shouted like that.

Ms. Duly stared at her. "Is there a problem?"

"My lunch," Taylor said. "I just remembered I left it outside. On the bench by the parking lot. It's tuna. It'll spoil. I really am such an idiot." A total lie, she realized—the lunch part, not the idiot part.

"I'm sure it will be fine," Ms. Duly said, studying Taylor with a look that said *Didn't you use to be my favorite student?*

Taylor slunk down in her chair and tried to speed up time. She also tried to ignore Gilbert's whispered chanting of "tuna brain."

Eventually, she got sick of his taunts and whispered one word at him—the word he'd stumbled on at the last spelling bee. "Psittacosis." Then she spelled it.

That shut him up for a while. But before the period ended, he said, "At least I'm not blowing social studies."

Taylor didn't have an answer for that.

When the bell finally rang, Taylor rushed to the library.

"See," she said, waving the book at Mr. Castlemayer. "I brought it right back. All safe and sound." She shoved the book in the waiting space and grabbed the volume for S.

"I'm such an idiot," she said again. There must have been thousands of gladiators. And plenty of gladiators in movies. Some of their names were easy enough to remember. Ben Hur. Maximus. She didn't think either of those was a legend. They'd been made up by modern writers. There were probably dozens of famous gladiators back in ancient Rome, just like there were lots of famous boxers now. But there was only one gladiator she knew of who'd become a legend. Taylor vaguely remembered watching a minute or two of a movie about him while flipping through the channels long ago. She turned the pages of the encyclopedia, scanning the guide words at the top until she found the name she'd been searching for. Her flesh tingled as she read the passage.

SPARTACUS. (born ?, died 71 B.C.) Gladiator who led the Slave Revolt against Rome. Originally a shepherd from the Thracian region of Greece, Spartacus was sold into slavery after serving in the Roman army. He and a small group of fellow gladiators escaped from gladiatorial school and took refuge on Mount Vesuvius in 73 B.C. They were joined, over the next two years, by more than 80,000 runaway slaves. Under the brilliant strategic leadership of Spartacus, the group managed to defend themselves against several assaults by Roman troops. Eventually, Spartacus was defeated by an army under the command of Marcus Licinius Crassus and killed in battle. His followers were crucified. In his camp, 6,000 captured Roman soldiers, held prisoner by Spartacus, were found, unharmed and well cared for.

More of Ryan's words came back to Taylor as she finished reading the entry. *They have no right to take this from us.* That's what he'd said when he'd walked past the park. She realized Ryan planned to reclaim the park from Snooks and his gang, leading his own revolt.

An image flashed through her mind, straight out of another movie—two armies clashed in fierce battle, fighting hand to hand. Soldiers screamed as they fell to the muddy ground. This was moving beyond a simple schoolyard brawl. She had to change Ryan's mind before someone got hurt.

She'd have a chance to catch him on the way to his health class. That was just one period away. Taylor went to music and plunked down in her seat.

"Hey," Ariel said. "I'm really sorry about before. I feel awful. I never should have said that stuff."

"It's okay," Taylor said, more out of reflex than understanding. She wasn't really listening. Her mind was still trying to free itself from battle scenes and the screams of the wounded. And it really wasn't okay. Not after Ariel had lashed out at her with all those hurtful accusations.

"Do you still want to do something after school? We could go to Smith's Ferry, or maybe see a movie."

"Not today," Taylor said. "I've got stuff to do."

Ariel didn't say anything more.

As class ended, Taylor rushed out to catch Ryan. On the way, she wondered whether she shouldn't have been so cold to Ariel. Maybe she should have allowed her to patch things up. It sounded like Ariel wanted to be friends again. But what kind of friend says so many awful things?

A moment later, Taylor forgot all about that.

She'd found Ryan. The instant she spotted him, she realized he'd gotten even stronger.

Appeal to Reason

The mob surrounded Ryan, filling the hall. They were all talking to him, calling him, trying to get close. He was careful to spread his attention equally through the group, not giving anyone cause to feel unfavored or superior.

"Ryan, wait!"

Beyond the crowd, a familiar voice shouted a name. Then she shouted again. But this time, she called out another name.

"Spartacus!"

"Let her through," he said quietly. His followers parted. They seemed eager to carry out his smallest wish. But the knowledge didn't bring him pleasure. It brought the burden of leadership.

"You've become Spartacus, haven't you?" Taylor asked when she reached him.

Ryan nodded.

"This is madness," Taylor said. "You can't start some kind of war. You're not a gladiator—you're a kid. Snooks and his gang don't play games. They fight for real. A whole lot of people could get hurt."

Ryan put a hand on her shoulder. "I have to do this."

"No," Taylor said. She grabbed his hand and turned it palm up. "It's not you. It's the disk. You aren't a fighter."

The last time she'd grabbed him, he'd been taken by surprise. This time, he gently pulled free from her grip. "We'll talk later. Right now, I have much to do." Around him, his followers clustered into orbit again as he marched away.

Taylor called after Ryan, but it did no good. Only Ellis remained behind as the mob left.

"Fear not," he said. "Ryan leads us. We can't lose. We're invincible."

"Not you, too," Taylor said.

Ellis shrugged. "There's something about him. Something that makes me want to follow him, wherever he leads me. On the other hand, I figure it can't hurt to be ready to run at a moment's notice. Ellis the Uncertain."

"Wise idea," Taylor said, glad that Ellis hadn't completely fallen under Ryan's spell. She just wished there was some way Ryan could run for safety when things turned ugly. But that wouldn't happen. Not while he was sharing his mind and body with Spartacus. Why couldn't he have become someone more peaceful? "Those disks have been nothing but trouble," she said.

"Well, at least I've got the rest stashed out of his reach," Ellis said.

"Where'd you hide them?" Taylor asked.

"Inside one of my new speakers," Ellis said. "The backs come right off. Nobody will find them there."

"Are they big ones?" Taylor asked, remembering what she'd learned about speakers in science class. Maybe Ellis had put the disks in the bottom of a large cabinet, far from danger.

"Nope. Small, but really powerful. I had to cram the bag inside. It barely fit."

"Oh boy," Taylor said. She could just picture the disks jammed up against the magnet.

"What's wrong?"

"Nothing." There was no point telling Ellis right now. He had enough on his mind. She realized Ryan had probably never warned him about magnets. Most likely, the disks were just powder. *We're better off without them,* she thought. Then she remembered her adventure on the high seas and felt a wave of regret at the loss. She'd never have a chance to be so totally free again.

Right now, she had other things to worry about. By lunchtime, Ryan's crowd of followers had swelled to more than thirty. Taylor couldn't get near him. But even from a distance she could tell he'd continued to grow stronger. Both his sleeves were in tatters. The rest of his shirt stretched tight against his body, turning the alien's mysterious expression into a look of wide-eyed surprise.

Ariel was already sitting at their table. *I'm really not in the mood for more insults,* Taylor thought. She took her tray to the other end.

Ariel glanced over and muttered, "Fine. I don't want to sit with you, either." She got up, crossed the room, and joined Kara's table.

"Yeah, go sit with the airheads," Taylor said.

"What's up with her?" Susan asked.

"We've lost Ariel to the dark side." Deena patted Taylor on the arm. "Write a poem about it. You'll feel better."

"I feel perfectly wonderful," Taylor said. She tried to remember whether that was her second or third lie for the day.

As her eyes wandered around the room, Taylor noticed that Coach Ballast had cafeteria duty. Normally, he just sat at a table sipping guava juice. But the unusual activity around Ryan was enough to draw him to the edge of the mob.

"That protein powder is incredible!" he said. "Look at those results. I'm gonna be rich." He danced back to his seat.

When Taylor headed out of the cafeteria at the end of the period, someone tapped her on the arm.

"Your brother's been working out."

"What?" Taylor asked, puzzled that Kara was talking to her.

"I never realized there was a hunk hiding under those baggy shirts," Kara said. "Has he been lifting weights?"

"All the time," Taylor said, amused at the idea of Ryan pumping iron.

"I can tell. You should invite me over this afternoon," Kara said. "You could introduce us."

"Invite you over?" Taylor asked. That was even crazier than the idea of Ryan lifting weights.

"Sure. Maybe then I won't spread the word about who I saw coming out of the boys' room with smelly Ellis. Not to mention all the other wonderful things I happen to know about little old you." Kara grinned and started to strut away. Then she stopped, glanced over her shoulder, and said, "Mayhew Street, right?"

"Right . . ." Taylor said as Kara slithered down the hall. Taylor felt her cheeks flush, both in embarrassment and anger. What secrets had Ariel spilled? There were so many possibilities, some bad enough that their exposure would make life at school unbearable. She had to find out. She scanned the cafeteria, but Ariel had already left.

Taylor gritted her teeth as she walked along the hall toward her Spanish class. Throughout the period, her anger grew. She broke two pencils while taking notes. Finally, the bell rang and she stormed toward math. *What did Ariel tell Kara?* The answer would be there. One seat to her left. Ariel had some explaining to do.

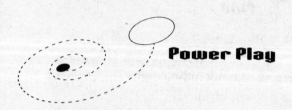

Power Play

Can you make it?" Billy asked Ace. He'd managed to find him at work, which was a break. Ace was on the road a lot.

"I'll be there," Ace said. "Looking forward to it."

"Solid." They'd be unstoppable now. Billy had one more place to go. There were some guys at the high school he could count on. He was pretty sure they'd be hanging out in the auto shop, so there wouldn't be any problem talking with them.

I'm a warlord now, for sure, Billy thought. He was gathering an army. And his army would crush all who stood in its way.

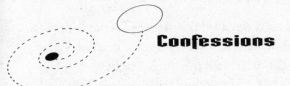

Confessions

The instant Taylor reached her seat, she spun toward Ariel and asked, "What did you tell Kara about me?"

Ariel's expression flashed from surprise to exaggerated innocence. "Nothing."

"You never told her anything at all?" Taylor asked. "Never even mentioned my name?"

"Well, sure I mentioned you. But just good stuff," Ariel said. "I mean, I'd never tell her any real secrets."

"Do you swear?" Taylor asked, staring straight into Ariel's eyes. *Please say yes.*

Ariel opened her mouth. Taylor waited to hear that everything was okay—waited to hear that her best friend in the world hadn't betrayed her. Ariel's eyes shifted away, breaking contact. She still hadn't spoken.

"I knew it," Taylor said. She felt as if someone had crushed her heart beneath a boot heel.

"It was just little stuff," Ariel said. "Nothing important. Little things . . . you know, girl talk."

Taylor shut the words out. She could picture Ariel and Kara and the others huddled together, gossiping and laughing. A lifetime of secrets was in Ariel's hands. Every item became currency with which to buy the false friendship of Kara and her crew of sniveling pawns.

Math class was a blur. Taylor was too angry to think and too hurt to care. On the way out, Ariel tried to say something, but Taylor ignored her.

She spotted Ryan again as she went to social studies. He still looked strong, but nowhere near as pumped up as he'd been at lunch. The effect was fading. Taylor wondered what kind of shape Ryan would be in after school. And what kind of shape he'd be in if he went through with this stupid fight.

She sat in social studies and watched the clock until the bell rang. As she gathered her books, a group of kids marched down the hall. The sight reminded her of a Civil War movie, where all the proud young men parade off to join the battle, only to return home broken and maimed, if they returned home at all.

"Taylor, could I see you for a moment?" Ms. Exeter asked.

"Sure." Taylor went up to the teacher's desk.

"I've been thinking about that test," Ms. Exeter said. "You're such a wonderful student. And you participate so well in class. It would be a shame to let a single bad score ruin your whole grade. I'm willing to give you another chance."

"Thank you. That's great." Taylor couldn't believe her luck. This was the first good thing that had happened in ages.

The teacher pulled a sheet of paper from her desk drawer. "In order to be fair, I really can't give you more time to study. You'll have to take the test now."

"Now?" Taylor glanced toward the door. Troops were still flowing past. How could she sit and take a test when Ryan was about to go to war?

Ms. Exeter nodded. "Now."

Taylor felt like her lungs had been clamped in a vise. She knew she had to make a decision. But there was no right answer. Whatever her choice, she'd lose.

All her hard work from the moment she'd started middle school was about to get flushed. If she stayed and took the test, she could still be first in her class. If she left, she'd be second. Worse, she'd be second to Gilbert, who'd gloat about it all the way through high school. Nothing she did, no spelling bee victory or other minor triumph, would match that. What would her father say? She heard his voice. *Second? How could you let this happen? I'm so disappointed.* And if she came in first? What would he say then? *Nice job. Keep it up.*

"Well?" Ms. Exeter asked.

Beneath Taylor's feet, the floor rocked like the deck of a pirate ship. The tightening vice, washed in ocean water, corroded and crumbled. Her lungs relaxed and she breathed a deep breath that seemed tinged with the faintest hint of salt air. "Thank you," Taylor said. "That's so nice of you. But you're right. It wouldn't be fair."

"You don't want to take the test?"

"No, I don't," Taylor said.

"Are you sure?"

"I'm sure." Taylor left the room, rushed down the hall past the marchers, and forced her way out the door. A wave of guilt tugged at her for tossing away an opportunity. But the wave fell back, replaced by a strange sense of freedom. "Second is pretty good," she said. No. It was a lot better than "pretty good." It was excellent.

She hurried toward Ryan, whose march had turned to a stagger. With each step, a bit of power drained from his body. Behind him, his followers didn't seem to notice that their hero was deflating. They were still caught in the spell he'd woven throughout the day, eager for the glories of combat.

"Spartacus," Taylor called.

He didn't look at her.

"Ryan," she said when she caught up with him. He stumbled along like a sleepwalker. "Let me see your hand." She reached out and grabbed his wrist.

Ryan didn't offer any resistance. Taylor examined his palm. The disk was now barely larger than a pencil point. As she watched, it vanished.

Spartacus was gone.

The legendary gladiator and leader of the Slave Revolt, the

brilliant tactician who could defeat vast enemy armies, had disappeared, leaving behind nothing but a thirteen-year-old boy with fifty battle-hungry followers. All thirsting for a fight. All ill-equipped to face a gang of experienced brawlers and thugs who loved to cause pain.

Thank goodness, Taylor thought. At least now she'd be able to talk him out of doing something stupid.

A Walk Toward the Park

"P hew," Ryan said as his hand flopped back to his side. "What a day . . ." *A nap would be nice*, he thought as he yawned and stretched.

"Are you okay?" Taylor asked.

"I'm fine. A little sleepy, maybe. What a day," he said again. Spartacus was gone, but the memories lingered. "It's been interesting. Did you know that troops on a mountainside can defeat a much larger force if they—"

"Interesting?" Taylor asked. "Is that all you can say? It's been *interesting*?"

"Yeah. What else should I say? I'm not the one who's always showing off a big vocabulary."

"Have you looked behind you?" Taylor asked.

Ryan was surprised to discover he was at the head of a crowd. "What are they doing here?"

"Following you," Taylor said. "You're their leader. Remember your little encounter with Billy Snooks? Remember *'meet me in the park'*? Do those words sound familiar?"

Ryan nodded. It was hard to sort out the old memories from the new ones in the moments after a disk wore off. "Oh yeah. We're going to fight the oppressors. Now I remember." He rubbed his face. "That's good. It has to be done."

"No it doesn't," Taylor said.

Ryan glanced toward the park. A crowd waited near the benches. Colosseum or park, gladiators or kids, one thing never changed—every fight drew spectators. "We can win."

"Forget it, Ryan," Taylor said. "Maybe you had a chance

before the disk wore off. But it's all gone, isn't it?" She gripped his arm with two hands.

Ryan tried to pull free, but Taylor held on. "See," she said. "You don't have any power. It's over. Give up."

"I can't. I talked them into this. I won't let them walk into a fight without me."

"Then talk them out of it," Taylor said.

Ryan checked over his shoulder. There had to be at least fifty kids on his side. That was more than enough. "We have a chance. A good chance." With a show of force like that, there might not even be a fight. Maybe Snooks would back down. There weren't that many thugs in the school.

"You just don't know when to quit, do you?" Taylor asked.

"You got that one backwards," Ryan said. "I know all about quitting." He sped up, eager to reach the park. When he was close enough to take a good look at the crowd by the benches, he discovered he'd been completely wrong about one thing.

The sight struck him like a kick in the stomach. It wasn't spectators who waited there, and it wasn't his supporters—not unless his followers had started wearing ripped denim and leather. Ryan realized he wasn't the only one who'd raised an army.

One More Time

This is madness, Taylor thought as she saw who was waiting in the park. A lot of kids were going to get hurt.

"You have any disks left at home?" Ryan asked. "Maybe you could run and get one."

Taylor shook her head. "We used the two I took from you. Don't you have any left?"

"I gave everything to Ellis to hold for me."

"Then I've got some bad news for you," Taylor said. She told him about the speakers and the magnets.

Ryan sighed. "I wish I'd brought one to school."

"Thanks to me, you didn't." *But I did.* Taylor remembered the disk she'd taken to school. Where had she put it?

"I should have left them in my closet," Ryan said. "They were perfectly safe in my jacket pocket."

"Pocket!" Taylor shouted, yanking her backpack from her shoulders. That's where she'd put it. She knelt and unzipped the small front pocket. For a frantic instant after she reached inside, she couldn't find anything. Then she felt the smooth, cool surface against her finger tips. The last time she'd held a disk, it had taken her away. The memory of those carefree moments drew her. She thought about saving the disk for herself. Ryan had already used plenty of disks. All she had to do was tell him she didn't have it.

Taylor glanced toward the park, where Snooks waited, then pulled the disk from her backpack and handed it to Ryan. "Let's hope it's someone who can fight."

"Yeah. That would be good." Ryan held the disk close to his

face and squinted at it. "One digit. This is going to be really short."

"Good luck," Taylor said as Ryan flipped. It took him three tries. Once again, she watched a disk bury itself beneath his palm. Though the sight made her sick, she didn't turn away. When the skin sealed over the disk, she studied Ryan's face, wondering who he'd become. She hoped to find the fierce scowl of Genghis Khan or Attila the Hun—someone powerful and nasty enough to smash Snooks into a pile of sobbing flesh.

Ryan gave her a gentle smile.

"Who are you?" she asked.

"Mohandas," he said.

The name meant nothing to Taylor. *You don't look very tough,* she thought as they walked toward the center of the park. Ahead, one figure detached himself from the waiting gang. Billy Snooks. Taylor's eyes swept across the mob behind Snooks. There were a couple of dozen thugs on his side—half the number of Ryan's forces, but more than twice as tough. They looked ready for battle. Some wore spiked wrist bands or belts made of chains. A couple had picked up branches from the ground. Taylor wondered what other weapons they'd brought.

Ryan's army was unarmed. Taylor saw Huey with his clarinet case. Stitcher had his skateboard under one arm. Nobody else carried anything more dangerous than an algebra book.

She searched Ryan's face for clues. *Who are you now? Are you tough enough?* He seemed maddeningly calm. "Can you fight?" she asked.

"Violence is not the answer," Ryan said. "Violence is never the solution to any problem."

"Right," Taylor said. Maybe there was still a chance to get him to leave. It sounded like he'd become someone who didn't want to fight. "I absolutely agree. So let's go before things turn violent."

Ryan smiled at her again. It was a smile filled with a sense of inner peace that almost erased Taylor's fears. It was a smile that said, *Everything will be just fine, my sister.*

"I must go forward," Ryan said. Then he spoke one indecipherable word. "Satyagraha."

"What?" Taylor asked.

She didn't get an answer. Ryan, smiling serenely, was walking toward Billy Snooks as if the two of them were old friends.

Snapshots: The Fringes

Ellis marched with the rest of Ryan's supporters. As the group reached the park, he slowed enough to let everyone else get ahead of him. He could see Taylor and Ryan talking together. Then Ryan and his army went on without her. Ellis decided it would be safe to join Taylor. He'd go that far, and no farther. Not with that gang of brawlers standing there.

Click

Kara stopped in the girls' room on the way out of school to freshen her makeup. There'd be a big crowd at the park. She wanted to look her best. Besides, she knew there wasn't any hurry. Boys never started a fight right away. They'd strut around. Then they'd talk. Call each other names for a while. After that, they'd push each other. There were all sorts of rituals they'd go through before anything exciting happened. Even if they weren't fighting over her, it would be worth watching. Especially if Ryan's shirt got ripped off. She pictured herself with him on the cover of a romance novel. Definitely hot.

I can't believe Tara tried to tell me Ryan wasn't my type, she thought. He was *so* her type. No more listening to anyone else. This time, she was going to get what she wanted. And Tara, who had to run off to some stupid orthodontist's appointment, wouldn't be there to give her any more bad advice.

* * *

Click
Revenge was so close now, Billy could nearly reach out and touch it. Everything was perfect. He had his troops with him. They'd get to see him smash that little creep. It was going to be so sweet. Then they'd tear up anyone else who wanted to tangle. Put an end to disrespect once and for all. Erase the bad thing. As Billy scanned the crowd, he saw the geeky kid. The one he'd started beating up yesterday. He wasn't finished with him. *Gonna snap you in half, tall boy,* he thought. But first, he was going to destroy that alien-loving freak.

Pass a Fist

Taylor stayed back as Ryan's army moved past her. They gathered several paces behind their leader, unaware that the gladiator they'd followed had deserted them. Taylor grabbed Ellis's arm when he reached her. Maybe he knew what the word meant. "Satyagraha?" she asked.

"You sat where?"

"No. Satyagraha. Ryan just said it. Do you know what it means? Or *Mohandas*?"

Ellis shrugged. "Sounds like some other language."

"Yeah, it does," Taylor said. "But not Spanish or French, or anything like that."

"India!" Ellis said.

"India?"

Ellis nodded. "My brother Jake was there last year. He sent me a couple of postcards. Some of the words on the back sounded like that. Guess there's no way to know what it means." Ellis hovered next to Taylor. She hoped he wouldn't risk going closer. There wasn't much chance he could do anything to help, and there was every chance he'd get hurt. The enemy looked unbeatable.

Taylor saw Snooks's usual gang from the middle school, and a bunch of high school kids. She noticed a truly scary looking guy sitting on top of a bench, watching Snooks and Ryan with an expression that betrayed no emotion. His dark hair was slicked back, and his arms, bulging through the short sleeves of a black T-shirt, were covered with tattoos, including an ace of diamonds impaled by a dagger. That had to be Ace. Taylor could almost imagine him battling in the Colosseum, clothed in iron-studded leather, slashing away with a sword in each hand. Two other tough guys sat there with him.

"Come on, Ryan," a kid called from the crowd. "Kick his butt."

Ryan turned toward the speaker, smiled, and said, "That is no answer." He turned back to Billy Snooks. "I did not come here to fight you, my friend." He spoke so softly that Taylor had to strain to hear him.

"Oh yes you did," Snooks said. "You came, you fight. No choice, loser."

"There are always choices," Ryan said.

"Hit him!" another kid yelled from the crowd behind Ryan.

"Yeah. Knock his head off!"

"Throw him out of the park!"

"Please. We can settle this without violence," Ryan said.

He seemed smaller. And older. He was so calm, Taylor wanted to scream. What kind of legend was against violence? Martin Luther King was the first name that came to mind. Who else? She sifted through the clues. Nonviolence ... India ... "Oh ... my ... God ..." The answer hit her with its own violence. This was bad. Especially now that Ryan was face-to-face with Snooks. He might as well have turned into Florence Nightingale or Tinkerbell.

"What's wrong?" Ellis asked.

"He's Gandhi," Taylor said. She remembered another movie from far in the past. Mahatma Gandhi had led the struggle for the rights of people in India. He'd preached nonviolent civil disobedience—putting himself at risk to win his cause. Nonviolence was a noble way of fighting against a government, but suicide in a gang fight. *Mahatma* must be a title, she realized, remembering he'd called himself *Mohandas*. Either way, this was not a change for the better.

"Gandhi?" Ellis said. "Oh no. He's history for sure."

A Peaceful Offer

He was surrounded by anger and hatred. It rose from the mobs like thick steam. Both sides were eager for bloodshed. They would be disappointed. He'd never lift a hand against a fellow human. Or any living creature. Instead, he lifted his hand above his head to silence the crowd so they could hear his message. This was not a time for shouting.

As the cries around him dropped to curious whispers and then silence, he faced the angriest one. "You are welcome to stay in the park. But it belongs to all of us. It was placed here for everyone's enjoyment." He held out both hands in a gesture of friendship. "Please. Let us share this lovely sanctuary in peace."

He waited to see if his offer would be accepted. The angry boy appeared to be thinking. That was good. Calm thought was an essential step toward peaceful solutions.

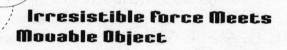

Irresistible Force Meets Movable Object

As she listened to Ryan's plea for peace, Taylor was sure it would work. How could anyone resist such a noble speech? Only a monster wouldn't be moved by this outpouring of grace and compassion.

Snooks's eyebrows had pulled together in confusion. But then he answered Ryan with a swear word and a punch. Taylor gasped as the bully smashed a hard right into her brother's jaw, shattering the peaceful mood. Ryan went down like he'd been hit from above with a concrete piano.

Snooks bellowed his donkey laugh, then shouted, "Who's next? Come on, suckers. Who wants to tangle? I'm just warming up." He sneered down at Ryan. "One punch? That's no fight. But it ain't finished. You still got a stomping coming."

Taylor wanted to rush over to her brother and drag him away. She wondered whether there was anything left of his jaw. Before she could move, Ryan rolled to his stomach, then got to his knees. He shook his head hard and rose to his feet. "I do not plan to leave the park," he said.

"Good. That would ruin my fun." Snooks lashed out with another punch, nailing Ryan straight in the nose. Taylor screamed and slammed her eyes shut. When she opened them, she saw Ryan climbing to his feet again. Blood gushed from his nose, flowing over the alien face on the front of his shirt. Taylor had never been this close to a fight before. The sight of all that blood—far more than she'd seen when Ellis came to the porch—made her stomach churn, flooding her throat with a sour, burning liquid. She fought against the nausea. And saw the first glimmer of hope.

The blood had slowed to a trickle.

He's healing. Taylor thought about how Ryan's poison ivy had vanished the first time he'd used a disk. Now, as Gandhi, he seemed to be able to absorb a large amount of punishment. Still, she couldn't believe she'd been so eager to see anyone get beaten up. The reality of the fight was far uglier than the fantasy.

Not everyone was impressed with Ryan's approach. A nervous murmur rippled through his followers. Taylor realized they'd expected their side to provide the beating, not receive it.

"Join me," Ryan called to the kids behind him. "Stand up for yourselves. You can find truth through courage. You can find strength through unity."

Snooks slammed a punch into the side of Ryan's head. Ryan spun halfway around as he fell.

"Stay down!" Taylor screamed.

"Get up, wimp," Snooks said. He drew back his foot and kicked Ryan in the ribs. "Come on. Get up!"

As Ryan crawled to his feet, Stitcher stepped from the crowd and stood at his side. So did another eighth grader. Taylor recognized the second kid. He was a wrestler, and pretty tough, though not anywhere near big enough to tackle Snooks. But at least Ryan no longer faced the enemy alone.

Snooks rubbed his right fist with his left hand and grimaced in pain. He shook out his wrist, then hit Ryan again, swinging so hard he grunted with the effort. As the punch landed, the sickening sound of snapping bone ripped the air like a rifle shot, drawing a cry from Taylor.

Ryan tumbled to the ground. But it was Snooks who screamed as he cradled his wrist in his left hand.

Ryan rose again, wobbling as if the bones had been removed from his legs. Another kid left the crowd and joined the group of nonviolent protestors. What was the point? As far as Taylor could tell, nonviolence didn't work any better than violence. Either way, people got hurt and the stronger side won.

Snooks right arm dangled at his side. He seemed puzzled, but that didn't stop him from throwing another punch. He hit Ryan with a looping left. Ryan dropped to his knees. His right cheek swelled up, forcing his eye shut.

As Snooks pulled back his fist, Taylor realized Ryan wouldn't even be able to see the next punch coming.

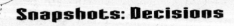

Nothing was going right. The kid should never have gotten to his feet. When Adam had pounded on him, Billy had always stayed down and curled up. Right now, he felt like he was in some kind of weird dream. His right arm was on fire. His left fist was starting to ache. At least the kid was on his knees. Maybe he'd go down for good this time. Billy put all his strength into the punch, hoping it would be the last one.

Click

Even if Ryan loses, I'm going out with him, Kara decided as she strolled from the girls' room. Besides, it was hard to imagine him losing. He looked totally pumped. She never thought a torn sweatshirt could be so hot. But he couldn't wear that kind of stuff to the nice places he'd be taking her. No matter—after they started going out, she'd help him with his wardrobe. It was one of her best things.

"Nothing is coming between us," she said out loud. "Ryan's as good as mine."

Click

Ellis touched the puffy spot on his lip. All his life, he'd been afraid of getting beaten up. Yesterday, that fear had become a reality. He pressed harder against the scab that covered the healing flesh and realized he'd felt just as much pain when he got his allergy shots. Maybe more.

It wasn't all that bad, he thought. The worst part was being trapped. Seeing them come at him and knowing he couldn't get away. That, and being alone.

He wouldn't be alone here. Besides, he'd always wanted a chance to be brave.

Click
    The punch smashed into Ryan's blind side. As his head rocked from the impact, he thought about falling to the ground and giving up. He could just lie there. Let everyone else fight. It would feel so good to quit. Taylor had been shouting for him to stay down. Maybe this time, he'd take her advice.

I quit, Ryan thought.

He'd failed at everything else. Failed at school. Failed at home. He'd even failed to go through a week without using the disks. *No reason this should be any different.* All he had to do now was let go. As he looked to his left at the spot where he'd fallen, he saw that Ellis had come forward to join the front line.

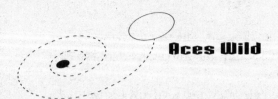

Taylor was surprised to see Ellis step forward. Then she forgot all about him as Ryan got hit again. The punch snapped his head to the side. Ryan, already on his knees, started to topple. It looked like the fight was finally over. But instead of falling, he stood up.

About half the kids were with him now. The others hung back. Taylor realized nonviolence wasn't as attractive to a mob as a vicious fight, no matter how much courage it took.

Ryan wasn't the only one getting support. Ace left the bench and walked over toward the fight. *We're dead,* Taylor thought. *We are absolutely, beyond any doubt, totally dead.* Ace was six inches taller than Snooks, and probably fifty pounds heavier—all muscle as far as Taylor could see. A scar running across his forehead, and another carved along his arm, showed he was no stranger to violence. She knew he could wipe out Ryan. He could probably wipe out everyone in the park, including Snooks.

As Taylor stared at Ace, he looked her way. She froze, caught in the grip of his cold eyes. Then, behind the chill, she saw a glint of something softer, as if the two of them shared a bond. Freed by that flicker of human reaction, Taylor tore her gaze away, wondering what she and this creature could possibly have in common.

She turned her attention back to the fight as Snooks swore at Ryan and said something about his mother.

Ryan smiled. "Actually, my mother is wonderful. She puts up with quite a lot."

Snooks hit him again, grunting when he threw the punch and then gasping for breath afterwards. Ryan staggered, but stayed on his feet. He barely moved at all when the next punch landed, or when Snooks followed that up with a double jab to the ribs. "No more playing around," Snooks shouted. "Time to pay the price." He fumbled inside his jacket with his left hand and extracted a dark, deadly bar of iron.

"No!" Taylor screamed as Snooks raised the tire iron over his head. Not even a legend could withstand a blow from that heavy weapon. She raced toward Ryan, though she knew there was no chance to reach him in time.

Snooks swung his weapon with his left hand. It was an awkward strike, but that didn't make it any less deadly. Taylor's scream rose in pitch as she reached out helplessly. In her mind, she could already hear the sickening smack of the bar making contact.

Ryan didn't move.

Ace did. He stepped forward and caught Snooks's left forearm with his own left hand, stopping the blow as if it had met a stone wall.

"Enough." One word. Both sides fell silent as he spoke. Ace lowered his gaze toward Ryan. "You've got guts, kid. Maybe no brains. But definitely guts." He glanced toward Taylor, then back at Ryan. "Friend of yours?"

"Sister," Ryan said.

"Thought so. She's all right," Ace said. "Nobody else ever bothered to hold a door for me."

Taylor stared at the red-eyed cobra on his left index finger. The jewels glinted in the sunlight, winking at her.

Snooks's body jerked as he tried to pull his hand free. Taylor could see the muscles bulge in Ace's arm. He was clearly far stronger than Snooks. "It's over," Ace said. "Let the little kiddies have their park." He squeezed tighter.

Snooks moaned and opened his left hand. The iron bar fell from his fingers and struck the ground with a muffled thud.

"You understand *over*, Billy?" Ace asked.

Snooks nodded.

"You don't hit this kid again. You already hit him enough. Whatever this was about, I say it's even. Right?"

Snooks started to protest. "But he—"

"Right?" Ace asked again, his voice growing firmer.

"Right," Snooks said.

"Tell him you're even," Ace said.

Snooks lowered his head and muttered, "We're even."

"I'm outta here." Ace nodded at Taylor. "See you around." Then he walked away. Taylor could hardly believe this was the same person who'd delivered the package to the pottery store. In a long-sleeved uniform that covered the tattoos, with his hair tucked beneath his hat, he'd been a different person.

No, she realized. He hadn't been a different person. She'd *seen* a different person.

The other tough guys followed Ace. Snooks stayed for a moment, staring at the tire iron. Finally, he must have realized he was badly outnumbered. Nearly every kid in the place had something to settle with him. He turned and hurried off.

The crowd cheered. Kids rushed toward Ryan, lifted him on their shoulders, and carried him around the park.

"I was going to go bop Snooks in the nose," Ellis told Taylor, "but I figured he'd had enough. That's what separates me from him. I'm civilized. Ellis the Merciful."

"Hey," Taylor asked as it dawned on her that the fight was over. "Did Ryan get in any trouble today?"

"No way. He had far too much charisma for that," Ellis said.

"Amazing." She thought about all that had happened since that morning. Ryan had gotten into two fights and spent most of the day raising an army, but still managed to avoid trouble. He'd actually made it through the week. Her father would have to keep his part of the bargain. And Ryan would have to accept that he could actually succeed at things. She wasn't sure which of them would be more shaken by the realization.

Taylor's smile faded when she spotted Gilbert. He had that look of evil delight she knew so well—the one that popped up every time he saw a chance to tell on someone. Taylor walked over to him and said, "Are you thinking of reporting this?"

"Fighting's against the rules," he said. "If you look on page twenty-nine of the—"

"Ryan didn't fight," she said. "And it's really important for him to stay out of trouble today."

"He was in a fight," Gilbert said. "It takes two to fight, you know."

"This isn't school property," she said.

"That doesn't matter."

The sound of his whining voice made Taylor want to punch him out. Then she thought about the fight she'd just witnessed. Violence had lost some of its appeal. "Listen, Gilbert," she said, stepping closer to him. "I'd really appreciate it if you didn't get my brother into any more trouble. He gets in enough on his own. Okay? Whatever competition there is between you and me, it has nothing to do with him. Can I count on you to give him a break?" She moved even closer.

"Why should I?" Gilbert took a half step away from her, his cheeks coloring slightly.

Taylor noticed that he was breathing more quickly, and that his eyes held a look she'd just recently become aware of when she talked to boys—a confused mingling of fear, awe, and interest.

"Because I asked," she said. She leaned forward and gave him a kiss, then turned and walked away.

That should shut his mouth for a while, she thought, grinning at her own boldness. She'd seen other girls use their charm, but had never dared to try anything like that herself. Mostly because she was sure it wouldn't work. She was delighted to discover that she was wrong. Gilbert had definitely been silenced for the moment. Maybe he'd even get so distracted, he'd blow a test or two. Life was certainly growing more interesting by the moment.

Self-Reliance

It was a strange experience for Ryan. They carried him all the way around the park. Then they carried him around again. He was sort of embarrassed by the attention, but he understood that they wanted to celebrate. Even after they put him down, kids hovered nearby, reliving the moment and telling him how great it had been to see someone stand up to Snooks. Though he realized "stand up" wasn't a very accurate description of his strategy. Finally, everyone drifted off.

"Are you okay?" Taylor asked.

"Fine." Ryan wiped his nose with the back of his hand. He flinched, then felt his cheek carefully. "But I think I might be hurting a bit for the next couple days. How do I look?"

"You ever see sausage before it's cooked?"

Ryan nodded.

"You look worse." She took his hand and turned it palm up. "The disk's gone. Thank goodness it lasted long enough to get you through the fight."

"I wish," Ryan said. He couldn't help smiling, even though it hurt.

"How long did it last?" Taylor asked.

Ryan tried to sort through the fuzzy memories to find the moment when he stood alone. "I'm not sure. It definitely wore off before he broke his hand on my face. I'll tell you, it's pretty loud when it happens right up against your head. At first, I thought my own skull had cracked. I'm still not all that sure it didn't."

"So Gandhi wasn't there when you were getting beaten up at the end?" Taylor asked.

"No. Unfortunately, I got to experience that part all by myself. But I figured it was too late to back out. Besides, he was running out of steam."

"I'm proud of you," Taylor said. "Even if it was pretty stupid to stand there and let him pummel you."

"Thanks. Believe me, if I could have pounded him, I would have," Ryan said. He was painfully aware that it was Ace's actions and threats, more than anything, that had saved the day. "You know, I'm pretty proud of you, too. It's nice having a smart sister. Especially a smart sister who makes friends with thugs and convicts."

Taylor shrugged. "Guys just like me, I guess."

"Ryan, did you see me?" Ellis asked as he joined them. "I was up there with you."

"I sure did," Ryan said. "It was the bravest thing I've ever seen. As a matter of fact, that's what gave me the courage to keep going."

"How about that?" Ellis said, grinning in delight. "Who'd have thought I'd ever be Ellis the Brave?"

freedom of Speech

s Ellis said *brave*, Taylor caught sight of Kara strolling toward the park. "I'll catch up with you," she told her brother. "I have my own battle to finish." And this battle, she knew, couldn't be won with a kiss.

"Looks like I missed all the action," Kara said when Taylor reached her. "But that's okay. Fights are boring. Besides, I'd rather get to know your brother somewhere less crowded. Speaking of which, after you introduce us, it would be nice if you took off so we could be alone. I'm sure you've got lots of reading to do or something like that. So, what time should I come by?"

Taylor hesitated, wishing she had some legendary hero inside to help give her courage. But she didn't. She was alone. Finding her own strength, she forced out the words: "Don't bother."

Kara's eyes widened in surprise. Her jaw dropped, revealing a piece of gum resting against her lower right molars. She emitted a tiny squeak, a far distant cousin of Ellis's terrier yelp.

Now that Taylor had started, the rest of the words came much more easily. "I don't like being threatened. And I don't like bullies—any kind of bullies. That's what you are, Kara. You're a bully. And a sneak. I don't want you in my house. Not now. Not ever."

Kara glared at Taylor. "I guess I'll just have to tell everyone some interesting stories about you. Is that what you'd like?"

"I don't care what you do," Taylor said. "I really don't. Tell people whatever you want. It doesn't matter." She walked away from Kara and headed across the park toward home. Much to her surprise, she felt great.

illy told his mother he'd fallen off his dirt bike.

"Promise me you'll be more careful," she said when they left the emergency room. "I knew that thing was dangerous."

"I'll be careful." Billy waited a moment, then asked, "Do you miss Adam?"

"Every day," she said. "He never writes. I'm afraid he isn't as thoughtful as you. Maybe with him being in that place for a while he'll have time to write."

"I miss him, too," Billy said, surprised at how easily the lie came out. "Maybe that's why I got hurt. I didn't have him around to keep an eye on me."

His mother nodded. "He did watch out for you. You two were so close. Even when you were little, he never minded taking care of you when I had to go out shopping."

"No reason we can't be close again," Billy said. "You ever think of that? Maybe we could move out near that prison. You could visit him. And see him all the time when he got out."

"That's a wonderful idea," she said. "You're so smart, Billy. And so thoughtful. You're always thinking about everyone else. Especially me." Then she frowned. "But what about all your friends—won't you miss them?"

Billy shrugged. "I'll make new ones." He hoped he could talk his mother into leaving right away. He really didn't want to go back to that awful school.

"It will be so nice to see Adam," his mother said.

"Yes it will," Billy said. He had at least six months before Adam got out. Six months more of lifting weights and working on the heavy bag while big, mean, lazy Adam sat in a cell and grew soft. "I can't wait."

R yan's not really my type, anyhow," Kara said as she left the park. She'd already lost interest in him, even before his loser of a sister had interfered. Those two were so much alike.

She had plenty of other guys around to choose from. Most of them were a lot hotter, anyhow. Maybe it was time for someone a bit wilder. Someone she could really have fun with. She pulled out her cell phone and called Tara. "You know who'd be perfect for me?" Kara said.

"Who?"

"Billy Snooks." She'd had her eye on him for a while, but the last couple of weeks he'd really caught her attention. He was so sure of himself. So powerful. All he needed was a bit of guidance in how to dress and how to act.

"*Ohmygawd*," Tara squealed. "That is soooo perfect. You'd be like Beauty and the Beast."

"Yeah," Kara said. "We would." The image appealed to her. She was looking forward to going back to school on Monday.

Sliding into Home

espite the pain in his face, Ryan felt good. For the first time in ages, he'd stuck with something. Maybe it had been stupid to let himself get pounded. Stupid or not, he'd seen the plan through, and everything had worked out. Even the bad news Taylor gave him didn't kill his mood. But Ellis was upset when Ryan told him about the disks.

"It's okay," Ryan said. "You didn't know magnets would ruin the disks."

"Yeah, but I still feel rotten," Ellis said. "Though, to tell the truth, I'm kind of glad to have you back. I missed you."

"Thanks." Ryan knew it was going to be hard to adjust to living without the company of legends. He'd gotten so used to fleeing from himself. He reached up and felt his right cheek. The swelling had gone down a bit, allowing him to peer at the right half of the world through a blurry slit.

"Be careful," Ellis said. "Your dad will probably buy you boxing gloves when he sees your face. How do you feel?"

"It could be worse," Ryan said. He touched his ribs and winced. "But I think I'm going to be a little stiff at tryouts next week. Hope I can swing a bat."

"Tryouts?" Ellis asked.

Ryan nodded. "Yeah. It might be fun to play baseball again." He thought about how great it felt to swing away without worrying that he might strike out. That was one gift Babe Ruth had left behind. And he thought about all the times he'd failed when he could have succeeded. He wasn't stupid. Looking back, he realized some of the things that had driven him to fail. And he realized how close he'd come to throwing his future away for the worst of reasons.

"Man, I can't believe you're thinking about joining the baseball team," Ellis said. "That will really make your dad happy."

"I know," Ryan said. "He'll be thrilled. There's nothing in the whole wide universe that would make him happier. But I can't let that stop me. I'm going to do it anyway."

The Best Kind of Make Up

As Taylor reached the far edge of the park, a familiar voice called after her, "Hey, wait up."

Taylor waited. She was still angry about a lot of things, but there'd been enough fighting for one day. Maybe even for one lifetime.

"I'm sorry," Taylor said when Ariel reached her.

Ariel spoke her own apology at the same time.

"I was a jerk," Taylor said.

Again, Ariel's words overlapped Taylor's. They both laughed at the coincidence. Then Ariel motioned for Taylor to go ahead.

"I shouldn't have gotten so angry," Taylor said.

"But you were right," Ariel admitted. "I told Kara some stuff about you. That was wrong. I mean, I didn't tell her anything bad. But you know how it is when a bunch of us start talking."

"I know," Taylor said. "It's okay. I might have done the same thing if I'd been with them. Hey, nobody's perfect." She paused and drew a deep breath. Then she asked the question that had been on her mind all day. "Am I really a snob?"

Ariel bit at her lower lip. "I didn't mean that."

"Come on," Taylor urged. "The truth. Please."

"Promise you won't get angry?" Ariel asked.

Taylor nodded.

"Sometimes you are. I mean, just because you don't care about cheerleading, you act like anyone who does is stupid or something. Brittany Loomis is on the squad, and she gets straight A's. Katie Williams gets good grades. So do I, for that matter. Danielle and Tiffany are really nice. They spent an hour the other day helping me learn a cheer. But you act like all my new friends are worthless and brainless. They aren't. They're people, just like you and me."

"Not Kara," Taylor said. "Or her little shadow puppet, Tara."

"Okay," Ariel admitted. "Kara's spoiled. But the girls that I like hang out with her, so I guess I'm stuck. I'll cope. I'm not as much of a sheep as she thinks. And you don't have to like her. Or any of them. But please don't make me feel bad if I like them. All right?"

"All right," Taylor said. She'd asked for the truth. Now that she'd heard it, she'd have to deal with it. "I'm sorry."

"Friends?" Ariel asked.

"Friends," Taylor said. She reached out and hugged Ariel. "I'd better get home and see how Ryan is."

"Wow, yeah. Ryan was amazing. He beat Snooks without even throwing a punch. I'll walk with you. Okay?"

"Sure."

"You think Ellis will be there?" Ariel asked.

"Probably," Taylor said. "Why?"

"I don't know. He's kind of cute. You notice the way he gets all flustered when he sees me?"

Taylor nodded. "Yeah. I've noticed."

As they left the park, Taylor glanced behind her, enjoying the sight of kids spread across the grass and sitting on the benches, back where they belonged. The rolling scrape of skateboard wheels drifted over from the tennis courts. Things were returning to normal.

"There's the hero," Ariel said when they got near the house. She pointed ahead to Ryan, who was sitting with Ellis on the front porch.

"Yeah, there's the hero," Taylor agreed. Ryan had just shared his mind and body with one of history's greatest peacemakers. She hoped some small part of that gentle legend would remain with him forever.

As she thought about Gandhi, Taylor almost regretted that she hadn't let Kara come over. It might have done the girl some good. Laughing at the image of Ryan teaching Kara the joys of peace and compassion, Taylor walked up the porch steps and sat down with her brother and Ellis.

"What's so funny?" Ariel asked.

"Have a seat," Taylor told her. "It's a long story."

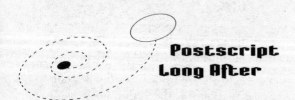

Eventually, the Nexulans returned to earth and recaptured the best of the legends they'd lost on their first trip, along with a nice selection of disks about humans who'd achieved fame in the decades since the last visit. The series was a huge hit.

They even created a disk about the inventor of the McKenzie Star drive. A noted physicist, and the first human to discover the principle of atomic imperfection, she was responsible for helping the Earthlings begin their journey beyond the solar system. In her spare time, she wrote humorous poems.

On a less galactic, though no less fascinating note, a childhood friend of hers went on to become both an Olympic gold medalist boxer and the most popular horror writer of his generation. Critics took a great deal of pleasure in saying that his stories packed a punch. Interestingly enough, on one occasion he returned the favor by punching a critic.

As for the physicist's twin brother, he went to college on a baseball scholarship. After graduation, he was offered a chance to play in the majors. He turned it down to dedicate his time to a project that helped get troubled kids involved in sports. Eventually, the project grew into a nationwide organization.

Though he helped thousands of kids, there's no disk to tell his story. He didn't meet the Nexulan definition of a legend. But the kids he worked with, and his friends and family, thought otherwise. They knew he was pretty remarkable. Whenever anyone asked him how he'd accomplished so much, he shrugged and said, "No big deal, sport. I just take a good, hard swing. And if I miss, I take another one."

Author's Note

Even aliens with advanced research technology are capable of making mistakes. The production crew did their best while compiling the disks. But remember, they're in show business. They were creating entertainment, not documentaries. So if you spot any flaws in the portrayal of the legends mentioned here, or question the inclusion or exclusion of any individual, don't blame me. Tell it to the Nexulans.

**Tor Books
READER'S GUIDE**

FLIp

by David Lubar

ABOUT STARSCAPE BOOKS

The richly imagined worlds of science fiction and fantasy novels encourage readers to hold a mirror up to their own realities, exploring them in a way that is secure yet challenging and demanding. Whether surviving in a complex alternate universe or navigating life on Earth in the presence of a strange, new discovery, the characters in these works help readers realize, through comparison and contrast, what it means to be a true human being. Starscape strives to encourage such critical discoveries by making the very best science fiction and fantasy literature available to young adult readers. From the works of David Lubar to Orson Scott Card and from Niel Hancock to Jane Yolen, Starscape books provide numerous unique universes through which young readers can travel on the critical journey to the center of their own identity.

ABOUT *FLIP*

An accidental space collision causes a set of Nexulan entertainment disks to drop into the earthly hands of eighth-grade twins Ryan and Taylor McKenzie. Ryan learns that the flip of a disk can transform a common kid into a historic hero, and a disappointing school day into an amazing adventure. He is Babe Ruth, Albert Einstein, Queen Victoria . . . even Elvis! Meanwhile, Taylor struggles to keep her top class ranking, to keep her best friend, Ariel, from abandoning her for the "popular" group, and to keep Ryan from flipping into too much trouble—especially with school bully Billy Snooks.

Taylor escapes from her stress by flipping into Captain William Kidd, accidentally setting the stage for Ryan's final confrontation with Billy. As the slave soldier Spartacus, Ryan sets off bravely, but the disk wears off. He flips another, only to become pacifist Mahatma Gandhi. Unwilling to fight, Ryan-Gandhi weathers blow after blow until a kinder member of Billy's gang intercedes to bring the battle to a definitive end.

After the fight, the twins discover that the remaining disks have been accidentally destroyed. But other parts of their lives have been repaired. Taylor regains the friendship of Ariel and loosens her grip on academic anxiety. Ryan begins to sense direction in his life and decides to try out for the baseball team. Perhaps most important of all, the twins realize that being somebody else for awhile is a pretty good way to find out how to be yourself.

ABOUT THIS GUIDE

The information, discussion questions, and activity ideas that follow are intended to enhance your reading of *Flip*. Please feel free to adapt these materials to suit your needs and interests.

WRITING AND RESEARCH ACTIVITIES

I. Science Fiction Facts

Go to your school library or online to research the phrase "science fiction." Then create a large, fact-filled poster about science fiction. Include a definition of the phrase, a short history of the literary form, and a list of notable science fiction authors and their books. If desired, add some facts about science fiction in film and television.

II. Extraterrestrial Explorations

As *Flip* begins, readers learn about Nexula, the "entertainment hub of the universe," and its citizens. Do you believe there is life on other planets? If yes, what might this life be like? Write a short answer to this question, then:

A. Create a survey including such questions as: "Do you believe in extraterrestrial life?" "Do you think we will ever make contact with extraterrestrial life?" and "What would you like to tell space visitors about human beings?" Survey at least ten people, then compile your results in a short report. What result most surprised you?

B. Search through old newspapers or scientific periodicals for articles about the search for extraterrestrial life. Read at least three articles. Write a short summary of each article on an index card. Include the source of the article, its author(s), and its main idea. If possible, display your index cards with the cards of classmates or friends. What do the articles lead you to conclude about the possibility of extraterrestrial life?

C. Imagine you have met an extraterrestrial in a local park. From what planet does it hail? What does it look like? Why has it come to Earth? What does it think of Earth and humans? What do you think of your new acquaintance? Write a short science fiction story that answers these questions. Include an illustration if desired.

III. Great Quotations
David Lubar uses a quote to begin each of the four sections of *Flip*. Start your own quotation collection. Include quotes from favorite authors, historical figures, newspaper or magazine articles, or even from people you know. Compile your favorite ten quotes into a booklet. Illustrate with drawings, photographs, or pictures cut from magazines.

IV. Heroes and Legends
Ryan, Taylor, and Ellis "flip" into the life experiences of some amazing people from world history including The Great Blondin, Albert Einstein, Mahatma Gandhi, Helen Keller, Captain William Kidd, Edgar Allan Poe, Elvis Presley, Babe Ruth, Spartacus, and Queen Victoria. Research the life of one or more historical personages from *Flip*, then:

A. Imagine that you have discovered a Nexulan disk containing an experience as hero or legend from *Flip*. You flip the disk . . . Write a 2–3 paragraph essay describing what happens to you and how it affects your life.

B. Imagine that you are a Nexulan talent scout. Based on your research, write a short list of criteria that an Earth hero or legend must meet to be included on one of your disks. Now, write a recommendation for a new hero (not found in *Flip*) that should be added to the disk set. Explain why this person qualifies as a hero or legend.

V. Books and Games

Outline a design for a computer or video game based on *Flip*. Make a list of characters, settings, and objectives for the game. Draw a diagram of one or more of the settings as it would look on a computer or video screen. Write a short paragraph describing the game.

QUESTIONS FOR DISCUSSION

1. Compare what you know about Nexulan entertainment disks to video games, reality television, books, or other types of Earth entertainment. To what type of Earth entertainment do you think the disks are most similar? Explain your answer.

2. At the beginning of the story, how might Taylor describe Ryan? How would Ryan describe Taylor? How do Ryan and Taylor each react to touching the "glob" in the woods? Do you think your reaction would have been like Ryan's or Taylor's? Explain.

3. Page through the story for descriptions of mealtimes at the McKenzie and Snooks homes. How are Ryan, Taylor, and Billy's dining table experiences similar or different? How do these scenes help readers better understand the story?

4. What does Ryan really do to make Billy Snooks so angry? What do Ryan's actions tell us about his character even before he begins flipping the disks? Is it surprising that Ryan, and not Taylor, makes the critical discovery about the disks? Why or why not?

5. Although in some ways very different, Kara and Billy are both bullies. Compare Kara's schoolyard powers with Billy's. Which character do you think is more dangerous

and why? Have you ever encountered a bully? Describe your experience.

6. Page back through *Flip* to create a list of the "Ellis the——" names that Ellis gives himself. What does this list tell us about Ellis? Is this accurate?

7. What happens to Ryan when he "flips" into Babe Ruth? Whose opinions of Ryan are changed by their encounters with Ryan during this flip?

8. What are some of the ways Ryan gets in trouble at home or at school? Is his behavior intentional? Do you think Ryan is responsible for the stressful dynamics of the McKenzie household? Can Taylor really do anything to improve the situation? Do you think the McKenzie household is normal? Explain.

9. At the end of the chapter entitled "Alienation," Ryan comments that his parents are going to "flip" when they find out about his multiple detentions. How many different uses of the term, or the idea, of "flip" are used in the novel?

10. Why doesn't Taylor tell her parents the truth about why she was not accepted into the summer program? How is this related to her decision to flip? Do you think her personality causes her flip experience to be different than most of Ryan's? Compare Taylor's flip to Ellis's.

11. Imagine you are a friend of Mr. and Mrs. McKenzie. Would you tell them that they are right to consider medicating Ryan? What advice would you give them about handling Ryan? What might you tell them about Taylor?

12. Find moments in the story when Ryan is betrayed by Ellis, and instances where Taylor is betrayed by Ariel. How are these betrayals similar? How are they different? Who is really responsible for each betrayal? What do the betrayals reveal to readers about these friendships?

13. Do you think it was lucky or unlucky that Ryan transformed from Spartacus to Gandhi during his fight with Billy? Who was the bravest during the confrontation on the playground: Ryan, Billy, Ace, or Ellis? Why?

14. What motivates Ace to stop the fight between Billy and Ryan? Who truly defeats Billy? After the fight is over, how is Kara also "defeated"? How do you feel about Billy and Kara at the end of the story? How do you feel about Ryan and Taylor?

15. David Lubar wrote *Flip* with many short chapters and with chapter titles that are often humorous or carry a double meaning. How does this style affect your reading of *Flip* and your understanding of its characters? What chapter titles do you find most significant or amusing?

16. Many kids dream about being a star athlete, a great performer, or another famous individual. Think of *Flip* as a story about getting the chance to become your heroes. What does this teach you? If you could "flip," what hero or legend would you choose to experience?

17. The four sections of *Flip* are entitled "Discovery," "Exploration," "Users," and "Battle." Explain two ways each of these titles might be understood.

18. The author begins each of the four sections of *Flip* with a quotation. Review the four quotes. How might the quotes apply to—or help readers understand—Ryan, Taylor, Ellis, Ariel, Billy, or Kara?

19. Reread the "Postscript." How do you think the Nexulans define "legend"? If you had a choice to become Ryan, Taylor, or Ellis "long after," whom would you choose? Would you like to become a legend or a hero? Why or why not?

20. If you could find an artifact from an extraterrestrial life form, what would you like it to be? Would you share your

find with your siblings or friends? Would you show it to your parents or teachers? What else might you do with your find? How might it affect your life?

21. One message of *Flip* might be that a few radical "flips" sometimes help put a life back in balance. Other than the disks, what "flips" happen in the course of the novel? Do you wish that any of these flips would happen in your own life? Why or why not?

ABOUT THE AUTHOR

David Lubar grew up in Morristown, New Jersey. His books include *Hidden Talents*, an ALA Best Book for Young Adults; *True Talents; Flip*, a VOYA Best Science Fiction, Fantasy, and Horror selection; the Weenies short-story collections *Attack of the Vampire Weenies, The Battle of the Red Hot Pepper Weenies, Beware the Ninja Weenies, The Curse of the Campfire Weenies, In the Land of the Lawn Weenies, Invasion of the Road Weenies*, and *Wipeout of the Wireless Weenies;* and the Nathan Abercrombie, Accidental Zombie series. He lives in Nazareth, Pennsylvania. You can visit him on the Web at www.davidlubar.com.